Praise for *Breathing Lake Superior*

"In Ron Rindo's gripping novel *Breathing Lake Superior*, a grieving man goes on a troubled religious odyssey.

"Sixteen-year-old John lives in suburban Milwaukee with his m~~t~ stepfather, Anna and Cal, and his stepsister. ̄ ̄ ̄ his family, seems to possess a special aura. F linked to both parents,' and his surprise vasectomy. . . . But when David drowns at the loc his family is overwhelmed by shock and sadness. (depression. And then Cal's despondency turns to spiri

"Though the novel begins with deceptive complacency, the events following Cal's conversion spiral into gradual madness . . . .

"Amid wondrous descriptions of rural, seasonal beauty, the novel *Breathing Lake Superior* examines moments of intimacy, love, and humor against a formidable biblical background."

—Meg Nola, *Foreword Reviews* (September / October 2022)

"Ronald Rindo's novel marks a very welcome addition to Wisconsin literature. Everything is here that you could want, love, loss, faith, doubt, joy, despair, plus the miracles of a faith healer—all set in an area of the state Rindo knows well."

—Anthony Bukoski, author of *The Blondes of Wisconsin*

"How is it that this novel's sister and brother are so profoundly understood that though I have no brother, I have *this* brother, *this* mother and father, *this* church, *this* farmhouse, *this* winter, *these* woods, *these* delights, *these* trials and *these* redemptions? We turn the pages of *Breathing Lake Superior* thrilled and suspended, and come away from them steeped in story, owned by rare wisdom. If there really is a Thin Place, where the earth gives way to its own mysticism, then to read Ron Rindo is to open a door that will lead you to it."

—Abby Frucht, author of *Are You Mine?*

"Set against the unforgiving backdrop of northern Wisconsin, *Breathing Lake Superior* explores the extraordinary depths of grief, love, and the astonishing power of magical thinking. Debut author Ron Rindo expertly narrates the stunning transformation of a Midwestern father into a self-proclaimed messiah through the eyes of his teen stepson, John. A new literary voice that exquisitely augments the Midwestern fiction genre."

—Eldonna Edwards, award-winning author of *This I Know*

"*Breathing Lake Superior* is a masterpiece of dramatic tension about the destruction and resurrection of a family. . . . a timely story, full of vivid imagery and unforgettable characters—a tragedy in a beautiful landscape.... Evocative, poetic description captures human emotion and landscape throughout the novel."

—Ruth Latta, *Compulsive Reader*

Breathing
LAKE SUPERIOR

Ron Rindo

Brick Mantel Books
Saint Louis, Missouri

Published by Brick Mantel Books, USA

Brick Mantel
BOOKS

www.BrickMantelBooks.com
info@BrickMantelBooks.com

An imprint of Pen & Publish, LLC
Saint Louis, Missouri
(314) 827-6567
www.PenandPublish.com

Print ISBN: 978-1-956897-11-1
e-book ISBN: 978-1-956897-10-4

Library of Congress Control Number: 2022936428

Printed on acid-free paper

Cover photo by David Mould

*This book is a work of fiction. Though the landscape, rivers, and
lake that appear in this work are real places (many of them likely
far more beautiful than I've been able to render them), the events
and characters here are entirely the products of my imagination.
Any resemblance to actual persons, living or dead, or actual
events, is purely coincidental.*

*For Jenna, and for Della, Tyler, Claire, Riley, and Noah,
with memories of glorious, sunny afternoons
gathering sea glass on Lake Superior's south shore.
Someday someone will find blue.*

PART I: WATER

That as I said, I say, take, Lord, they're thine.
I piecemeale pass to Glory bright in them.
I' joy, may I sweet Flowers for Glory breed,
Whether thou getst them green, or lets them Seed.

—Edward Taylor,
"Upon Wedlock, & Death of Children" (1692)

Chapter 1

L **ike many stories we cannot forget, this is a story about belief.**
Even before God spoke to him—in the way He summoned
Nat Turner in a Virginia cornfield—my stepdad, Cal, always told us
that *miracle* was not a word to be used lightly, if at all. Like the word
tragedy, it was not to be spoken or written unless it carried the precise
meaning for which it had been intended. In all of human history, he
said, few people had ever experienced anything *truly* miraculous or
tragic. Modern culture had abused both words so often, they had long
been drained of meaning.

But I know of no other words that fit our set of circumstances
these past fourteen months. If not tragic and miraculous, I don't know
what our lives have become.

* * *

We were a normal family once.

Sometimes when my stepsister JJ said this, as we lay submerged
in alfalfa, sucking sweet nectar from the purple blossoms amid the
honeybees, or while we sat cross-legged, reading books aloud to
one another, we both felt like crying. Sometimes we started laughing. And sometimes we didn't do anything. I just repeated what she
said, emphasizing a different word, "normal," sometimes, or "were," or
"once," and we would both nod and shrug, because that one sentence
was both question and conclusion.

Who really knows what we were or what we are? We're never
really the same from one day to the next. Each hour, we slough off
a blizzard of skin cells and hair. Red blood cells die and regenerate.
Damaged by storms seen and unseen, our brains erect dikes or boil
over, flood new territories. Each time we blink we're someone different, and our eyes behold a new world.

Not that long ago, though, our family at least *seemed* normal—normal *and* as boring as watching a dog shit, JJ always said. Comfortably middle class, three children, two parents, we lived in West Allis, Wisconsin, a working-class suburb of sidewalks, square blocks, and alleys, where the sign that greeted you as you drove into the city announced how many days had passed since anyone working in one of the local factories had accidentally lost a finger or an arm or an eye. ("Great," Cal had said, years earlier, when we moved there from a duplex on the south side of Milwaukee, "a neighborhood full of Polacks and Germans missing body parts. We'll probably move in next door to some guy called Lefty.") My sister and I attended West Allis Central High School, hung out at the mall with our friends, cruised with them in noisy cars dragging mufflers that sent sparks down Greenfield Avenue on warm Saturday nights. We wore baggy cargo pants, Abercrombie and Fitch T-shirts, and tennis shoes with air in the heels—whole wardrobes, Cal pointed out, made in Far-East sweatshops by child laborers working for sixty cents a day. We grudgingly went to church with our parents on Sunday mornings and cheered for the Green Bay Packers on our big-screen TV on Sunday afternoons. We shopped at Kmart, Wal-Mart, and Target. We had "blended family values up the ass," Cal said. We were a monosodium glutamate–tolerant, TV-watching, traffic-jam-cursing, run-for-the-ringing-telephone family, living the American dream ten blocks from the interstate.

Most evenings, we ate supper together—Mother and Cal, JJ, me, and our little brother, David—sitting around the table quietly scraping our plates with our forks, staring at Sportscenter or The Learning Channel on the kitchen TV. David would eat quickly and then disappear into the living room to continue work on some elaborate construction project he had going, utilizing Legos, TinkerToys, and Lincoln Logs. "Look at him," Cal would say, proudly. "The next Frank Lloyd Wright." At four years old, David had built a recognizable model of the Eiffel Tower using fettuccine noodles and masking tape. At five, with Legos and TinkerToys, he'd constructed Notre Dame Cathedral (based upon a picture in Cal's ancient copy of *Europe on Five Dollars a Day*.)

Because David had been conceived two years after my stepfather's vasectomy—what Cal euphemistically referred to as his "vase-stuck-to-me"—Mother often called David her "miracle baby." Cal's vas deferens had been bombed like the bridge over the River Kwai, but somehow a single sperm had crossed the great divide and made its way to the Promised Land. "No—it was no miracle," Cal always retorted. "The doctor just botched my ball job. Hurt like hell, too. Felt like I got kicked in the nuts for a week." Even so, as the Final Straw, the Last Hurrah, the Grand Finale—nicknames JJ and used to tease him—our half-brother David glowed with the aura of the treasured youngest child, and the only child biologically linked to both parents in our unremarkable family.

Sometimes at supper, Cal would mute the television to ask JJ and me what we were doing in school. JJ and I would take turns muttering a few things, hoping to get by with brief generalities. He'd ask for elaboration, and we'd mutter a few more things, and then the TV volume would return and everyone would go back to their pork chops or their tuna casserole. We'd learned to keep our explanations vague to help avoid the almost certain lecture from Cal that would come if we took his request seriously.

In the spring of my sophomore year, I got into trouble for a research paper I'd written in my Honors English class, "The Heavy Metal Guitar Solo as Male Masturbatory Fantasy." My stepsister had sketched the cover page for me, a beautiful colored-pencil drawing of a honey-haired heavy-metal rocker playing electric guitar, the neck of the guitar shaped like a man's erect penis. A series of musical notes spewed from this erection like a geyser.

When my turn came to read the paper aloud in class, I had read only the title and the opening line, "Male rock guitarists have traditionally carried their instruments slung low so that the wooden neck of the guitar projects from their pelvis like an erect penis," when Mr. Kleefish, my English teacher, interrupted and sent me to the principal, someone who knew me only as JJ's stepbrother. (JJ herself had spent considerable time in the principal's office over the years for what Mother called her "independent nature.") Fortunately for me, the principal had two sons in a local rock band. She smiled at me and said while she could not *condone* the repeated use of words such as *penis*, *erection*, and *ejaculation* in a high school English paper, she believed the paper was insightful and, undoubtedly, true. "Really made me think," she'd said. Nevertheless, the principal supported Mr. Kleefish, to a degree, by requesting that I write a different paper, one more befitting an audience of students my own age.

At supper that night, when Cal asked how school had gone, I pulled the essay out of my backpack and began reading. I wasn't allowed to read beyond the opening line at the dinner table, either.

"John!" Mother interrupted. "Is that any way for a young man to talk?"

"What?" said JJ, coming to my defense. "'Penis?' He can't say 'penis' in his own house? It's an anatomical fact. Boys have penises."

"Beanis!" David, who was five then, yelled gleefully. "Beanis, beanis, beanis!"

"David, please," Mother said, looking to Cal for support. Cal shrugged. "Mother's right," he said. He winked at David.

"About what?" JJ asked.

Cal shrugged. "About whatever she just said."

"You weren't even listening!"

"Darling, I was listening," Cal said. He winked at me. "Use a different word, John. Use schlong, or schwanz, or tricky Dickie."

I laughed.

"That is so bogus!" JJ said. "Your paper *kicks ass*, Johnny. The principal always sticks up for the teachers, even when they're wrong. It makes me sick."

"When I was a kid," Cal said, "we wrote essays about the Founding Fathers, about the US Constitution, about how a bill becomes a law, that sort of thing. I got so bored I thought my eyes would melt out of my face. At least your teacher's trying to make the subject more interesting. You can't blame her for that."

"So he shouldn't have to rewrite it," JJ said.

"Not in an ideal world," Cal said. "Does this look like a perfect world to you?"

"But John's essay is great!" JJ said. "Even the principal said so."

"Darling, that's how life works. Even a smart kid like your brother has to take it in the shorts on occasion. Best get used to it."

JJ glared at him, then jumped out of her chair and stormed up the stairs to her bedroom, her long hair flying over her shoulders. She slammed the door.

Mother pursed her lips and shook her head slowly. Cal shrugged his shoulders at her. "What?" he asked. "What'd I say? Why's she so sensitive?"

"She's fifteen," Mother said.

Cal looked at me and rolled his eyes.

I grew up wanting to be a writer, and Cal had a lot to do with that. Back before any of us children were born, he had been working on his PhD in American literature. He had completed everything but his dissertation, which was to be a book-length study of the poetry of Edward Taylor. A Calvinist minister and poet in Puritan New England who served his congregation in Westfield, Connecticut, for over fifty years, until his death in 1729, Taylor secretly wrote hundreds of poems which went unpublished and unknown until someone discovered them in storage at the Yale University Library in the 1930s. Taylor had fathered fourteen children—he needed a vase-stuck-to-me, Cal noted—but five of his first eight children had died in infancy. When Cal married his first wife—JJ's mother, who died of pancreatic cancer when JJ was three years old—he quit work on his dissertation and took a full-time job teaching English at Waukesha County Technical College. Cal never went back to finish his degree, but his passion for early American literature and Taylor's poetry stayed with him.

At the technical college, Cal occasionally got to teach American literature, and he would sometimes read to us from the thick worn anthology he used while he prepared for his classes. Mostly, though, he taught writing courses, multiple sections of what he called "English grammar for semiliterates." In the evenings, watching Cal grade his students' essays was like seeing a man read a long, poorly written letter filled with bad news. He'd sit at the kitchen table, a rumpled stack of papers before him, half as high as the label on his bottle of beer, and he'd shake his head, he'd groan, he'd grimace.

"Think!" he would yell suddenly. "Does that point make any sense at all? You couldn't win an argument with a tree!"

"In your thoughtful opinion, marijuana should be legalized, because it doesn't give you a hangover like alcohol does?" His head would fall back and he'd stare at the ceiling in disbelief. "Did the moron train stop and unload every passenger into my beginning argumentation class?" Of course, when he came to an essay that met his standards, his face beamed. "A thesis sentence!" he'd announce. "Evidence in support of assertions! The English language used with conciseness and precision!" He'd kiss the paper, give it an A, and drain the remaining beer from his bottle.

The ordeal of grading papers aside, Cal loved teaching. He loved an audience and a good argument, but he also believed in the value of what he did. Yes, he taught English to future mechanics, welders, and plumbers who would possibly never read another book in their lives, and who would one day earn far more money than Cal while unclogging his drain or repairing his automobile, but he took his job seriously. "They'll still have to read the newspaper," he'd say. "And they'll have to write estimates. They can do it with style and precision."

In addition to his love for the English language used well, Cal had other passions.

One of them was his obsession with Black music and musicians. He had a collection of record albums that numbered in the hundreds: Lead Belly, Ma Rainey, Bessie Smith, Mahalia Jackson, Elmore James, Howlin' Wolf, Muddy Waters, Blind Lemon Jefferson, Louis Armstrong, and his favorite, Duke Ellington. Sometimes in the summer he'd clear the kitchen floor after supper on a Saturday night. He'd set up his old stereo turntable—he detested CDs, preferring, he said, "the authentic sound of music being made," which could be heard only on vinyl records—he'd open a quart bottle of St. Ides Malt Liquor, and then he'd put on Wilson Pickett, Otis Redding, the Temps, sometimes my favorite, Little Richard. He'd turn the volume up and grab Mother in his arms, and they'd dance on the kitchen floor. David would sit on the kitchen counter, clapping his hands, spilling a bottle of root beer down his chin. Sometimes JJ and I would join Mom and Cal on the dance floor, spinning together and sweating, holding hands, knocking knees, laughing, singing the chorus of "na na"s during the "Land of a Thousand Dances," or shouting "womp bomp alu bomp a womp bam boom!" between verses of "Tutti Frutti."

Sometimes Cal would take David up on his shoulders and hop around the room, David's sticky hands locked under Cal's chin, giggling and drooling into Cal's hair, and the two of them would laugh so hard the tears would roll down their faces. Perhaps because David's conception had been so unexpected—a surprise gift is more treasured than an expected one—Cal took David everywhere, fed him meals in his high chair as a baby, held him on his lap to eat as David grew older, and insisted that David sit beside him at dinner as a toddler and beyond. By the time he was five, David knew the words to several R&B songs by heart. Cal would stand him on the kitchen table, and with his mop of blond hair flopping, David would clap his hands and dance, singing his own version of the lyrics in his tiny voice.

When our family dances ended and the cool night air drifted in through the open windows, Cal would collapse into his chair with David on his lap. He'd open his shirt and button David right in against his skin while he read the newspaper or watched late-night TV. David would fall asleep there, and Cal would hold him buttoned against his chest, David's fluffy hair up under Cal's chin, until he and Mother went upstairs to bed.

But that seems like a long time ago, now. I can't speak for JJ— her name is Jennifer Joy, a name she despises ("call me Jennifer Ambivalence, Jennifer Rage, Jennifer Despair," she says, "but *never* Jennifer Joy"), so we call her JJ—cannot narrate the images that pass behind her eyes when she closes them to remember the moment our lives changed, the point when our family stopped seeming remotely like anyone else's, and Cal moved us to a farm in northern Wisconsin he named New Eden, six miles south of Lake Superior, a hundred miles or more from anywhere worth being. It was a time when Cal fell into a darkness he thought was light; a time when temptation crawled inside JJ and me like the bud of some mysterious, irresistible flower, waiting to bloom; a time when Mother, the anchor we'd always counted on to keep Cal tethered through the most maniacal of his storms, drifted away from all of us.

And I only, as Job said in the Bible, escaped to tell thee.

The moment our lives changed is like a vision through antique glass: clear enough to be known, but too distorted to be known well. It's the kind of glass you find in old houses, full of bubbles and other imperfections, like new ice on a pond. You lay on the black ice, hold your breath to keep from clouding your view, and you can see bubbles and other things—dead fish, weeds, bugs, sometimes—frozen right into it, as if the water's slow movement from liquid to solid had surprised them. The glass in some of the windows of our house in New Eden looks like this, with bubbles and slices and other opaque imperfections, and when the sun hits certain parts just right, the windows cast little rainbows against the wall. Granted, you can't see through those windows very well, but I've learned that deceptive clarity is usually less preferable than a more opaque, functionless beauty.

Some windows are manufactured so well, with double panes and argon gas sealed inside, sometimes it doesn't appear as if you're looking through anything at all. One night at a party during my sophomore year, I saw a drunken high schooler run through a glass patio door. He fell screaming on the concrete, trailing ribbons of skin and blood. But that's not even the greatest danger. Looking out their beautifully clean windows, people think they can see the real world without actually letting any of its trouble inside. That's the illusion that traps everyone sooner or later. Because trouble gets in, regardless.

Ours arrived on the third of July, 1999. We were all looking forward to fireworks the next evening, to writing our names in the air with sparklers, blowing up Coke cans with firecrackers, and sending bottle rockets whistling over neighbors' houses—celebrating the Declaration of Independence American-style, with lots of noise and flash and just enough chance to blow your fingers off to make it interesting. I'd built a special model rocket—the Mercury Atlas, thirty-three inches tall—to launch in celebration of the holiday, a long two-stage rocket that held five C6-5 engines. David had helped me paint it silver, and we were excited because we'd never launched anything with so many engines of that size. We figured if it got up into the wind, it might drift as far as Lake Michigan before parachuting down again. We planned to put a note inside with our name and address on it, so that whoever found it might write to us, or mail it back.

I'd been building and launching model rockets for many years, and a number of my best models hung at 45-degree angles from my bedroom ceiling, suspended by fishing line. I'd painted the ceiling a glossy black and pasted dozens of self-stick, glow-in-the-dark stars on it, carefully arranged in familiar constellations—the Big Dipper, Orion, Gemini, the Pleiades—so that at night, with the window shades down, when I opened my eyes in bed, it looked almost as if I were sleeping in space.

Sometimes, if JJ got mad at me for something, or she wanted to get a rise out of me, she would sneak into my room and rearrange my stars. She'd spell the name of a girl I liked or, if she were angry at me, she'd cuss me out. I'd walk in and look up, and my ceiling would say something like, "John loves Amber," or "Kiss my ass," and I'd have to take the stars down and put up the constellations again. To retaliate, David and I might tie her underwear to a long piece of kite string and hang it out her second-floor window or draw smiley faces on the cups of her 32B bras with colored chalk.

The day our lives changed started out as an ordinary summer day. While Cal was teaching summer school and Mom worked at a factory assembling lawn mower engines, JJ and I stayed home with David, who had just turned six. The only air conditioner in our house, which looked like everyone else's house (they were squeezed together in straight lines like dominoes ready to fall, JJ always said), was a clattering, leaking Sears model hanging from Mother and Cal's bedroom window. The rest of the house felt like a steam bath. Condensation dripped from the toilet tanks, the spigots, even from the cold-water pipes in the basement, where we sometimes went for relief. Lime deposits sprouted from the basement's rock and mortar walls, and salamanders, shiny and wet-black as patent leather shoes, gathered in dark corners and near the floor drain behind Mother's washing machine. Upstairs, on the most humid days, you sweat just standing still.

Like most kids in the neighborhood, we spent those sweltering summer afternoons at the local pool, and that day after lunch, JJ, David, and I put on our swimming suits, grabbed our beach towels, and walked to Rainbow Park, David skipping ahead of us, a Batman towel draped across his shoulders, humming Ray Charles's "Unchain My Heart."

JJ spent the afternoon sunbathing with three of her girlfriends on the balcony that overlooked the diving boards. They rested on their bellies on beach towels spread across the hot concrete, the strings of their bikini tops untied, their long hair pulled up and pinned off their necks. A small boom box rested near their heads. Earlier, the four of them had gone together into the women's bathroom to get high. Amanda, who had her belly button pierced and a tattoo of Bart Simpson above her left ankle, led the way. I could see the white tip of a joint and a pink disposable lighter poking out of her hand as they passed me. I imagined them standing barefoot on the wet floor in one of the stalls with the door closed, passing the joint around, giggling, and ten minutes later I watched as they returned to their towels, munching popcorn by the handful, the whites of their eyes spoked red.

I stood at the rail beside them, pretending to watch the pool down below, where David splashed and swam somewhere with hundreds of other noisy children. I stole glances at JJ's friends, at their thin, sun-tanned legs and shiny ankle bracelets; the creamy, wrinkled whiteness of the bottoms of their feet, the firm arcs of their barely covered bottoms, the narrow strips of colorful fabric that passed between their legs. Perspiration glistened on their backs and necks and beaded in the golden hair on their arms. Sometimes one of them would lift herself to the elbows to light a cigarette, or to reach for the stereo to change CDs, and I would glimpse crescents of white breast flattened against a towel.

Occasionally, one of JJ's friends would glance over at me, and they would whisper to one another and laugh. They talked about music, their parents, about various boys in school, and once in a while I'd hear JJ refer to me, to "Johnny," as she called me. Mostly, though, JJ and her friends talked about the lifeguards, muscular, master-race types who wore mirrored sunglasses and baseball caps and sat in high white ladder chairs with their knees spread apart ("as if their balls were the size of coconuts," JJ said, "and they needed the room.") They reclined in their chairs like kings, twirling silver whistles by red lanyards looped over the tips of their index fingers. A skinny, bookish, rising junior that fall, and not yet 16, I didn't merit much consideration from JJ's friends, who were two years older than me, or from the lifeguards they simultaneously insulted and coveted. Because the lifeguards lusted after JJ and made crude, admiring comments to me about her ass and breasts, they more or less left me alone—didn't pull my swimming trunks down or hold my head in one of the locker room toilets while the others pissed in my hair, like they did to some boys they didn't like.

Because of the lifeguards' reputation and standing, all of the children who swam in the pool were either afraid of them or in awe of them. When a lifeguard blew his whistle to stop a chicken fight or to keep someone from running or to order everyone out of the pool for the lunch or supper break, activity stopped and heads turned. Those shrill whistles could stop time.

And on the afternoon of July 3, 1999, they did.

The piercing, sustained blast of one whistle, then several others, followed by orders to evacuate the pool, shouted through bullhorns, sent children splashing from the water. The urgency in the lifeguard's amplified voices hung like humidity in the air. This wasn't simply a playful, half-hearted order to stop a chicken fight. Everyone sensed the difference. JJ and her friends' heads bobbed up to watch as the pool cleared. The lifeguards jumped down from their chairs and ran—ran!—around the pool to the twelve-foot end directly below us where something—a pair of khaki pants, a deflated pool toy, could be anything, I thought, rested on the bottom along the wall. While one of the lifeguards ran to the beach house, two of the others dove into the pool, one of them still with his hat and sunglasses on, and even before they returned to the surface, holding whatever was on the bottom between them, young girls started screaming, and frantic mothers with dimpled, gelatinous thighs began running in circles, their faces twisted in panic, calling the names of their children.

But all of their children were safe. Because when I leaned over the rail to see what was going on, I watched them pull David from the pool, his body limp and boneless as a water balloon.

I couldn't breathe. For a while, I couldn't even move. White dots spread against a black background before my eyes, and I choked back my own vomit. And then I heard the sound of my stepsister screaming David's name, and I found myself running to the side of the pool, where David lay on his back. His eyes had glazed over, drops of oil on water. His lips were the purple of old bruises. His skin looked mottled and gray, the color of fog. Two lifeguards bent over him. One of them pushed with straight, muscular arms against his skinny chest, the palms of his hands crossed over David's heart. Tears streamed down the lifeguard's face as he counted out numbers between clenched, chattering teeth and watched the cage of David's ribs flex under his hands.

"Come on, kid," he said, each time he stopped counting. "Come on, kid. Come on, kid." The other lifeguard, his eyes wild with panic, pinched David's nose closed and breathed, at intervals, into his mouth.

Sirens wailed.

"His name's David," I said.

"You know him?" the lifeguard asked.

"He's my brother." It's the last thing I could say.

All around us, people hugged one another and cried. JJ held two clenched fists to her mouth and swayed from side to side, sobbing. Sometimes she put a hand on David's leg or shook one of his little feet between her fingers, as if she were trying to wake him from a deep sleep. I noticed only then that she had run to David without retying the top of her swimming suit. Her small breasts were white against her suntanned neck and stomach, her nipples pink and dimpled, like raspberries. No one seemed to notice she wasn't dressed, not until one of the paramedics wrapped a sheet around her shoulders as we rode with David in the ambulance to the hospital.

We waited along the wall outside the emergency room for a long time, rubbing our backs against the textured wallpaper, shivering, our lips quivering in cold and fear.

"We should have been watching him," JJ said.

I nodded.

"We should have been watching him!" she said, her face twisting into a long, choking sob.

A blue curtain separated us from the doctors and nurses bent over David. We could hear them shouting, could see the rustle of their legs and feet beneath the curtain. My head and neck throbbed. I had to keep swallowing to ease the stinging pain of withheld tears burning in the back of my throat.

Mother and Cal came in separate cars from work and they waited with us, their faces masks of pain and dread. We waited until a thin young doctor with disheveled hair came out to say that he was so sorry. So very sorry.

The sound that came from JJ's throat was like no human sound I'd ever heard. Disbelief, horror, rage, and agony all mingled together in my ears as I pulled JJ to me, wrapped my arms around her and locked them, too frightened to let go.

Mother and Cal insisted on seeing David, and Mother lifted his cool, stiffening body from the gurney and clutched him to herself, pressing his head against her shoulder, rocking him. His arms and legs drooped toward the floor, and if you didn't know better, you might have thought he had simply fallen asleep in front of the television and was being carried up to bed.

Cal rubbed David's back, the tips of his strong fingers moving the cool skin as he absently traced small circles there. Mother passed David to Cal, and Cal slid to the tiled floor with David in his arms. Cal pulled off his tie and undid the buttons of his white dress shirt. Then he pulled David's cool body against the skin of his warm, hair-covered chest and held him there, sobbing into David's hair. JJ and I stood against the wall, near one another. Her whole body shook in violent, jerky spasms. Her teeth chattered. She retched, gagging up air and bile, and a nurse brought a towel for JJ to hold over her quivering lips.

Mother knelt on the floor next to Cal. She pressed her lips to David's cheek, put her nose into his hair. We stayed that way for a long time, Mother, Cal, and David a tableau of sorrow on the floor.

Chapter 2

Grief poured into our house, blew in through window screens like the cold front preceding a thunderstorm. Cal closed David's bedroom door immediately when we got home, and everything inside remained untouched, exactly as it had been that afternoon when we left for the pool. I sat alone on the floor of my room. A hollowness, a numbing ache, filled my chest and throat.

The rest of the late afternoon and long into the night, Mother and Cal made telephone calls, spreading the awful, heart-rending news. Often, Mother could not finish her opening sentence, and Cal would wrest the phone from her hand and announce the shocking details while Mother sobbed. I could not bear to listen. JJ sat outside on the front steps, alone, still wearing her bathing suit bottoms and one of my T-shirts, mosquitoes humming around her head. I sat down beside her, put my arm across her shoulders, but she would not be consoled.

"It's all our fault," she said through her tears.

"I know," I said.

"Why weren't we watching him?" she asked. "I would gladly die if we could just go back and start this day over." She put her head against my shoulder. "Why weren't we watching him?"

At supper that night, nearly ten o'clock, with only four chairs around the table, in the mechanical silence of clicking forks and plates, and pasty mouthfuls of leftover chicken casserole—"we have to eat something," Mother had said, calling us together—JJ's shoulders, and then Mother's, started shaking, and then their sobs drove Cal from the table. He dropped his silverware, pushed back his chair, and slouched into the living room with a beer in his hand.

"I'm sorry!" JJ said. "I said was sorry! How many times do I have to say it?"

"Oh honey," Mother answered, "you know we don't blame you. It's not your fault."

"It *is* our fault," JJ said.

"Where the hell were you two?" Cal said, coming back into the kitchen. "Why weren't you keeping an eye on him?"

I stared at my plate, my stomach churning. "We didn't see him, Cal," I mumbled.

"We're *sorry!*" JJ said, crying loudly.

Cal said, "I just don't understand how this could happen. Hundreds of other children in the goddamned pool, lifeguards all over the place, our own kids up on the balcony, parents everywhere, the water clear as gin, how could it happen? How could this goddamned *happen?*"

"We said we were *sorry!*" JJ screamed.

"I'm not blaming you!" he said. "I just need to know what the hell happened. I just want to understand it."

"You *know* what happened," JJ said. "You're blaming us just by asking! Can't you see that?"

Cal ran a hand through his hair and shook his head. He looked at me, expectantly. What could I say? That instead of watching over David I was trying to cop a peek at the tits of JJ's girlfriends? That talking to my friends was more important to me than the life of my little brother? That I sometimes resented having to drag David along with us when we went to the pool? "I don't know how it happened," I said. I looked down at my plate. "I'm sorry, Cal." I began crying, too.

Cal walked around the table until he stood behind me. I could sense his weight against the back of my chair. He put his hands softly on my shoulders. "It's all right, John," he said. "It's just—" he paused. "This morning David was sitting right here, he was just right *here.*" He started sobbing again and left the room.

I couldn't fall asleep that night. Even with the windows open, the air in my bedroom was hot and sticky. I kept seeing David being pulled from the water, kept smelling the hospital emergency room, kept hearing Mother crying, repeating David's name over and over. Sometime after midnight, JJ came into my room, and without saying anything, she crawled into bed beside me. She had never done this before. She lifted the sheet and slid her legs in against mine, put her arm over my chest, and started sobbing.

Sometime later, JJ got out of my bed and went down the hall. Just after four o'clock in the morning, she returned to my bedroom and sat down on my bed.

She whispered, "I can smell David." She put her fingers under my nose. "I went into his room. I pushed his pillow into my face, and it was like I breathed in a picture of him." She grabbed my hand. "Come here."

We walked into David's bedroom and closed the door. JJ turned on the light, and I covered my eyes with my fingers until they adjusted to the brightness. All around us, we saw David's clothes scattered where he'd left them, his Power Rangers figurines in a shoebox on his bed, his other toys, his little shoes. My Mercury Atlas rocket stood on his dresser.

"He's here," JJ said. "Can't you smell him?" Her voice grew louder. "Maybe he left his soul behind to forgive us, Johnny." She seemed frantic. She sat down on David's bed. "I can feel him!" she said. She started to cry. "I can feel him right here. I can smell the chocolate on his breath. Come here, Johnny!"

David's bedroom door opened and Mother appeared, her eyes glazed, her face sagging and wrinkled. In our family, Mother had always been the calm, organized one. She exuded a stability that was comforting amid the more clamorous spontaneity offered by Cal. Where he was all energy and physical movement, she was stillness and softness, a storm petrel calmly hovering over riled waters. Even her hair, cut short in waves over her ears, always stayed the same. Their marriage was, in many ways, a union of opposites—the shy, studious bookworm riding off with the wild boy on the noisy motorcycle. The woman afraid of heights marrying the skydiver.

JJ ran to Mother and thrust David's pillow into her face. "David's still in here!" she said. Mother tried to hug JJ, but JJ ducked under Mother's arm and closed David's door. "We have to keep this closed!" JJ said.

"Jennifer," Mother said, looking at her.

"Can't you feel him?" JJ asked. "Come on, Anna! At least try!"

Mother shook her head and broke down crying. She reached for JJ, but JJ backed away.

"No!" JJ said. "Get out of here. You're making him go away!"

Mother looked at JJ a long while, then took me by the shoulder and led me from David's room. She closed the door behind us. On the other side of the door, we could hear JJ talking. Mother went back to her room and closed her door, and I went back to my bed.

After a few days we had a funeral, driving behind the white hearse in a long row of cars with their lights on in broad daylight, driving through red stoplights without getting stopped by the police, leaving David's small white, silver, and gold casket behind, perched up on a metal rack at the cemetery under trees because for some reason they don't actually let you watch them filling in the grave with dirt.

We had to sit through an agonizing luncheon afterward, where strange men in suits shook our hands and women wearing too much perfume hugged me and JJ, told us repeatedly it wasn't our fault (each time repeated, the lie grew more painful to hear) and asked us about school, even though it was summer. And then finally everybody left, and we were back home alone again in our haunted house.

Each small sound exploded like a rifle shot. Each spoken word, in the silence of our grief, startled and surprised.

Cal didn't return to work for several days. He called the department secretary and canceled his classes. He sat in his chair in the living room, a framed picture of David balanced on his lap. One morning Mother told him he needed to put the picture down and go teach his classes. Cal looked surprised, but he did as she asked. He put on a shirt and tie and left the house. But he went to the cemetery, sat with his back pressed up against an oak tree near David's grave. Mother found him there after she called the college to speak to him and was told he hadn't come in to teach. When Cal returned home that night, the back of his white shirt was crisp with dried blood. He had an open wound in the middle of his back where he had rubbed it raw against the bark of a tree. Mother fussed over him with gauze and antibiotic ointment, but Cal sat expressionless, staring at the floor.

Chapter 3

JJ began to keep her feather pillow stuffed inside of a Teenage Mutant Ninja Turtles T-shirt she had pulled from David's dirty-clothes hamper. She carried a pair of his dirty white sweat socks in her pocket, and sometimes she wore them stretched over her hands when she ate. She stopped talking to her friends on the phone, stopped wearing makeup, stopped combing her hair, stopped showering, even. One afternoon, she dragged the mattress from her bed down the basement stairs and stayed there.

To sleep, Cal drank St. Ides Malt Liquor by the gallon, and Mother took Valium, which had been prescribed by her doctor. I sometimes snuck one of the small pills out of the bathroom cabinet for myself, and I welcomed the reliable buzz in my brain, the near paralysis of arms and legs, the thickness of my tongue and difficulty swallowing, even, as I fell asleep. Without Mother's Valium, I would lie awake for hours, my legs twitching with energy I didn't have, thoughts racing behind my eyes like an endless line of ants crawling through the maze of veins and arteries in my brain.

We stopped talking about David. No one discussed it openly, but it seemed as if we'd all decided our lives might go on if we did not speak his name. David's bedroom door had been closed and now locked. Each time I passed it, I tried not to look. But of course, my self-consciousness only made passing the closed door more obvious. It is as if the harder you try to forget something, the more easily it stays remembered.

JJ and I continued to have trouble sleeping, JJ especially, who would wake up at one or two in the morning and be unable to fall asleep again. I'd open my eyes and find her sitting cross-legged on the floor in my room, crying, staring at me, wanting to talk but not able to speak coherently about anything. Sometimes I'd go to bed at ten o'clock and I wouldn't fall asleep until two or three in the morning.

Even if I felt exhausted, my brain always filled up with things—memories, scenes, conversations with David—to keep me awake.

Mother took us to a bereavement counselor named Dr. Crawford in downtown Milwaukee. Looking out of her window, which was on the twenty-second floor, we could see the Allen-Bradley clock tower, the sewage treatment plant, and Lake Michigan. To the west, we could see the slaughter yards, the Mitchell Park Domes, and, almost just below us, the tangle of the Marquette interchange, where the whole Milwaukee freeway system came together. It looked like tapeworms in a jar of formaldehyde.

"Pretty weird for a shrink to have an office up so high," JJ said. "Sort of like Weight Watchers meeting in a room above the Ambrosia Chocolate Factory or something."

Dr. Crawford was a well-dressed woman in her 50s with long, thick gray hair pulled back into a ponytail. She kept half-moon glasses on a gold chain looped around her neck, and brought them up to her nose when she needed to read something. She wore lots of makeup and gold jewelry over her darkly tanned skin, and she talked slowly, in a soft voice, the way cowboy actors spoke to spooked horses on television. JJ and I sat down nervously in overstuffed black leather chairs which had been arranged in a small square around an oriental rug in her office, and Dr. Crawford asked us questions about ourselves, how old we were, what school we went to, what we liked to do in our free time, whether or not we were sleeping, eating, attending to daily activities. The whole time, JJ sat with her arms crossed defiantly, giving the briefest answers possible.

"In days not that long ago," Dr. Crawford said, "before antibiotics, before childhood immunizations and other improvements in public health, nearly every family could be expected to lose a child, some even two or more. Of course, it still hurt, terribly, to lose a little brother or sister. But chances were good that others you knew had also gone through it, usually many others. It was simply understood as a terrible thing most people had to go through, and because the pain was shared by so many, it seemed to be less unfair." She looked at me, then at JJ. "It's really, really hard to lose a little brother."

"He's not 'lost,'" JJ said. "He's dead. If he were lost, we'd be out looking for him."

Dr. Crawford ignored JJ and focused on me, her more willing patient. I thought then that I was weaker than my sister. This did not prove to be true in the end. "How are you doing, John?" Dr. Crawford asked. "What are you feeling?"

"I feel sad," I said. "Guilty. Like I'll never be happy again."

Dr. Crawford nodded. "Of course. You're alive and he's not. Survivor's guilt, we call it. People who survive airplane crashes, for example—"

"No!" JJ shouted, almost leaping from her chair. "It's not 'survivor's guilt' or whatever fancy thing you want to call it. We should have been watching him, and we weren't, and he drowned. We killed him."

"But you didn't kill him, sweetheart," Dr. Crawford said softly.

JJ said, "If we'd been watching him, he'd still be alive."

"But that may not be true," said Dr. Crawford. "We always think we could have done something, or should have done something. *Everyone* thinks that. It's human to expect better of ourselves, and it's human to feel we've failed. David's death was an accident."

"Aren't you supposed to be listening to what we're saying?" JJ asked. "Isn't that part of your job?"

Dr. Crawford turned to me. "John, what do you think about all this?"

I started crying. I couldn't even speak, it hurt so badly. My heart felt like a ball of ice.

"Great," JJ said. "You must have gone to college a long time to be able to do this." JJ sat down on the arm of my chair and put one hand on my shoulder. Then she squeezed down into the chair next to me, with one of her legs thrown over mine, protectively.

Dr. Crawford put the palms of her hands together, and put them to her lips. She sat without speaking for some time.

"Sweethearts," she said, finally, "let me help you through this, okay? Will you let me help you?"

I nodded. JJ sat stonily, saying nothing.

Dr. Crawford scheduled a second appointment and also arranged for our family to join a bereavement group, a regular meeting of families who had lost children or parents. When the evening came for the meeting, Mother, JJ, and I attended, but Cal refused to go.

We went to the group twice, two consecutive Tuesday nights in the basement of a small Catholic church. We sat in a circle in metal folding chairs, with bronze plaques depicting the Stations of the Cross, in bas-relief, hung on walls around the room. Dr. Crawford led the discussion. We had to introduce ourselves, and then she asked us to talk about our losses, and how we were feeling. There was one other family there who had just recently lost a child, an eleven-year-old daughter, to leukemia. They brought her picture to pass around, a framed eight-by-ten of a cute blonde girl with butterfly-shaped barrettes in her hair. The other people there, the ones who didn't cry as often, had had children die more than a year earlier. And there was one couple there, a man and a woman who looked to be in their fifties, whose son had died some fourteen years earlier in a motorcycle accident. They were there, Dr. Crawford said, to remind us that while the pain of the loss would always be with us, its hold would gradually weaken, and we would one day be able to step more confidently into the future.

Dr. Crawford explained that suffering the loss of a child put us all on a suspension bridge over deep waters, a bridge many of us would take a long time to cross completely. Beneath us would be the memories of the child we'd lost, both the happy memories and the grief. At first, we'd just stand on the bridge, looking down, lost in the depth of grief and memory, unable to move. A few people, she said—very few—would find the grief too unbearable. She never said what happened to them, but of course they're up high on a bridge, so she didn't need to spell it out. In time, though, she said, all of us would take a few steps, and eventually we would start walking forward, looking straight ahead, moving through our lives. But every once in a while, without warning, we'd look down and remember where we were, and where we'd been.

"The brain builds calluses over difficult memories," Dr. Crawford said. "It doesn't mean they won't always be there. It means someday they won't be so painful. It just takes some time."

Going to the bereavement group was not easy. When Mother told the group what happened, when she explained, in a soft, quivering voice, that her six-year-old son, David, had drowned in the local swimming pool, JJ reached over and grabbed my hand and refused to let go. Mother didn't tell anyone that we had been at the pool with him and should have been watching him. When Mother had finished, Dr. Crawford looked at us and asked if we wanted to add anything, and we both shook our heads.

"Maybe sometime," she said to us, "when you're ready."

But after two sessions, we stopped going to the group. Dr. Crawford called us several times. She urged us to continue counseling, if not with her, then with someone else. But we never went back. JJ returned to the basement. I went back into my room. The medicine Dr. Crawford had prescribed helped us sleep. Mother started going to work regularly again, hoping, I think, that the routine would serve to restore some order to our lives. I tried to return to a life hanging out with my friends, but I always felt distracted, and they seemed uncomfortable, too, the great silence of David's drowning a wall between us. It was a hot summer, and they spent a lot of time at the pool. I would never return to that pool again.

Chapter 4

All this time, Cal mourned the loss of his youngest son with a fierceness none of us fully understood. At first, we didn't notice anything other than grief. His anger stayed inside, building, a change that came slowly, the way a long fuse sizzles as fire makes its way toward a waiting charge of dynamite.

Like the rest of us, Cal had trouble sleeping and had lost interest in things that had once given him pleasure. He no longer listened to music, no longer cleared the kitchen floor for Saturday night dances, didn't invite me outside to shoot baskets in the alley. He didn't read for pleasure, didn't tell off-color jokes during supper or talk about ridiculous mistakes his students had made in their essays. He lost weight. He wore his baggy pants cinched tightly with a brown leather belt, leaving accordion folds of material around his waist.

At supper, he would push his food around on his plate, eat a few bites, and then excuse himself. He'd wander into the living room, sit down on the sofa, and close his eyes. Sometimes he'd try to read, usually from his copy of *The Poems of Edward Taylor*, *which* sat on a shelf with his abridged two-volume edition of the *Oxford English Dictionary*.

Behind the closed door of their bedroom, I could sometimes hear Cal and Mother arguing. But Cal's silence was the most unusual thing. All of that brooding stillness in Cal seemed to be incubating something. He was like a gas leak inside a warehouse, waiting for a spark.

It came on a late Saturday morning. We had just left the house to drive downtown to a Milwaukee Brewers game. Mother had purchased the tickets. She wanted to get Cal out of the house doing something he had always enjoyed doing before. We lived only a few miles from the stadium. In past summers, Cal would take David and me and we'd sit in the lower grandstands in the sun, along the first baseline, and take in the game. He'd buy us big pretzels and ice-cold Pepsi, and he'd eat peanuts by the bagful and drink a cold beer every time someone on the Brewers hit a home run, which in those days practically put him on the wagon. If it was a Friday evening game, after a week of teaching and grading papers late into the night, and if the Brewers had hit two or three home runs, he'd slouch in his seat after the seventh-inning stretch and fall asleep. David and I would sit quietly, smiling at one another, waiting to see whether or not Cal would wake up before the rest of the people in the stadium had gone home.

But that afternoon Cal didn't want to go to the game. He tried to make JJ and I go, but Mother had insisted we go together, "just the boys." And so we left.

Merging onto the freeway, Cal floored the gas on the Ford Escort, and the engine whined as we entered traffic. We passed two cars on the on-ramp. When the speedometer hovered above eighty-five and the car started to rattle, I said, "Cal, what are you doing? Slow down."

He glanced at me but didn't answer. We merged into the right lane. A car in front of us loomed close. Cal swerved wildly to the right shoulder, two wheels going down into the grass, and then Cal steered us back on the freeway. The driver of the other car leaned on his horn, but Cal only looked into his rear-view mirror and frowned.

I grabbed my shoulder belt and pulled it around me, snapped it tight. "Cal," I said, "The speed limit's fifty-five here."

But he didn't slow down. The Escort engine whined. He rolled his window down and the warm air outside blasted against our faces. Our car weaved through traffic. We passed Miller Park and the long line of cars slowly exiting the freeway to enter the parking lot.

"Cal you missed the exit. You have to go back."

But before he could respond, a police siren sounded. The red-and-blue flashing lights were about six cars behind us, and closing. Cal glanced in the rear-view mirror.

The police car weaved through traffic and pulled in behind us, headlights flashing, siren screaming, lights whirling.

"Pull over, Cal," I said.

Cal nodded. He slowed down, turned the car to the shoulder, and stopped in the shade of an overpass with the squad car immediately behind us. The police officer got out of his car. Just as he reached the rear bumper, Cal shifted into gear again and took off.

"Cal!" I screamed at him. "What are you doing?"

He jammed his foot on the gas, looking into his rear-view mirror. "Buckle your seat belt, John," he said to me.

According to JJ, who read about us in the newspaper the next morning, Cal reached speeds of nearly one hundred miles an hour. ("In a Ford Escort?" JJ had said. "It's a miracle.") Cal looked at me. With his right hand, he reached over and slapped my thigh lightly, the way he always did when he was happy about something.

"This is better than a boring old baseball game!" he shouted at me. "Having a good time?"

I shook my head. "No, not really," I said. I gripped the edge of the seat with my fingers. "Should we just go back home?" he shouted.

I nodded. "Yes."

A second squad car had joined in the chase, screaming down the on-ramp to my right as we passed it. With two police cars behind us, Cal exited I-94 East, crossed over the freeway bridge, and got back on I-94 West, headed toward home. A third squad car joined in pursuit. By this time, however, Cal had slowed to fifty-five miles per hour. With the squad cars tailing us, one in each lane, the cars ahead of us pulled over to the shoulders, brake lights glowing red, and Cal and I moved through traffic on the interstate like Moses and the Israelites through the Red Sea. We exited on Seventy- Sixth Street, a four-car parade, crossed Greenfield Avenue, and turned toward home.

We pulled into the alley behind our house and stopped the car by the garage. The police arrested Cal on our lawn. Four men rushed him, knocking him to the ground. On his belly in the grass, Cal looked worried and confused as they bent his arms to cuff his hands behind his back. Mother emerged from the house.

"What in heaven's name is going on?" she cried. She looked at me, panic in her eyes. "What did he do?"

One of the officers helped Cal up to a sitting position. Another of the police officers, one of the older ones, explained to Mother exactly what Cal had done. Her mouth dropped open, and she shook her head. The officer asked her if Cal had been taking any drugs or pre- scription medications, or if he had been drinking. Mother answered no to everything. "He's never even had a parking ticket." She struggled to keep from crying.

Cal sat cross-legged in the grass with his hands cuffed behind his back, looking down toward his ankles. He looked as if he might be counting blades of grass.

When asked if there might be any reason Cal had behaved so strangely, Mother nodded. "We lost our son a few weeks ago," she said.

As she said this, Cal's head slowly dropped. His chin fell against his chest. His shoulders began to quake, and we could hear him sobbing.

The district attorney agreed to drop the most serious charges, but Cal was still fined over six hundred dollars for speeding and reckless driving. As part of the plea bargain, he was also sent to the county hospital for a mandatory psychiatric evaluation.

When Mother brought him home, he was as angry as I'd ever seen him.

"Manic depression!" Cal shouted. "No shit! You don't need a goddamned diploma on the wall to figure that out." He stomped up the stairs to their bedroom and closed the door.

He had come home with a prescription for Prozac, which both embarrassed and infuriated him. Mother carried the bottle in her hand. Twenty milligrams, once a day, to be taken in the morning. The doctor who had examined Cal believed he was suffering from a major depressive episode. Mother put Cal's medication on top of the refrigerator and smiled at JJ and me.

"If he won't take it, I'll take it," JJ said.

Mother shook her head. "Don't joke about something like that, Jennifer," she said.

"I wasn't joking," said JJ, softly.

Cal was arrested for speeding on I-94 twice more the following week as he drove home from teaching—the first time, radar clocked him at eighty-two, the next night at eighty-five. One more infraction and he would lose his license.

"What's happening to him?" I asked.

"He's grieving," Mother said.

JJ said, "I think he's losing his mind."

"Keep those thoughts to yourself please, Jennifer," Mother said.

A few days later, on a Friday morning at the college, in some illogical rage, Cal lost control. He had cut loose with an hour-long rant in the classroom—criticizing politicians, television, the Milwaukee Brewers, America's obsession with celebrity, the commercialization of almost everything—and then had returned to his sixth-floor office, opened his windows, and tossed his computer and monitor into the street below, followed by his printer, his files, his filing cabinet, his desk drawers, and assorted other office equipment. Students had gathered below the building to watch the carnage, some of them applauding as each new item sailed out the window, until they were moved across the street by university officials and local police. A television news crew from Milwaukee arrived in time to see a wooden office chair and four long fluorescent light bulbs explode on the concrete in front of them.

The dean called Mother to apologize, but said he'd had no alternative but to let Cal go. He said the college had repeatedly tried to enroll him in their employee assistance program, which would have provided free psychiatric services, but Cal had refused. He had become a danger to himself, to his students, and to others working with him. He had refused a leave of absence. He had destroyed thousands of dollars' worth of property.

Then that Sunday, Cal disrupted morning services at St. Paul's Lutheran Church. In disagreement with something Pastor Whittier had said during his sermon on Ecclesiastes, Cal stood up on the pew and shouted at the minister while the rest of the congregation buzzed in shock and disgust. I looked at JJ, who stared back at me, wide-eyed. We sank in our pews in embarrassment. In a frenetic rage, Cal began throwing hymnals toward the altar, and church elders hurried to our pew and struggled to pull Cal to the floor. Mother fell to her knees next to him, wrapped her arms around one of his legs, and held on tight, her eyes pinched closed in tears.

At home, Cal locked himself in the bedroom. Mother called the doctor who had performed Cal's psychiatric evaluation. The doctor wasn't yet certain what was wrong with Cal, but his dosage of Prozac would be gradually reduced and then eliminated. At that point, perhaps, a new drug would be prescribed. In the meantime, we would have to try to help Cal in any way we could.

"He's cracking up," JJ said, as we sat together on her mattress on the basement floor. She lit a joint, inhaled, and held her breath. She offered the joint to me but I pushed it away. She exhaled and sprayed into the smoke with a can of lemon air freshener. Her eyes were bloodshot. She leaned forward and kissed me on the cheek, then lay down on her back and covered her face with her pillow, still stuffed into David's T-shirt. Her clavicles looked like sticks, and her ribs showed through her T-shirt. Her dirty clothes hung loosely from her body. Her hair, unwashed, hung in thickly tangled ropes across her shoulders. Her skin smelled sour.

"Do you think we'll ever stop thinking about David?" I asked her.

"Nope," JJ said.

Later that afternoon Cal got into his car and drove away. Ten o'clock came, then eleven, and Mother became frantic. She drove out to check the cemetery, but Cal wasn't there. She came home and called everyone she knew. No one had seen Cal. She called the local police to report him missing. She even called Pastor Whittier.

Then just after one o'clock Monday morning, a police car pulled up to the curb and two officers got out of the car. JJ saw them coming. She'd been sitting outside on the front porch. Fighting tears, she ran upstairs to wake me. "The cops are here," she said. A knot tightened in my stomach, and I went to find Mother. But she was already awake.

She met the police officers at the door. We followed behind her, stood back in the shadow of the doorway, listening.

Cal had been in a car accident on the interstate north of Madison. From what they could determine, he had deliberately driven into a concrete bridge abutment at a high rate of speed. The car careened back into traffic and was struck by an eighteen-wheeler, fully loaded. At impact, Cal's car was cut in half.

Mother began crying.

The officer smiled. "Ma'am, he's going to be fine. He's at Memorial Hospital, but they said he's up walking. I imagine he's got some bumps and bruises. It took a long time to cut him out of the car, but he wasn't badly injured."

Mother composed herself. "Was anyone else injured?"

"No ma'am," they said.

We drove to Madison immediately, a trip of just over an hour at that time of the morning. We entered the hospital, asked for the location of Cal's room, and went to find him. We thought it a good sign that he wasn't in the psychiatric ward.

We found him sitting contentedly on the hospital bed with the light on, wearing a blue hospital patient's smock, reading a hospital Bible. I assumed this was because it was the only reading material in the room. Cal read whatever he could get his hands on. Mother rushed to him. Cal wrapped his arms around her back and buried his face in her neck.

"I'm sorry, honey," Cal said. "I'm so sorry."

Mother leaned away from his arms and Cal smiled at her. He noticed me and JJ, then, and waved. "Hi, John," he said calmly. "Hi, darling. You didn't need to come all this way. I'm fine."

Mother asked him what happened.

"Well, I'm not really sure. I was going about ninety, and I remember hitting the concrete. I didn't see a bright light, nothing like that. It just felt like someone was holding my hand, leading me off the highway. We walked into this beautiful green field covered in a fine mist, like fog, a huge oak tree in the middle of it, with a gorgeous stretch of dark woods in the distance. In my head, I heard words." He lifted the Bible on his lap. "I think it was the Psalm Twenty-Three, King James version. Beautiful writing! I was in the valley of the shadow of death, being made to lie down in green pastures.

"Anyway, as I walked out into this beautiful field, I looked down at my body, and I had blood all over me. My legs were missing. One of my arms was gone. But then suddenly I felt this wash of heat, like a warm wind, against my face, and when I looked back down at my body, the blood was gone, my legs were back, my arm was fine. I was awake, hanging upside down. Outside the window of my car, I could see someone sawing through the door. It sounded like a thousand screeching cats. Sparks were flying."

"You were unconscious," Mother said. "You must have a concussion."

"Yeah, they said maybe that was the case," Cal said.

"What else could it be?" Mother smiled softly. She reached over and placed her hand against Cal's forehead. "I'm just glad you're all right," she said.

"When that man finished cutting through the metal, my door dropped off. I unhooked my seatbelt and climbed out of the car. People stared at me like they were looking at a ghost. One of the paramedics reached out to me with one finger, like he expected it to pass right through."

"You were so lucky," Mother said.

Cal nodded. "I'm no holy roller, you know that, honey. I go to church for you, and for the kids, mostly. Religious hocus-pocus makes me cringe. But look at me. I'm not even scratched! There is just one piece of that car left behind that's any bigger than a television, and it's the piece I was sitting in. How could I have survived something like that?"

"I don't know, but you did. That's all that matters."

"The priest on duty here said the ways of God are a mystery to even the most devout believers, and the ways of men can be just as mysterious."

"Which means what, exactly?" Mother asked.

Cal shrugged. "Which means I might have been saved by God, or I might just be the luckiest son-of-a-bitch on the planet."

I laughed and Mother smiled at him. Cal winked at me. I had to admit he seemed more like himself than at any other time since David died. His voice sounded like him again. He had a spark in his eye.

"Can we take you home?" Mother asked.

"I'm ready if they'll let me go," said Cal. "But you better drive."

Chapter 5

And so by walking away from a car accident that should have killed him, Cal returned to us. Though he cried when he did so, he started speaking of David's death openly, laughed through tears remembering David's dancing, and his fondness for root beer and chocolate. Cal began to eat with us again, too, and along with his returning appetite came his desire to read, to listen to music, to go outside in the yard and cut the lawn. He began sleeping through the night. Whether it was the accident or the result of some other factor unknown to the rest of us, Cal seemed more like himself again, and we were all grateful and relieved to have him back.

Every so often, he'd rattle the newspaper at us as he used to, critical of the writing he found even there. "Look at this!" he said, holding up the advertisement run by a local automobile dealership. "'*Pre-owned*' *cars!* What in the hell does that mean? *Used* is what it means! Might as well call people who are divorced *pre-married*. Call convicted felons *pre-innocent*. No one uses the language with precision anymore, least of all the charlatans selling things in this country."

But the change most noticeable to all of us was Cal's sudden interest in the Bible. After each meal, he'd do some reading, as he always did, but now he'd pass over his beloved *OED* and the collected poetry of Edward Taylor, and he'd pull the Bible he'd pinched from his hospital room off the shelf. It made sense, of course, in a clichéd way, for someone who suffered a terrible loss to turn to faith for comfort. But Cal wasn't like that. He'd frown on such behavior precisely because it was clichéd, because it was too easy, because it represented a level of hypocrisy he was too proud to allow in himself. Even so, his accident, and the peculiar manner of his survival, directed him to the Bible, if only to read, again and again, the language of the twenty-third psalm, which he insisted he'd heard in his head. He read every day as if the Bible were a text open to his interpretation and critique, shaking his head, nodding and muttering to himself, often with a yellow marker in his right hand, for highlighting passages he found particularly noteworthy or beautiful.

Then one morning we woke up and found Cal and our van gone, and he remained away from us for three days. He stranded us at home without a vehicle and left without leaving any notice of where he was going or when he'd be back. At first, Mother was only fearful, but as the days passed, she became angry, then hysterical. She called all of our friends, our extended family in other states, the police, anyone who might know where Cal could be. When he came home again, arriving in the evening just before supper, he walked in the door with a smile on his face, as if he'd only been gone for an hour.

Mother smothered him with hugs but spoke sharply. "Where in the hell have you been?" she asked. "I've been so worried. You can't just leave without telling me where you're going. You have to stop doing this."

"I'm sorry," Cal said. "Really. I'm sorry. I didn't mean to worry you."

"Didn't mean to worry me?" Mother said angrily. "You've been gone *three* days."

"Was it that long?" Cal asked. He seemed genuinely puzzled. His hair was disheveled, and his face glowed red with sunburn.

"Where the hell were you?" Mother asked.

"Let me take a shower, and then we can sit down for supper and I'll tell you all." He motioned to the chairs around the kitchen table. "I've got a story you are not going to believe."

At dinner, Cal boiled over with energy. "Remember when I had my accident, and I told you that someone had taken me by the hand and led me away?"

"Your dream," Mother said. "Yes, I remember."

"That's right," Cal said, nodding. "Whoever took my hand led me to a field, a beautiful, peaceful place in the bottom of a shallow valley, with a row of trees in the distance."

Mother nodded. Cal smiled at her. "I found that field!"

"I thought it was the valley of the shadow of death," JJ said.

Cal laughed. "I thought so, too, darling," he said. "But turns out it was an alfalfa field. In northern Wisconsin, a few miles from Lake Superior."

"Is that where you've been?" Mother said.

"That's where I've been." Cal looked at each of us. "I've been reading the papers, looking to buy some land. Just sort of idle dreaming, you know, thinking about starting over out in the country somewhere. And the other day in the Sunday papers I found an ad for an old abandoned farm up north. I cut it out and put it into my pocket. I tried to forget about it, but I couldn't. And the other night, when I couldn't sleep, I knew it was because I had to take a look at that property. I got on the freeway and kept on going north, drove all night, arrived about four-thirty in the morning. Got myself so thoroughly lost I didn't even know if I was in Wisconsin anymore. The last ten miles or so I went up a gravel road. I had no idea where I was, but up above me, you could see every star in the sky." Cal smiled at me. "Anyway, I passed an intersection and came through the other side, and there it was. I mean, there it was! That very field." He spread his arms excitedly. "Alfalfa, overgrown, with a row of tall evergreens along the north side, and a single white oak in the center, a huge white oak, its limbs spread like a giant umbrella."

"The exact same field you saw in your dream," JJ said skeptically.

"The very one," Cal said.

"I don't believe it," JJ said.

"When I look into your beautiful face, darling, I know it's you," he said. "When I saw that oak tree, it was just as familiar to me. My heart started pounding so hard I had to stop the car. Thought I might have a heart attack. I walked through alfalfa knee-high, all the way to that oak tree, and I stood under it and looked up through the branches at the sky. I walked toward that row of pine trees, and by this time the dew had completely soaked through my pants and my shoes. I pushed through the boughs of those trees and found myself standing on the driveway of an old abandoned farm. A house, a barn, a machine shed, and a silo stood there in the dark, quiet as fence posts. There was a busted-up windmill by the driveway. And out in front, almost covered by tall grass, was a For Sale sign." Cal smiled.

"You didn't!" Mother said.

"Oh, it's contingent on the sale of our house here and a couple other things, including whether or not you'll like it. But yes, I did. I signed the offer papers late this morning, and then I drove like a maniac to get back home by supper."

"We're moving?" JJ asked.

"I didn't know anything about this, Jennifer," Mother said. She looked at Cal. "This is something we usually talk about, right? We make this kind of decision together."

"I realize that," Cal said. "But this is a little bit different."

"How is it different?"

"I've been saved for something," Cal said. "And whatever it is, it's going to happen on that beautiful land. I have to go there. I don't have any choice. And I want you all there with me."

JJ looked at Mother. "He's crazy," JJ said.

Cal laughed. "You might be right about that, honey, who knows? All I can tell you is that something has taken hold of me, and it just won't let me go. Something was pulling me along that highway, flying north like a Canada goose in the springtime. It was as if the path had been cleared for me. After I wandered around the yard a bit, I walked back to my car, pulled in the driveway, and waited until morning. I fell asleep, slept like a baby. And you know who woke me up?"

"God?" JJ asked.

Cal shook his head. "A real estate agent! I opened my eyes and saw a woman in a blue pantsuit standing there, wearing enough makeup to paint a house, knocking on my window. She was holding a sickle, intending to trim that tall grass so people could see her For Sale sign. I introduced myself and asked if the property was still available. She said absolutely. I pulled out the sign and put it in the trunk of her car."

"Honey, if we move all the way up there, how will we make a living?" Mother asked. "What kind of jobs can we find?"

"We'll be farmers," Cal said.

"Farmers!" Mother said. "What do we know about farming?"

"We'll read some books. We'll learn!"

"And what will we raise?"

"We'll raise the roof, darling."

JJ laughed. She laughed softly at first, and then the sound she made seemed like laughter, but it wasn't.

Cal frowned. "Oh, give it a chance, honey. We can simplify our lives, live with a sense of purpose. We can't afford to stay here, anyway. I don't have a job. Your mother's lost her job. We can't even make our house payments anymore."

"You lost your job, Mom?" I asked.

She nodded. "I didn't want you to worry, honey," Mother said.

"Jesus Christ," JJ said. "This house has turned into a loony bin."

"Jennifer, please," Mother said. "That is no way for a young lady to talk."

But I found the whole idea intriguing. I imagined looking at open expanses of sky and stars unhindered by the lights of the city. I thought of open fields where I could launch my rockets without fear of them landing on neighbors' rooftops. And, guiltily, I thought of a place where I wouldn't be reminded of my little brother's death every minute of the day.

It might seem odd that we didn't really talk about it much. Inertia is like a disease, I suppose, and Cal seemed to be the only one with enough energy to carry on, pulling the rest of us with him. We decided, more or less that night, to go ahead with Cal's plan. He raved about it in his energetic, enthusiastic way, sold us on it, really. He talked about how beautiful it would be, how there would be tall grass prairies filled with wildflowers of every color; woods filled with rare orchids, songbirds, black bears, and deer; and birch trees that seemed to glow in the dark at dusk.

"It's like the Garden of Eden," he said. "I'm serious. It feels like paradise. Through the back corner of our far forty runs a little creek, and get this—" he paused for effect, "—it's full of fish. Trout, I think."

"A stream with fish in it," JJ said flatly. "It's a miracle!"

"We'll raise ducks, and keep chickens for the eggs, and we'll get a cow or two for the milk, and we can plant a huge garden in the spring. We can raise goats, and sheep, and cut off the wool and clean it and spin it and make our own coats and blankets. We'll grow raspberries and apple trees and our own strawberry patch."

Just as she had as a younger woman, Mother came under Cal's spell, smiling and shrugging as he talked about the possibilities. But before she would agree to this adventure, she demanded that Cal take her up to see the land for herself, and he did. When they returned, Mother, too, seemed convinced we should move.

"What's it like?" JJ asked. "Tell the truth."

"Well," Mother said, "the house will need a lot of work." She sighed. "I mean, *a lot of work*. But the land is beautiful. It really is."

"So we're moving," JJ said.

Mother nodded. "Yes, honey," she said. "I'm sorry. It won't be easy. But I think it's the right thing to do."

In less than a month, our lives in West Allis were over. Cal put an ad in the paper to sell everything we didn't plan to take north with us. On the day of the sale, he erected a sign in our front yard, "Estate sale! Everything must go!" He also put up a second smaller sign that said, "Now all who believed were together, and had all things in common, and sold their possessions and goods, and divided them among all, as anyone had need. Acts 2:44-5." People flooded our house, hauling away our possessions like discovered treasure: the televisions, the VCR, the stereo, the La-Z-Boy recliner and most of the other furniture, books, CDs, our computer and Nintendo 64, all of Cal's records, pretty much everything, really, that JJ and I couldn't hide. Many of the smaller items Cal gave away for free. He even took off his wristwatch and gave it to a young boy, who pulled it up his arm over his elbow, and left it there.

Our house was purchased later that day at auction by a young couple with four children, all of them under the age of eight, who scattered like cockroaches when their parents came to the house for their final walk-through, the day before they were to move in, on the fourth of September. They paid cash for the house, inherited by the young woman, whose mother had recently passed away at a condo down in Florida.

Cal backed a small U-Haul truck up the alley, and we loaded it with our few remaining possessions—our clothing, our mattresses and dressers, the things Cal thought were necessary from our old, complicated lives. Pictures of David were packed, still in their frames, inside a box, and the box was taped closed and loaded in the U-Haul. The next morning, our friends came to say goodbye to JJ and me. They stood around awkwardly in the alley, watching us put the last of our belongings into the truck then sadly hugged us goodbye.

"Drive carefully, sweetheart," Cal said, as we got into our vehicles to leave West Allis behind.

JJ slammed the door, still crying. She pulled a cassette tape from her back pocket, shoved it into the tape player, and cranked the volume. She lifted a joint from her shirt pocket and put it in the ashtray for the drive.

We drove throughout the day, stopping only for gas and at rest stops to use the bathroom. We drove almost four hundred miles, the final fifteen straight north on an unnamed gravel road with potholes so deep the differential on the U-Haul Cal and Mother drove in front of us bottom-centered and threw sparks. We pulled off the road into a dirt driveway with weeds three feet tall between the tire paths and came to a stop. JJ and I sat together in the mini-van behind the U-Haul and stared. All around us were green woods, thick with vines and undergrowth. In every direction were miles of rolling fields, rotting gray fence posts, and rusted barbed wire. The gray skies sagged with thick clouds, made you want to crouch beneath them.

"This is the middle of nowhere," JJ said.

We had moved to Bayfield County, Wisconsin, just south of Lake Superior, on land bordering the Chequamegon National Forest, because Cal believed he had been called to a new life on eighty acres of woods and farmland he had seen in a dream.

"Look at that freaking house!" JJ said, finding her voice. "Needs some work, my ass! It needs to be condemned."

The one-and-a-half-story house looked uninhabitable. Some of the windows were broken or cracked, and the tin roof and metal chimney pipe poking through it were streaked with rust. The lapboard siding was a weathered, unpainted gray. Cast-iron wood stoves in the kitchen, living room, and upstairs hallway were flaked orange with rust. Upstairs, the ceilings were water-spotted, and pigeon shit and feathers covered the carpeting in the hall. The house had only two bedrooms, so JJ and I would have to divide and share one of them, a prospect that did not thrill either of us. Downstairs, trails of tiny mouse turds led everywhere. A raccoon or opossum had been living beneath the kitchen sink. A barn swallow's nest hung like a turban over the front porch light, with congealed droppings piled beneath it.

The barn was in better shape than the house. It, at least, had recently been painted red, the metal roof watertight. There were about fifty bales of old alfalfa hay in the loft. The concrete silo beside it was empty but solid. And a smaller barn, a machine shed, really, was also in good shape. It was spacious and bright, with large windows made of old bubbly glass. The little hen house across from the barn was full of dirty feathers, dusty straw, and dried, hard chicken shit.

A huge overgrown garden the size of half a football field grew behind the house, with volunteer tomato vines, pumpkins, zucchini, and squash all weed-choked and tangled together. The zucchini were so dark green they looked black, and most of them were as thick as logs and split open, the flesh-toned scars revealing rows of seeds. Ants ran in and out of the squash and pumpkins. In the front yard, two apple trees sagged with worm-eaten fruit. Beneath it, in the tall grass, yellow jackets buzzed around rotting windfalls and tunneled into their sweet, sticky flesh.

In the center loop of our dirt driveway stood an old windmill, its steel legs rusted and covered six feet high at the bottom by a thick tangle of raspberry canes. On top, half of the fan blades were missing.

Before we unloaded anything, we wandered the property together. Flying grasshoppers bounced off of our legs and buzzed in the field grass just ahead of us. Mosquitoes whined in our ears.

"*This* is where we're going to live?" JJ said.

Cal smiled. "If the Pilgrims could land at Cape Cod in 1620 in the middle of winter and start from nothing, we can certainly handle this place. We'll be self-sufficient. We'll grow our own food and raise our own animals."

"Cal, we don't know how to farm," I said. "We don't know the first thing about it."

Cal winked at me. "We'll learn, John."

"Where's the high school?" JJ asked. "Are we going to have to ride the bus for an hour?"

Cal glanced at Mother and smiled. "Your mother and I have talked that over, and right now the plan is to homeschool you. We're going to need your help here on the farm, at least in the beginning."

"No school?" I said.

"I didn't say that," Cal said. "We'll get your books from the district, and we'll go from there."

"What if I want to go to school?" JJ asked.

"Let's just see how it goes."

JJ looked at me and I shrugged. A few more months without school didn't sound too bad to me.

Across the fields, I looked back at the barn and silo, the shed, the little decrepit house. Beyond that, to the northwest, a wall of dark clouds rolled in, and streaks of lightning flashed through the clouds. The low murmur of thunder followed. A cool wind swirled around us. It rippled the fields from end to end, as if someone had passed over them with a giant comb. The wind smelled like water and, faintly, like fish.

"Looks like a storm's coming in." Cal lifted his face to the sky and said, "'Let us now fear the Lord our God, Who gives rain.'" He smiled. JJ rolled her eyes. "That's from Jeremiah," Cal said. "A wild guy, that Jeremiah. Bet he could sing and dance like James Brown. Well, we best start getting that truck unloaded before the storm hits."

All night, as JJ and I tossed and sweat on uncovered mattresses on the floor in our sweltering room, the rain pelted the house and dripped rhythmically through the roof, bleeding into the plaster ceiling above us. We kept one window cracked open. JJ reclined on her mattress in a T-shirt, sweating. Each time the lightning flashed, I could see her silhouetted there, on her back, her head propped on a pillow. The smell of marijuana drifted across the room. When she inhaled, I could see the tip of her joint glowing orange. A loud clap of thunder made JJ call out.

I said, "You okay?"

She rolled toward me. "No," she said weakly. She seemed to be crying.

I left my mattress. I crawled across the wooden floor between us, and JJ moved to the side of her mattress to allow me room beside her.

As I lay beside my stepsister, shoulder to shoulder in the heat, rain lashed the house and poured over the gutters. I don't know if JJ slept at all, but when the thunder and lightning finally rolled into the distance, I drifted away.

The cooing of pigeons nesting inside the eaves woke us to sunshine the following morning. And then the sound of footsteps on gravel pulled me from bed to the open window. I squinted to see in the sun.

Outside, Cal stood alone on our driveway, looking up at a gray pigeon perched on the windmill. Slowly, Cal extended his arm and opened his hand, palm up. Like a mirror, his palm seemed to reflect the sun. He pursed his lips, let out a calming, mournful whistle. The pigeon cocked its head. Cal whistled again. The pigeon dropped from its perch, and in a fluttering of wings, extended its pink feet and landed softly in the center of Cal's hand.

PART II: FIRE

In silent night when rest I took
For sorrow near I did not look
I wakened was with thund'ring noise
And piteous shrieks of dreadful voice
That fearful sound of "fire!" and "fire!"
Let no man know is my Desire.

—Anne Bradstreet,
"Verses upon the Burning of Our House, July 10th, 1666"

Chapter 6

After breakfast we stood in the weed-choked driveway, basking in the sweet, earthy morning-after air left behind by the thunderstorm. Rainwater glistened in tire ruts, in potholes, in sunken areas of distant fields. It dripped rhythmically from tiny holes in the clogged gutters, flowed in thick muddy rivers along the ditches. Rain had fallen with such force the orange flower heads of day lilies growing near the road had been pounded into the grass. But the air pulsed with the fresh scent of a world washed clean. All around us echoed the crisp singing of birds and the calling of morning insects. Beyond the barn, the leaves on a small stand of quaking aspen fluttered and glowed like pieces of silver.

Cal said, "I feel as if we've just stepped out of Noah's ark."

"I'm sure the ark was more watertight than this house was last night," Mother said.

"And less full of animal crap," said JJ.

Cal laughed. He was in a soaring, delirious mood. "We'll get the house in order, don't you worry," he said. "But we've got to finish unloading this truck so I can get it back to town." Unloading the U-Haul, Cal and I beat a path through the long wet grass from the driveway to the front door. Every step taken in the grass brought clouds of fierce mosquitoes that swirled annoyingly around my head and whined in my ears. JJ and Mother remained in the house, sweeping the floors, washing out kitchen drawers and cabinets with soapy water and disinfectant, brushing spider webs from the walls and ceilings. They opened all the windows, some of which had no screens, and every few minutes a mop or broom would emerge through the wall to be shaken, and a cloud of dust and debris would drift away in the breeze.

The house as yet had no running water. "No flush toilet!" JJ had screeched. "You've got to be kidding me!" But Cal calmly assured her that one would be forthcoming. Eventually. No electricity ran to the property, either. The nearest lines ended a quarter mile down the road. Fresh water had to be drawn from a well using an iron hand-pump that stood waist-high in the yard, just outside the kitchen door. The pumped squeaked and groaned as we worked it, but the water came up from deep underground, shockingly cold and delicious.

During the afternoon, Mother took breaks from her inside work to wander around the house with gardening gloves on, pulling weeds from overgrown flowerbeds, exposing the wild daisies, black-eyed Susans, Queen Anne's lace, and other wildflowers we could not name that grew along the rock foundation on the south side of the house. Along the southeast corner, near the driveway, she found a stand of bright yellow sunflowers and shorter stalks of millet that had sprouted and grown beneath a dilapidated bird feeder mounted on a steel pole. Two rows of white spruces, the tallest of them perhaps sixty or seventy feet, grew in a windbreak along the field on the north side of the house, with feathery white pines bobbing in the breeze to the west of them, near the ditch. All along the driveway stood dainty-looking blue chicory and thick-stemmed bull thistle six-feet high, with stalks as big around as my wrist, their thorny green shoots thick with fuzzy pastel-purple blossoms the size of baseballs.

"Who lived here?" I asked Cal. We'd just carried one of the heaviest of our belongings—Mother and Cal's bedroom dresser—from the truck into the house, and were sitting in the grass, resting.

"I asked the realtor that very question," Cal said. "Some old hermit. A snowmobiler found him back in February. He was on the floor in the living room, his golden retriever curled up beside him, both of them frozen solid. The guy broke a hip outside on the ice, crawled into the house, and froze to death."

"Geez," I said, "how awful."

"He was ninety-one years old, living on his own," Cal said. "He didn't have electricity or a furnace, but he did have a cell phone, I guess. Sitting right on the end table next to his body."

"Are we getting a phone?" I asked.

"I don't know. We've got the mailbox. A phone gets you out, but it lets an awful lot in, too. That old guy had a telephone, but when he broke his hip, he didn't even call anyone. He didn't want to get carted off to some hospital, where they'd stick him full of needles, cut him up, make him bleed out his last dollar paying for it all. He just curled up with his dog and waited to die. More peaceful than coding in a hospital ward."

Cal shrugged and looked up at the roof of the house. "We didn't pay much for this place. But we own it clear. And we have money left over for food, seed, farm equipment, animals. We're going to make it work, John." He paused, looked down at the ground. "Listen," he said, holding up a hand for silence.

"What?"

"Can you hear that?"

"Hear what?"

"Nightcrawlers," he said. "It's so quiet you can hear them crawling around right under your feet."

I laughed. "Yeah, right."

"No really," he said. "Sounds sort of like the bass guitar riff on 'Pretty Woman.' Roy Orbison's version."

We both laughed. I looked up at the kitchen window and saw Mother smiling, watching us. I waved, and she waved at me and disappeared.

"John, let me ask you something," Cal said. "Do you believe that God talks to people?"

"What do you mean? Like out loud?"

He shrugged. "No, not exactly. I mean he comes into your head and you hear him, not with your ears but with your brain, maybe."

"I don't know. I have no idea."

"Okay, then let me ask you this. Do you believe God spoke to Nat Turner, or to Joan of Arc?"

"Who's Nat Turner?"

"He was enslaved in Virginia. In 1831, God spoke to him in a cornfield, told him to lead a slave insurrection. So Nat Turner led a group of fellow slaves in a revolt across Southampton County. They got maybe ten miles, killed about fifty slaveholders before they were caught. They hanged him and displayed his knuckles in a store window, but not before Nat Turner served notice that slavery would not be abided any longer. You never heard of that?"

I shrugged. "Maybe they cover Nat Turner junior or senior year," I said.

Cal laughed. "I swear, people don't know shit if they haven't seen it on *Oprah*. At least she's got people reading books, I'll give her that, but my God, the idiot box has completely taken over this country."

I nodded and remained silent, always the best response if you wanted to cut Cal short when he went on one of his rants.

"Well anyway," he said, "God spoke to Joan of Arc—you have heard of her, at least—and Nat Turner in some way. I don't want you to tell your mother or your sister about this, because there's no need to get them all riled up over something I can't even explain. But at night sometimes, when I'm trying to fall asleep, I believe I can hear God speaking to me."

Cal looked hard into my face to try to gauge my reaction. I kept my composure. I shrugged. "You hear voices?"

"No!" he said. "Not like that. I'm not schizophrenic! Are you listening? I'm not hearing voices. It's more like your brain is a tilled garden and God is dropping seeds in the furrows. It's like some kind of tactile language, one you feel."

"So what does he say?" I asked.

"That's the thing," Cal said. "That's what's got me puzzled. I'm not sure. I get just bits and pieces. I feel like David has something to do with it, but I don't really know. At times I can almost understand. I feel as if maybe I'm being asked to build something, something big, but I can't quite see what it is."

"Not an ark, I hope."

Cal laughed. "I sure as hell hope not! It's hard to explain, John. It's like I can almost see what it is, but I'm seeing it through thick fog."

"Didn't Joan of Arc get burned at the stake?"

Cal nodded. "For heresy," he said. "When God speaks to people, often not too long afterward the shit hits the fan."

I almost said, "Anything's possible," but he might have corrected my sloppy logic. Anything, he would have pointed out, isn't possible. Clichés muddy our thinking. I shrugged instead.

Cal smiled at me and put a hand on my shoulder. "I think it's possible that God might be speaking to me. To *me*." He put a hand to his chest. "To tell you the truth, it scares the crap out of me. But I'm going to listen."

I laughed. "All right," I said.

He nodded. "I'm going to listen," he said, again. He put a finger to his lips, to remind me to keep that to myself. He got to his feet, and we walked back into the U-Haul to finish unloading our belongings.

Chapter 7

Our initial days and weeks at New Eden were a haze of new experiences and hard labor. I worked and sweat like I'd never worked before. Some nights, after washing up with water Mother had heated on the gas stove, I collapsed on my mattress, too exhausted to even take off my socks or my pants. I really didn't mind the work. It distracted me, served in part to make me forget all the things I missed—the television, the radio, music, the computer, trips to the mall with my friends, the telephone. I felt as if I had been addicted to those things, and in idle hours I suffered a painful withdrawal. The silence, too, could be unnerving. It seemed eerie to be in a house without a television on somewhere. The lack of music, especially, was difficult. JJ and I had brought along our CDs and boom boxes, but without electricity in the house, they were of little use to us. We used batteries for a while, but when those went dead, we didn't buy more.

Cal continued to read the Bible after each meal, particularly after supper, and he had begun to read aloud to us while Mother, JJ, and I did the dishes. He started at the beginning, in the Old Testament, making his way through Genesis, Exodus, Leviticus, Numbers. He read enthusiastically, as if he were reading a good novel, changing his voice when he got to dialogue, pausing at dramatic moments, reading faster during the most exciting sequences. Editorializing in his own, inimitable way.

JJ did not adapt as quickly to our new life as I did. Her insomnia returned. Often, at two or three in the morning, I'd wake to find her sitting downstairs on the sofa in the living room, crying, idly scraping the cuticles from her fingers with a sharp fingernail or the blade of a steak knife until they bled. At other times she'd just stare out the window, her body rocking from front to back as if she were a tree blown by gusts of wind.

"I heard David," she'd say, sometimes. "I thought he was calling me."

"You were dreaming," I'd tell her.

In the morning I'd usually find her in our room again, sitting with her knees pulled to her chest in the corner, looking out the window, the tips of her fingers encrusted with dried blood. Sometimes we'd find her outside in the yard under one of the apple trees, her body pocked with the round swollen blisters of mosquito bites, yellow jackets hovering around her tangled hair. Mother would walk her back inside, dab at the mosquito bites with a cotton ball soaked in rubbing alcohol. Sometimes afterward, JJ would fall asleep on the sofa for an hour or two, but in the evening, she would wander the house again.

Though it was difficult initially, I got used to the rustic conditions. It took a lot of energy and resourcefulness to make our house habitable, but each day, things improved. We replaced the broken windows with new glass, put in new screens, tore up the soiled carpeting, sanded and painted the floors and the walls. We cleaned and sanded the cast-iron wood stoves, hauled out buckets full of wood ash, applied a coat of black stove paint to each of them. One sleepless night, JJ scrubbed clean the large cast-iron claw-foot bathtub in the tiny washroom downstairs off the kitchen, and we found her asleep in there the following morning. We boiled water on the stove and took turns bathing in that tub in the evening, draining it each time through a hole in the floor. Sometimes JJ would pull up three or four wild mint plants that grew in a corner of the garden, their roots kinked and bright white, and she'd float the plants in her bathwater. She'd emerge later, her wet hair smelling like peppermint.

When we drained the bathtub, the wastewater flowed through a black drainage hose Cal had stretched to the vegetable garden. He intended to recycle everything, to make use of "natural technology," as he called it, whenever possible. Sometimes when it rained, Cal stood naked behind the machine shed with a bar of soap, and showered. When the wind blew from the west, he opened the doors on both sides of the barn and watched the dust blow out.

The privy was connected to the house through a door on the west side, and it took the most getting used to. The room was maybe six feet wide by eight feet deep, with a wooden box mounted to the floor against the back wall, and a black toilet seat mounted on top of that. A small oil lamp and box of matches rested on a table next to it, for evening visits. A small bucket of powdered lime and a plastic scoop rested on the floor. The pit below had to be almost eight feet deep, and initially it took some nerve to actually sit down above it and attend to business. In the afternoons, when the sun beat on the west side of the house, shining through the privy's only window, the temperature inside soared, and clouds of black flies would swirl up out of the pit, buzzing incessantly against the window glass. So to avoid the heat and smell of the outhouse on the hottest days, I became accustomed to walking far out into the fields or woods to relieve myself.

Cal's ingenuity was on display often, and I frequently assisted him in making whatever improvements he had in mind. He rented a well-drill to put in a new well point, and he ran a line from the well to the kitchen sink, so we'd have running water in the house. He buried the lateral line six feet deep so it would not freeze in winter. He purchased solar electricity panels and installed them on the south-facing roof of the house and a bank of batteries to store the power for cloudy days. Along with a five-thousand-watt gas generator, for emergencies, this would produce just enough electricity to run our water pump, our small refrigerator, and a chest freezer. We lit the house in the evenings with candles and kerosene lamps. With no washing machine or dryer, we washed our clothes by stirring them with a broomstick in a bathtub filled with soap and boiling water, wringing them out by hand, and hanging them outside on a clothesline to dry. Cal hoped to stay completely "off-grid," so we'd never have to pay an electric bill, though he agreed that if we needed more electricity than we could provide for ourselves, he would pay to have the electric company run power to the house, and would wire the inside himself, when the time came.

To supplement firewood already split and stacked just off the porch, Cal and I cut down about twenty dead oak, maple, and birch trees from the woodlot on our property, cut them to length with a chain saw, and split them with an ax and a wedge until we had a stack of firewood that would have filled the Rainbow Park pool from end to end and clear up to my chin.

Cal traded in our mini-van for a used one-ton red Chevy pickup truck with four-wheel drive, and he used it to haul whatever supplies we needed and to drive along the fenced boundaries of our farm, putting up wooden signs he painted on old barn board—bright green letters against a white background—that read: "NEW EDEN FARM." On the rare occasions we all went into town as a family in those early days—the closest town of consequence was Iron River, about thirteen miles south—JJ and I had to sit in the extended cab behind the truck's front seat, on small fold-down platforms, face to face, our legs and feet tangled together.

We met a few people in town, introduced ourselves to the cashiers at the grocery cooperative, the hardware store, and the gas station, but because we lived so far out, we didn't have any real neighbors. Our closest neighbors, dairy farmers who lived about four miles south of us in a house that looked even more run-down than ours, had stopped by just once in a battered pickup to introduce themselves shortly after we moved in. Their names were Bill and Eunice Hall, and they seemed to be nice enough, though they were awkward, socially, the kind of quiet, reserved people who respected others' privacy, and expected theirs to be honored as well.

Bill Hall was a tall man with tiny eyes that never seemed to stop moving. A thick black beard clung like moss to his weather-beaten face, and he wore a soiled blue baseball cap with an American flag on the front. He carried a small pistol in a leather western-style holster that he wore around his waist and spoke softly, in brief carefully measured phrases, barely opening his mouth when he did so.

His more talkative wife, Eunice, was short and stocky, with a round face that seemed permanently flushed, short brown hair, and large glasses that made her look like an owl. She wore a blue sweatshirt emblazoned with decals of red cardinals, her favorite bird, as she told Mother. Both of them wore black rubber boots that smelled like cow manure.

Cal and Bill talked about the weather, about where we used to live, about the work we'd been doing on the house. Cal pointed to Bill's pistol.

"Little thirty-eight," Bill said. "Coyotes got two of our calves last spring."

"Or maybe wolves," Eunice said, nodding.

"Could have been wolves," Bill said.

"There are wolves around here?" Cal asked.

"Some," Bill said. "But they're protected." He smiled when he said this.

"We see a lot of black bears, too," Eunice said.

Bill nodded. "They make nice rugs," he said.

They talked awhile longer, until the conversation trailed off.

"Well," Cal said, finally, "it is nice to meet the neighbors." He shook Bill's hand.

"Likewise," Bill said. Mother and Eunice shook hands. Bill and Eunice got back into their truck and closed the doors.

"If you ever need anything," Bill said, out the open window.

"Thank you," Cal said. "I'm sure I'll be asking for your advice sooner or later."

Bill nodded and smiled. "Farmers ain't ever short of that." They drove off.

"A little unusual," Mother said, as we watched them rumble down the road.

"Country people," said Cal.

Once the barn and chicken coop were prepared, and the pasture fences repaired and tightened, Cal began to buy some animals. His initial purchase was three dairy cows, all of which he acquired for just three hundred dollars, delivered, a price so low, he said, he had to buy them all. We let them wander in the small five-acre pasture south of the barn, and they returned to the barn at nightfall, where we'd lock them in their stalls with a supply of fresh water. Each morning I'd let them out again, refill the water, and shovel manure from the stalls, hauling it to the garden in a wheelbarrow. Because they were the first cows we'd ever seen up close, or touched, we were afraid of them. They were beautiful, with large splotches of black against a background of white, but could be skittish and unpredictable. They were huge, too, and prone to sudden loud mooing that could raise the hair on your head if it caught you by surprise.

"When do we milk them?" I asked Cal, the second or third day we owned them.

"I don't know," Cal answered.

The Halls sold us an extra rooster and a small starter flock of chickens, a mix of Plymouth Rocks and Brahmas, which they said weathered the winter cold better than other breeds. The chickens spent a lot of time cautiously exploring their new surroundings, picking gravel along the driveway, and wandering through the garden eating, from what we could tell, just about everything. After a few days, we discovered a few brown eggs in some of the nesting boxes inside the coop.

Cal also bought a few white turkeys, which we kept fenced behind the barn, with an old straw-filled doghouse inside for shelter, and four Rouen ducks, two males and two females. They looked like large mallards as they waddled around the yard. The turkeys seemed to be afraid of everything. If a chipmunk ran through their enclosure, they'd squawk wildly and pile into a corner, huddled there until the danger passed. The ducks wandered everywhere together, and they seemed most happy when it rained. They'd stand in a large puddle with their beaks pointed to the dripping sky, water running off their feathers, their eyes squinted in duck ecstasy.

An old John Deere tractor had been left behind in the machine shed, and it came included with the property. At a farm auction over near Washburn, Cal bought a plow, a planter, a hay cutter and baler, and other assorted implements we'd need to begin farming. The next spring, he planned to put in a huge vegetable garden to grow enough produce to last the year, but he had not yet decided what cash crop to put in. He leaned toward soybeans, but wasn't yet certain.

It took him a few days, but through trial and error, he figured out how to cut our alfalfa field, and he finished baling the alfalfa during a light fall rain. We got soaked as we hauled the bales to the barn in the back of the pickup truck, ten at a time, a chore we didn't finish until well after dark. In the morning, we had a large sweet-smelling stack of more than eighty alfalfa bales drying in our barn, enough, we hoped, to feed our cows through the winter.

By mid-October, as the nighttime temperatures dropped below freezing, we had the house and property in good repair. We gave the appearance of a family of farmers who knew what they were doing. It would not be long until this appearance proved to be illusory.

Chapter 8

We had finished eating dinner. Cal had opened the Bible to begin reading, but he paused, turned his head to the side. I noticed it, too, a strange glow fluttering against the windows.

"Where's that light coming from?" he asked.

Mother got up from her chair and went to look out the kitchen window. Her knees seemed to buckle. She gripped the sink for support. "The barn!" she screamed.

The dance of light against our windows was fire.

Cal leaped to his feet. We all rushed to pull on our boots and coats and ran outside into the cold to discover our barn engulfed in flames. Smoke billowed out of the cracks of the sliding doors and poured from the vent in the peak of the roof. Our cows bellowed madly from inside. From behind the barn, I could hear the turkeys screeching.

"John!" Cal screamed. "The cows!"

He tugged open the sliding door, and thick black smoke billowed into his face, concealing his body. He crouched and moved inside, and I followed him, the smoke so thick we could barely see. Cal headed for the stall along the back wall of the barn, and I moved toward the other two, which were closer to the door. The pungent scent of smoke made me retch. I could feel the intense heat against my face. Sweat beaded on my forehead and under my clothes. Bales of burning hay and loose bedding straw crackled all around me, snapping like pine knots, and the flames had already spread up the walls, crawling up the thick wooden support posts that reached to the roof. I heard Cal shout, and one of the cows broke from her stall and ran bellowing through the barn, knocking me down as she passed. She was on fire, her hide smoking and glowing orange.

I found the other two stalls and opened one of the gates. The cow inside bellowed but wouldn't run out. Her eyes bulged, and she kept jumping wildly into the wood at the back end of the stall. She'd already bloodied her nose and one of her eyes. Blood glistened on her chest. I slapped her on the rump as hard as I could then leaned a shoulder into her hip to spin her around. When she spotted the open gate, she broke for it and ran out, her mouth open and dripping. The other cow was equally frightened and refused to leave her stall. I stood behind her and wrenched her tail over her back, leaned against her hindquarters with all of my strength. I swung a boot into her ass. This got her attention, made her jump forward, and when her shoulders were free of the stall, she ran out, swerving wildly to avoid the flames licking at the wood.

I ran out of the stall and crouched along the wall again, choking on the smoke. Cal was already outside with Mother. She held a garden hose with her thumb over one end, a weak stream of water spraying ten feet up the side of the barn.

"Let me," Cal yelled. "You kids get back."

The fire blazed, hissing and huffing like a living thing, and though the outside temperature was below freezing, the heat felt like the summer sun against our faces. I stood back with JJ beside me, my hair damp, my clothes and skin blackened. We glowed in the bright light. Tips of orange flame poked through the barn roof and flicked, like small forked tongues, through the gaps in the burning boards.

Cal stood as close to the barn as the intense heat would allow, the tiny stream of water falling almost uselessly on the flames. It was like trying to put out a forest fire by pissing on it, but he stood his ground, shrouded in mist and smoke, the water blowing back over him. Ice formed on his beard and in his hair and shone in a thin crust on his pants and boots.

The hayloft caught fire, the old hay crackling like lightning spreading across the sky, and suddenly the whole barn seemed to be a wall of flames. The heat drove us back. Cal turned his back and angrily threw down the garden hose. The fire roared and crackled and breathed, sucking everything inward as the superheated air rippled high above the barn, orange embers rising into the night sky like tiny comets.

"Son of a bitch," Cal said.

For fifteen or twenty minutes, we sat together in silence, watching our barn burn. South of the farm, from down the road, we heard the wail of a siren. We looked up and saw a single fire truck approaching, red lights flashing. Someone, the Halls, we learned later, had seen the flames and called the volunteer fire department. Just as the fire truck reached our driveway, the rear wall of the barn collapsed, and the roof dropped into the smoke and fire with a thunderous roar. I could see the burning barn reflected in the clear panes of the windshield as the fire truck turned in.

The flashing lights made our whole yard pulse red. Two men jumped down from the fire truck, pulled the hose across the driveway, and trained it on the flames. The engine roared as the pumps kicked in, and a wall of water hit the fire, sending plumes of white smoke into the sky. The silver reflective tape around the arms and torsos of the firefighters' yellow parkas glowed in the light as they moved from side to side with their hose.

More headlights came up the road, and Bill and Eunice Hall's truck entered our driveway and came to a stop. They hurried over to us, shook their heads sympathetically. Eunice looped an arm around Mother's waist. We watched as the water slowly beat down the flames, but by the time they had the fire under control, nothing was left of the barn but its rock-and-mortar foundation, a handful of charred beams, a few dozen half-burned boards, and the twisted, blackened steel panels that had once served as the roof. The fire truck would remain parked in our driveway for nearly two hours after the fire was out, waiting to be certain the fire would not rekindle, the remains of the barn smoking.

We heard a noise behind us, and one of our cows staggered out of the darkness, her head hung low. She'd been burned terribly. Large bloody patches of flesh oozed along her sides. Her tail looked like a blackened stick. She also seemed to be blind. Bill Hall said something to Cal, then walked to his truck and came back with a rifle. He put the muzzle of his rifle to her head, and pulled the trigger. At the report, the cow dropped belly first in the grass.

None of us slept well that night, the smell of smoke on our skin, our hair, and our clothes. In the morning, we walked outside, saddened by the sight—the charred rock foundation, the twisted steel of the roof, the thick wooden beams, virgin timber, perhaps a century old, now blackened and useless. Small rivulets of smoke still swirled from embers buried in the rubble, as they would for days afterward. Our dead cow bulged grotesquely, a heap of charred, bloody flesh. Because she seemed too large to bury, Cal dragged her around back of the barn foundation with the tractor, doused her with gasoline. She smoldered most of the day until all that remained was a patch of ash and tiny fragments of bones.

All of our turkeys died in the fire, too, though our ducks and chickens survived. Our two remaining cows wandered aimlessly around the outside of the barn, hungry, confused, and frightened. Soot covered their bodies, but they didn't seem badly injured.

Bill Hall returned in his truck and trailer, volunteered to care for our cows until we had a new shelter for them. Cal and I helped him load our cows into the back.

"I suppose something like this will keep their milk back awhile longer," Cal said.

Bill shook his head. "You won't get milk from these two," he said.

"What do you mean?" Cal said.

"They're old and dry," Bill said. "You think they were springing heifers?"

Cal sighed and shook his head. He looked disappointed. "I don't know what I thought."

"They're old now, only suitable for eating. You can butcher them," Bill said. "It's not a total waste."

Cal waved an arm at the smoking pile of rubble that had once been our barn. "I don't know what happened here," he said. "What causes something like this?"

"Hard to say," Bill answered.

"We didn't have any heaters going, yet," Cal said. "I don't know how that fire could have started."

"You put your hay up wet?" Bill asked.

Cal glanced at me. "It was raining when I finished baling it," he answered.

"You let it dry out in the field before putting it up?"

Cal shook his head.

Bill nodded. "Spontaneous combustion, most likely," he said. "Wet hay gets hot enough, it'll light itself on fire."

Cal shook his head, angry and disappointed. "Damn it," he said.

Bill shrugged. "Lessons learned the hard way are the ones we don't forget. I got extra alfalfa hay if you need it."

"I appreciate that," Cal said.

Bill Hall drove away with our cows, and Cal and I went to work building stalls on one end of the machine shed, using boards we salvaged from the old barn.

Cal had said we would learn farming by trial and error. Our first error had been a large one. It was only the first of many trials to come.

Chapter 9

The loss of our barn had been a setback, but Cal recovered quickly. We built stalls in the shed, got our elderly cows back from Bill Hall, purchased enough alfalfa to get them through the winter, and turned our attention to completing work on the house.

One morning Cal woke up in a noisy mood, bursting with energy, and our plans changed. He grabbed Mother, lifted her in his arms, and spun her around in circles. He crowed like our rooster, flapping his bent elbows against his sides.

"What has gotten into you?" Mother asked, laughing.

Cal sat down on his chair at the kitchen table and smiled at us. He winked at me, then announced that he'd had a vision.

"A vision?" Mother asked.

"A revelation." That night, he said, something, or someone, had come to him and told him to stop everything he was doing and build a church. It wouldn't be an ordinary church but something never before seen: a small cathedral built completely of logs, relying on the architectural integrity of the hexagon for its shape and strength.

"God has given the bees an instinct to build hexagonal honeycombs, and this is the shape that has come to me. If the Egyptians could build pyramids without bulldozers or cranes, we can certainly erect a hexagonal log cathedral."

"A church," Mother said.

"That's right," Cal said.

Mother's face fell. She eyed him cautiously. "Honey, what are you talking about?" she asked.

Cal raised his hands. "I know it sounds ridiculous," he said.

"You dreamed this?" Mother asked.

"Not exactly," Cal said. "I can't really explain it. It's more of a strong feeling than a dream. But I could see the structure in my mind."

Mother sighed. "Why don't we just join a church in town?" she said. "We could join a congregation in Iron River."

"I don't want to join a church," Cal said. "I want to build one."

"Why?"

"I've already told you."

"How are you going to build a church all by yourself?" Mother asked.

"It would be more the size of a large chapel," Cal said.

"Even so."

"John can help me."

Mother protested, but Cal remained steadfast. We'd finished most of the necessary work on the house, he argued, and we weren't even in the full grip of fall yet. He had the time. We had the tools and the wood. This was something he needed to do.

"When God asked Noah to build the ark, did Noah say, 'Ah, hell, the old guy's crazy. I'm not going to do that.' No he didn't. He did as he was asked."

"That was Noah," Mother said. "That was a long time ago."

"You don't believe God talks to people now?" Cal asked.

Mother's eyes teared. "Cal, I don't want to argue."

"We're not arguing," Cal said. "Don't cry, honey! Why are you crying?"

"What are we going to do with a church out here?" Mother asked. "Just tell me that."

"I don't know."

"It doesn't make any sense."

"I realize that," said Cal. "But it will in time. I believe that. I do."

We began by cutting down thirty maple trees, removing the limbs, and dragging them, chained to the back of the tractor, out into the field where Cal intended to erect his church.

"You think this is crazy, too?" Cal asked me, as we worked.

"It's not *un-crazy*," I said.

Cal tipped his head back and laughed. "Such a politician!" he said. "You'd make a good diplomat, John." We worked without any written plan or blueprint. Cal didn't even bother to sketch a picture. We moved the largest logs into the center of the others, arranged them into a series of crossing supports and girders, and tied them into place temporarily with rope or baling twine until Cal stood at the top of a tall ladder and joined them to one another, drilling holes by hand and pounding in maple pegs stripped of their bark and dipped in vegetable oil. For several days, we raised these logs one at a time using the tractor and a block and tackle Cal had rigged to lift each log into place. Then he'd tie them off and put in the pegs that would lock them permanently together. The initial shape of the structure did not inspire confidence.

"Cal," I said, looking up at him as he drilled a hole through one of the logs, "are you sure you know what you're doing?"

"Nope," he said, laughing.

"How do you know this just won't collapse or fall apart?"

Cal smiled. "'Faith is the assurance of things hoped for, the conviction of things not seen.' That's from Hebrews. It means, relax, John. Give it a chance."

In the beginning, Cal's cathedral looked like a pile of logs someone had dropped from the sky. Trees stripped of their branches crossed in every direction, like a forest decimated by a tornado. Logs angled toward the center in some places, and toward the outside in others. When Mother and JJ came out to watch, JJ compared it to the picture of a web spun by spiders on LSD, which she had seen in a psychology textbook.

Cal smiled at her. "I can see how you'd think that," he said. "But wait until we get the walls up. Then it will all come together."

We arranged the first layer of shorter logs into an interconnected hexagon on the ground, to see how they fit together, then began joining them to one another with wooden pegs as we stacked them along the beams we'd previously constructed. We leveled the first layer carefully, digging beneath those that were too high, stacking large flat rocks beneath those that needed to be raised.

As each new layer of logs was stacked upon the one beneath it, I could begin to see the shape of the building. Seen from the air, it would look almost as if it were a single cell of a honeycomb, or a kind of crown, with other logs radiating from it like shafts of light. But the walls also bulged outward at the bottom, and then inward at the top, where they would meet at the roof in a six-sided spire. Because of the unusual structure, the building would require no columns inside for support, but some of the rafters would emerge through the walls outside, and would angle into the ground, like the flying buttresses of an old stone cathedral.

"The triangle is what gives any structure its strength," Cal said to me. "Bees know that. Paper wasps know it. A hexagon is just two pairs of triangles put together, and that's what we've got here. It's a series of trusses, really, arranged in several directions. When we're finished, this thing will stand up to a hurricane, a flood, even an earthquake."

"How did you learn to do all this?" I asked him.

He shrugged. "I don't really know."

"You must have learned sometime."

He nodded. "Well sure," he said. "I knew how to drill a hole, that's true. I knew how to cut trees down with a chain saw."

"But what about building something like this?" I asked. "When did you learn that?"

Cal smiled. "I wish I could tell you, John," he said. "The truth of it is, I don't know. How does a moth learn to make a cocoon? It's a mystery."

We were nearly halfway to the top when we'd exhausted the supply of trees already cut, so Cal drove alone into the woods with his chain saw to cut more. He told me to take a break for a couple days. He cut trees through the day and well into the night, the sound of his chain saw buzzing in the distance. As the walls grew higher, he rigged up a taller block and tackle, using the tractor to pull against a cable that went up through the pulley, thereby raising each log into place.

Bill and Eunice Hall stopped by once to look at the building, which they could now see all the way from their farm. Eunice brought along a loaf of freshly baked wheat bread and gave it to Mother. They stood on the driveway talking, but Bill wandered out to the field and walked slowly around the structure, carefully examining each wall, inside and out.

Cal stood on the top of the wall, preparing to begin raising the logs for the steeple into place. "It's a church," Cal shouted down.

Bill nodded but didn't speak.

"More of a chapel, I guess," Cal said.

Bill looked up at him. "You a preacher?" he asked.

Cal shook his head. "No."

"Christian?"

Cal shrugged. "I suppose. Yes."

Bill nodded. He stood still for a moment, as if lost in thought. Then he lifted the belt of his leather holster—he wore his pistol, as always—and reached into his back pocket. He pulled out a piece of paper, slowly unfolded it. "Then you might be interested in this," Bill said. He held out the paper. "A revival. Eunice and me are going. Couple days. We got a young man down the way to do the milking for us."

"Sounds interesting," Cal said, though to me he didn't sound sincere.

Bill looked at me. "Kids are welcome."

Cal nodded. "Maybe we'll do that."

"Well," Bill said to Cal. "You're busy." He handed the paper to me.

"Thanks for stopping by," Cal said.

Bill raised a hand, then returned to his truck with Eunice and drove away.

I looked down at the paper in my hand. "CHRISTIAN PATRIOT REVIVAL," it said on top, in large bold letters. I folded it and put it into my pocket. When we finished work, I gave it to Cal and went into the house to wash before supper.

The next morning, Cal handed the paper to Mother. "Bill brought this over yesterday," Cal said. "I thought maybe we could all go, get away from here for a couple days, see what it's all about."

"That guy's a strange bird," Mother said.

"He's different," Cal said.

Mother read the paper and then stared at Cal with a pained look on her face. "You got this from Bill Hall?" she asked.

"That's right."

Mother shook her head. "Why would we want to go to something like this?"

"Aren't you just a bit curious?" Cal asked. "It might be nice to take a drive, have a little vacation."

"We could certainly take a drive," Mother said, "but we don't have to go to this. I don't think these are the sort of people we want to be associated with."

"What sort of people might that be?" he asked.

"What are you guys talking about?" JJ asked.

Mother passed the paper across the table to JJ and me. Across the top of the page, as I'd seen before, were the words, "CHRISTIAN PATRIOT REVIVAL!" On each corner of the paper were little pictures of angels, and beside them, little hangman's nooses. The angels on the top were blowing trumpets. The ones on the bottom were carrying rifles. On the bottom of the page, in the center, was a graphic of the US Constitution. Beneath that were the words, "For Love of God and Nation!" Almost every phrase on the poster was followed by an exclamation mark. The revival, sponsored by the Michigan Militia, would take place that weekend in the Hiawatha National Forest, located in Michigan's Upper Peninsula.

"Cal," Mother said patiently, "these people are kooks. These are the people you see on TV with their heads shaved, goose-stepping in parades."

"You don't know that," Cal said.

"Yes I do," Mother said. "You have no use for people like this."

"Bill and Eunice invited us," Cal said. "It wouldn't be neighborly to say no."

Mother sighed and looked at the flyer again. "Honey, these people are racists. They're bigots. They're violent. You're nothing like them, and neither am I."

"We've never been to upper Michigan," Cal said. "It'll be beautiful this time of year. I've heard there's sand beaches along the Lake Michigan side and beautiful rock formations along the Lake Superior side."

Mother shook her head.

"Could be an adventure," Cal said.

Mother frowned but started to cave in. "I don't want to associate with people like this," she said. "With this kind of idiocy."

Cal shrugged. "If it's idiocy, we'll find out soon enough," he said. "We can just pack up and come home. Okay? I promise. Wouldn't it be nice to get away for a couple of days? Have a little adventure?"

Mother sighed.

"I'm going to go, honey," Cal said. "I'd like the rest of you to come with me. Please."

Mother looked at JJ and me.

"It's pretty boring around here," JJ said.

Mother looked at me.

"I think so, too," I said.

"All right," Mother said. "All right. I'm outnumbered."

So against Mother's better judgment, the following morning we packed a tent and sleeping bags in the back of the truck, along with food and water and some other camping gear, and we climbed into the truck for the drive east into upper Michigan.

The entrance to the campground was a swirl of bright red-and-blue Confederate flags and modern nylon tents in every conceivable color. A large canvas sign, "WELCOME PATRIOTS," hung over the gravel road. The final hundred yards to the campground, traffic slowed and ran through a gauntlet of police and sheriffs' cars. Their lights weren't flashing, but their presence was ominous enough. Mother shook her head as we drove past them. "I don't like the looks of this."

"We'll be all right," Cal said.

As our turn in line came, Cal stopped the truck and a thin man wearing a camouflaged uniform and black boots beckoned to him with a clipboard.

"Afternoon," the man said. "How are y'all today?" One of his front teeth had been capped in gold. He had the word LOVE tattooed in blue on the back of his left hand.

"We're all right," Cal said.

The man held a clipboard through Cal's open window. "We're getting names and addresses of folks who might want information about future revivals, mailers, things of that nature. If you're interested."

Cal pushed the clipboard back and shook his head. "Not interested."

The man took the clipboard, and Cal slowly pulled the truck forward. Mother looked tense.

"Come on now, darling," Cal said. "Where's your sense of adventure?"

Mother shook her head. "We'll stay one night," she said. "But if there's any funny stuff, I will walk out of here with John and Jennifer."

Cal nodded. "All right," he said. "Fair enough."

Our tires popped along the gravel as we drove through the grounds, searching for an open campsite. Each of the campsites came with an electrical outlet mounted on a wooden pole, where you could plug in your trailer, if you pulled one, and a blackened square barbecue grill mounted on a concrete base.

We found an open site next to one that held a large Airstream trailer, rounded and bright silver, shaped like the fuselage of an airplane. An old man and woman wearing cowboy hats sat on lawn chairs beside a campfire, with a cast-iron pot of water smoking over the grate. The man wore a pistol in a shoulder holster and seemed to be chewing tobacco. The woman wore a T-shirt that said, "I LOVE MY COUNTRY," in the front. When she bent over, we could see the back, which said, "I HATE MY GOVERNMENT." It looked as if she had a sword hanging from a strap against her hip. An American flag, flying upside down, had been tied to a sapling behind the trailer.

"Oh great," JJ said, "We're next to Ma and Pa Kettle."

"Judge not," Cal said to JJ. He waved to the old woman and she smiled and waved back. She looked as if she had no teeth.

"A dentist would have a field day here," JJ said.

We set up our tent as activity buzzed all around us. Jeeps of men in camouflaged uniforms passed by on the road, and rag-tag groups of men and boys my age, many even younger, walked along single file. Some of them had camouflaged grease paint in greens and browns on their faces. We tried to watch without staring or laughing. I felt too frightened to laugh, though JJ often bowed her head, her shoulders shaking.

"Did you see that?" she asked. "That bald guy had the Confederate flag tattooed on the back of his head!"

In the late afternoon, when his wife was in the trailer, the old man camping next to us wandered over.

"Hey, neighbor!" he said, raising a hand. Mother and Cal relaxed by our campfire in the sunshine. JJ and I rested on our backs in a rust-colored bed of dead pine needles, nearly asleep.

"Hello!" Cal said.

"Where you from?" the old man asked. He shook Cal's hand and smiled at Mother.

"Wisconsin," Cal said. "You?"

"Idaho," the old man answered.

"We eat your potatoes," JJ whispered.

"Idaho!" Cal said. "That's a long drive."

The man nodded. "It is. Idaho's a long way from anywhere, but it's a White people's state. It's pure, like the water. We used to live in Arkansas, and we hated it. Too many Coloreds there."

Cal's face tensed. The muscles in his jaw tightened. Mother put a hand on his arm and squeezed. "I grew up with black-and-white TV myself," Cal said, "but I prefer colored now, to tell the truth."

The man frowned, confused. "No, no, not TV. I mean *Coloreds*, the *Nigras*."

"Ah," Cal said. "We don't have any of those in Wisconsin," Cal said.

"No?"

Cal shook his head. "Not one. I've never seen one, as a matter of fact. Not in all my life."

"I'll be goddamned," the man said, "ain't that something?" He looked puzzled. "Not even on TV?"

Cal shook his head. "Not even on TV."

"Damn!" the man said. "You're lucky."

Cal pointed. "What are you carrying, there?"

The man unsnapped the strap on his holster. "It's a forty-four. I call it Clint Eastwood." He raised the gun at the sky, closed an eye, and aimed at some imaginary target. "'Make my day,'" he said. Then he lowered his arm and smiled, sheepishly. He held the gun out to Cal, who examined it for a while before nodding and passing it back. The old man returned the gun to his holster and snapped the strap again.

"You coming to the meeting tonight?" he asked.

"Maybe," Cal said. "Where's it at?"

The man motioned with his arm and pointed down the road. "Over that hill. There's a clearing and they've got a tent set up, looks like a big circus tent. You should come. Bring the wife and kids."

Cal nodded. "We'll probably do that."

"Good enough," he said. His wife emerged from the trailer carrying a bowl of sliced potatoes. She walked to the pot of water over the fire, dumped them in, and stirred the water with a stick.

"Supper's starting," the man said.

"All right," Cal said. When the man had gotten out of earshot, Cal said, "Racist ignoramus."

"I told you," Mother said.

Well after dark, we followed the stream of people carrying flashlights to the tent the man had told us about. It covered an area the size of a large basketball court, and was nestled in a small clearing sheltered by a semi-circular stand of towering red pine trees, twenty or thirty of them, all more than a hundred feet tall. In front of the tent, beneath a series of propane lanterns hanging from wires, were four picnic tables pushed together to create a makeshift stage. People sat facing this stage, those in front on the grass, others in lawn chairs they had carried in, still others on other picnic tables arranged randomly beneath the tent. About every ten feet or so on both sides of the tent, a lantern hung from a wooden pole, lighting the tent from the inside. From the outside, the canvas glowed like a lampshade. Huge black speakers sat on wooden boxes in each corner.

The four of us walked in together. I recognized some of the boys I had seen that afternoon marching in formation toward the woods. A few of them now had black eyes, dried blood beneath their noses, dirt streaked down their faces. JJ and I sat down on the grass beside one another near the edge of the tent. I could lean back and see the sky. Shimmering etches of lightning, what Mother called heat lightning, flashed in the distance, illuminating the darkening clouds. It looked like the cracks in the glazing of old porcelain. Mother and Cal sat on the bench of a picnic table behind us, their backs to the table.

Within a few minutes, we saw Bill and Eunice Hall. They sat in lawn chairs about twenty feet in front of JJ and me. Bill looked back and saw us, and then he whispered something to his wife. Eunice turned around and waved at Mother. Mother smiled and nodded.

A thin man in blue jeans and camouflaged shirt climbed up on the stage and raised his hands. Gradually, everyone stopped talking. When the crowd was silent, he asked everyone to bow their heads, and he said a brief prayer. Then he started talking. He started slowly and quietly, but in a few minutes he gained speed and volume. He paced back and forth on top of the picnic tables, shouting things. He carried a wireless microphone but it didn't seem to be working, because it was possible to hear him clearly only when he shouted. Sometimes he shouted something and got most of the other men in front to shout back, pumping their fists in the air like kids in the mosh pit at a metal concert. Someone tapped him on the leg and told him to turn on the microphone. He clicked a button, popped the microphone against the palm of his hand, and the noise reverberated through the speakers.

"Can you hear me now?" he said loudly. Everyone nodded.

"All right!" he said.

He gave a rambling speech that seemed united only by its anti-Semitism and its criticism of America's federal government. He said America had been overtaken by something he called ZOG, the Zionist Occupational Government, which controlled the world economy and international banking, and which had infiltrated and now controlled American government at the highest levels.

"What a moron," JJ said.

I nodded but really wasn't listening. I kept looking outside, watching an ominous wall of clouds slowly move in, like a huge ship arriving from the west. Inside the tent, moths fluttered around the lanterns, and sometimes one of them would accidentally fly inside and burst into flames, and all the young boys would rise to their knees, gleefully, to watch.

After about ten minutes or so, the first man finished speaking. Everyone clapped politely. I looked behind us and found Cal, but Mother was gone. I elbowed JJ, who looked back and then faced me. "She must have reached her idiocy quota." JJ whispered.

A hush came across the crowd again as another man got up to speak. He was large, with a thick beard, huge arms, and fierce, wild-looking eyes. He dressed completely in camouflage, with his pants tucked into shiny black leather boots. The sleeves of his shirt were rolled up. He had blue tattoos in the shape of crosses on his forearms. A knife at least a foot long hung in a leather sheath from one hip, and a canteen hung from the other. Something that looked like a small black machine gun hung from a strap across his back. He removed his cap as he climbed on top of the picnic table, tucking it into a back pocket. He slapped the microphone against his palm. The sound boomed through the speakers and some of the people winced and briefly covered their ears.

"Patriots!" the man shouted, the speakers whistling with feedback. "Christian Patriots! Brothers of the Michigan Militia, the Free Militia of Wisconsin, and other God-fearing brothers and sisters in arms! I thank you for this opportunity to speak to you tonight."

"This must be the Grand Pooh-Bah," JJ whispered to me. I nodded.

"I stand before you a soldier, a veteran, a husband, a son, and a brother. It has been wonderful to meet so many patriots like yourselves, people who are committed, as I am, to turning back the corruption that is swallowing this great nation. Zionists on the West Coast and in the big cities, socialists in Washington, immigrants at home, and foreigners abroad are sucking our blood and robbing our children of their rightful inheritance of a White, Christian, English-speaking heritage. How is this happening? Well I'll tell you.

"First, we're being taxed to death. Read the *Communist Manifesto*, people! The second plank in communist doctrine is the income tax, and the IRS is our government's secret police force empowered to collect it. The Soviet Union had the KGB, and we have the IRS. There's no difference. Let me say that again: there is no difference! We work harder and harder for our daily bread, and the federal government takes more and more of it to give away to leeches at home and to foreigners overseas. Are we just going to stand by and let that happen?"

"No!" shouted a few men in the audience.

"Yes!" JJ said, laughing. People nearby stared at us, and I put my hand over JJ's mouth.

"Are we going to let the IRS come into our homes and rob us of what we've sweat and toiled to earn?" the man asked.

"No!" a few more men shouted.

"Are we going to let them take our farms and our trucks and our homes away from us?"

"No!" was the reply.

"You're goddamned right we're not," he said. "Other men among us here are experts in this area, and they are going to teach us how to keep from paying most of our taxes to the feds in Washington. If we all listen, we can stop the flow of our blood to Washington, DC.

"But that's not the only problem in this country. We have greater problems to solve here, brothers. Washington, DC, has turned our beloved Christian Republic into a secular socialist shithole. What does that mean for you and me? I'll tell you. In a Christian Republic, the *individual* is sovereign—individual liberty is absolute. To ensure that this remains so, county governments have been granted the only legitimate power, and that power is to be used solely to ensure that individual sovereignty is not breached. That's what the Founding Fathers created, people. The Articles of Confederation are based upon the holy Bible, my friends, and the US Constitution is based upon those Articles of Confederation. God's hand was at work in those founding documents.

"But in a socialist shithole, which is what this once-great nation has become, individual sovereignty has been destroyed. The central tyrannical government in Washington, DC, and the smaller, no less tyrannical state governments have given themselves the power to regulate our lives, to tax us, to require birth certificates and licenses and Social Security cards and dozens of other forms to ensure it can keep track of us and the money they wish to steal from us every April fifteenth. Are we going to just sit idly while we are regulated and licensed and tagged like cattle going to slaughter?"

"No!" everyone shouted.

"No we're not!" the man said. He went on to criticize other enemies, and other things about America that needed changing. He said that all amendments added to the constitution after the Bill of Rights, particularly the Sixteenth Amendment, which initiated the federal income tax, were nonbinding, because they'd been introduced by legislative bodies without the authority to make such laws. He railed against the Federal Reserve Act, which enabled the government to make money out of paper and ink, and the Gold Act. The government's introduction of Federal Reserve notes—paper money—as the only legal tender was its way of ensuring that it could create all the money it ever needed.

He argued that the civil liberties of everyday Americans were under attack by our own federal law enforcement agencies, particularly the FBI, the CIA, the DEA, and the Bureau of Alcohol, Tobacco, and Firearms. He ran through what he called the roll call of shame, dozens of names of American militia martyrs whose civil liberties had been violated, and some whose lives had been taken, by federal law enforcement officers.

"It won't be easy, my friends," he said. "Great power is aligned against us. Plans may already be in the works to set off a world economic crisis, and every day, God-fearing Americans like you and me will be rounded up to work in government camps to build the gulags that will be used to imprison us. And just over the horizon is something else people need to see coming, and that is a one-world government. The UN is working toward that end. Clinton the anti-Christ is with them. You and I know that's true. Borders are breaking down. In Miami, Florida, and in much of Texas and California, Americans are already strangers in their own land. You go through the Miami airport, friends, and you don't even hear English over the PA system anymore. Bad enough with all the blacks on welfare, but now you got foreigners taking over America, reproducing like rats, and the federal government's quota system makes it happen."

JJ elbowed me in the ribs. "What a load of crap!" she said aloud. The people sitting next to us frowned and JJ stuck her tongue out at them. "Dog shit for brains," she said, "if you believe this crap."

"If we do nothing," the man said, "then all will be lost. A life of true liberty, the kind of life our Founding Fathers fought for, will no longer be possible. A life lived in decency, in fear of God, a life free from tyranny, will no longer be possible.

"Christian patriots!" he shouted. "What we really need is a revolution!" The man opened his arms wide and stared out over us, like the gun-loving Charlton Heston in *The Ten Commandments*, parting the Red Sea. "Brothers! What do we need?"

"Revolution!" Men and women leaped to their feet.

"What do we need?"

"Revolution!" they shouted.

"What will save this great nation?"

"Revolution!" The word resounded again and again in response to his calls. Gradually, the people shouting grew tired and sat down. The man abruptly stopped talking. He stepped forward and began to stare. He looked as if he were staring directly at JJ and me. One by one, then in small groups, people in front of us turned in their chairs to look back. A general murmur of disgust trickled through the crowd. Women covered their children's eyes and pulled them toward their chests. But they weren't looking at JJ and me. They were looking behind us. And when JJ and I turned around, we found Cal standing on top of the picnic table, his pants and underwear down around his thighs, the back of his shirt lifted, his bare, hairy white ass shining for everyone to see.

"Holy shit," I said.

"Daddy's going to get us killed," said JJ. She tried to stand but I held her arm.

Cal pulled up his pants and turned around to face the front again.

"Brother, you got a problem?" the man up front said, into the microphone.

Cal stepped down from the picnic table past JJ and me and began to snake his way through the lawn chairs to the front.

"Oh my God!" JJ said.

"Sit down!" an angry voice said, from somewhere in front of us. Cal ignored it. He made his way to the front of the tent, climbed up on the picnic table, and approached the man with the microphone who stood much taller, and looked much stronger, than Cal.

Cal held out his hand. The man shook it. Cal kept his hand out, reached for the microphone. To my surprise, the man handed it to him.

Cal turned to face us. He wore blue jeans and a buffalo plaid flannel shirt. He had not shaved since we moved to New Eden, but his beard was still short and rather sparse, a mix of gray and black. His hair was longer than it had ever been, long enough for a short ponytail, if he'd chosen to wear it that way. He put the microphone to his lips.

"My name is Cal Franklin and I believe God sent me here," Cal said. People shouted and booed and raised middle fingers at him. He paused to let the noise die down. "I'm telling you it's just as big a surprise to me as it is to you. Listening to what's been said tonight, particularly the hateful words directed toward my African American brothers and immigrants, I'm thinking maybe God was drunk at the time." This was greeted by more angry shouts and gestures. "I have to tell you, God doesn't like what he's hearing here.

"Look, people, I love freedom just as much as you do. But do we have to hate our brothers and sisters to live free?"

The crowd roared its disapproval. It looked as if some of the men sitting in front were reaching for Cal's legs to try to pull him from the table. The larger man who'd just been speaking, however, reached for the microphone. He pulled it from Cal's hand.

"Brothers!" he shouted. He waited for silence. "Let's let this man speak. If he has something important enough to say that he wants to get up here and share it with us, we should let him talk. Freedom of speech, friends. Our forefathers died for it." He handed the microphone back to Cal.

"Thank you, sir," Cal said, and smiled. He turned back to face the crowd. "Now look. The truth of it, I believe anyway, is that Black people are more American than most Americans. Think about it! Their people have been here a lot longer than most of us, except the Indians, of course, and we sure as hell didn't do right by them, either, but that's another story. It's a simple fact friends: as slaves and laborers Black Americans did more to build this country with their bare hands than anyone else." He paused. "And what about music and sports? Can anyone here really imagine the NBA without Black players? Who would want to watch a bunch of White guys shooting set shots?"

"Sit down!" a man in front of me shouted.

Cal smiled. "And what about music? What about Louis Armstrong, Duke Ellington, and Little Richard? I can imagine a world without them in it, but I wouldn't want to live in that world!" Cal put his left hand out and moved his fingers as if he were playing the piano. He tipped his chin down and began humming Armstrong's "What a Wonderful World." As he hummed the melody he did a little dance, walking, twirling, and swaying his hips from side to side. Some people looked around at one another, their anger now tempered by confusion. A few people even started laughing.

"This is embarrassing," JJ whispered.

The noise level in the tent grew. Cal began to shout into the microphone. "I haven't known a single Black person to do anything to make my life more difficult. And the Jews, well, unless your brain is so full of holes it looks like Swiss cheese, you know they were put through a hell in Hitler's Europe as bad as slavery. So when I heard folks up here saying hateful, ridiculous things about these people, I realized why I'd been sent here tonight. I've been called here to speak the truth, to set you free."

At this point, several men rushed the table and shook their fists at Cal, their faces contorted by anger. The tent once again convulsed in a loud uproar. Men shouted and waved their arms, some in anger, some trying to restore order. The large man walked over to him but just stood with his arms crossed, glaring. Though JJ and I were mortified, Cal didn't even look frightened. He stood calmly, even serenely. He caught my eye and winked at me.

And then at the peak of the chaos, when the noise had reached its greatest volume and a riot seemed imminent, Cal suddenly looked up at the top of the tent and raised both of his hands over his head. He reached his hands to the sky and closed his eyes. I saw it, JJ saw it, everyone saw it. Within seconds, and this is the truth, within seconds, a bolt of lightning slashed out of the night sky like a sword, accompanied by a deafening, thunderous explosion, like a massive bomb had gone off, and one of the pine trees just outside of the tent, not thirty or forty feet from where Cal stood, burst into a fireball.

Instinctively, everyone inside the tent ducked. The white flash temporarily blinded me, and the percussion of thunder felt as if someone had hit me in the chest with a pillow. Beneath my feet, the ground felt alive. My legs and arms tingled. The hair on top of my head, and along my arms and legs stood on end.

General panic followed. Children broke into wild, fearful screaming. People leaped from their chairs and shoved against one another, some falling to the ground as others rushed from the tent. They ran for the shelter of the hardwoods or for their tents or their trailers.

Above us, fanned by the wind, the fire spread from the top of one red pine to the next, the needles crackling, glowing orange, the sap snapping, until the whole stand of trees blazed, illuminating the clearing. Sparks and glowing bits of debris began to fall to the white canvas roof of the tent, and soon dozens of tiny fires erupted there as well. Through all of this, Cal stood calmly, his eyes drawn to the flames and smoke above him.

Great gusts of wind followed, and the roof of the tent huffed and billowed like a sail. Rain began to fall, lightning flashed, and thunder erupted all around us. Cal dropped the microphone on one of the picnic tables and hurried back to JJ and me.

"I thought they were going to kill you," I said.

Cal shrugged. He put an arm around JJ. "Let's find your mother and get the hell out of here before they know where to find me."

We jogged through the driving rain to our campsite, where Mother was waiting. We pulled up the stakes of our tent, tossed it in the back of the truck, and left. The rain fell in blankets, driven by wind, flooding the campground. As we pulled away, we could see Confederate flags plastered to trees like wet tissue paper.

"Never again," Mother said angrily as we left the campground, the wipers darting across the windshield like angry black snakes. "I don't know why I let you talk me into this."

"You should have seen him," JJ said.

"I saw enough."

"You didn't see this."

"Cal *mooned* them," I chimed in.

"He did what?" Mother asked.

"He mooned them, and then he told them all they were so full of shit it was turning their eyes brown."

"I've been called, darling," Cal said to Mother. "It's all starting to make sense to me. We're building a church, and I think I know why. I think I'm supposed to start preaching."

"Preaching? What do you know about preaching?"

"Not a thing!" Cal said, and laughed.

Mother shook her head. "You haven't been to a seminary. You have to study to become a minister, Cal. It takes years."

Cal shook his head. "I don't mean to become a minister," Cal said. "I just mean to preach."

Mother sighed. She turned her face toward the window, rested her head against the glass.

JJ and I looked at each other. Neither of us rolled our eyes. Cal might not be completely normal, we knew that, but he had just stood up in front of more than a hundred angry and heavily armed people and told them to pull their heads out of their asses. And while it was probably just a fantastic coincidence, he seemed to have called lightning down from the sky.

God, Cal said, had spoken to Joan of Arc and Nat Turner, and he believed God was now speaking to him. I would be there, watching closely, to see exactly what the results of that conversation would bring.

Chapter 10

All around us, as Cal completed work on his church, the land underwent a slow metamorphosis, its color changing from vibrant greens to the fire-red and oranges of fall maples and oaks, and the golds of poplar and birches. In the swamps, the tamaracks turned a bright, feathery yellow. Shoulder-high groves of sumac sprouted pointed pyramids of magenta seeds, and their leaves turned dark pink, and then red, before falling, leaving only the elegant gray skeletons of their branches.

Each morning, we'd wake to find our land dusted by frost, and moist breath would pour from our bodies like smoke in the icy air. I was rarely bored. I spent more and more of my time exploring, wandering our fields and woodlots. I watched whitetail deer bound into the woods, and I saw red foxes slink across fallen logs and disappear into swampy marshland. I split open the drying pods of milkweed to watch their downy seeds rise on invisible currents of warm air. I thought a lot about David, and how he would have loved running in our fields and playing in the woods. And I watched JJ sink ever more deeply into a sadness and a hopelessness from which I could not seem to rescue her.

In early November, scattered snowflakes drifted like downy feathers from still, gray clouds almost every afternoon. Flocks of Canada geese in broken Vs passed southward, their mournful honking echoing in the cold air; sometimes, flocks of mallards soared above us, too, their wingtips whistling, stirring up the ducks in our yard, who looked skyward and ran around in circles, flapping their useless wings. When the first geese passed overhead, we all ran outside to watch as flock after noisy flock passed over the house. Even at night, after we'd been in bed for a while, we'd hear them fly over, and we'd push our faces to the cold glass of the windows to see them pass across the night sky. Sometimes Cal would crawl out his bedroom window and lie on the porch roof inside a sleeping bag to watch them. Gradually, though, we got used to seeing geese, and after a week or so, their noisy passage overhead became commonplace, like the background noise of a television back in West Allis while we ate our dinner.

Cal finished his church, hauling the small wood-burning stove from the machine shed for heat, which he mounted and leveled on a platform of flat rocks. He didn't really want to heat the church, he said, but didn't feel as if he had any choice. The ground had frozen before he could finish chinking the openings between the logs with mud and straw. The building would likely be too drafty to be serviceable in the winter without the stove, anyway. He put up small shelves on each of the chapel's six sides, upon which he would place candles, or lanterns, for light. In the old days, he said, churches weren't heated, and they were lit by beeswax candles. In our church, eight hay bales served as benches, and bales in front, covered with boards, became the altar. In the end, the church featured about four hundred square feet of floor space, equal to a room twenty feet wide by twenty feet deep, and the top of the steeple, which Cal had capped with a cross carved from maple, reached thirty-five feet high.

Cal named his church the New Eden Church of God with Signs Following, and he painted those words on a small sign and posted it above the door. Above that, he placed another sign that said, simply, The Cathedral of David. He drove into town the third Wednesday of November and posted signs around Iron River announcing the church's installation service, which he'd scheduled for that coming Sunday. He also placed a flyer in Bill and Eunice Hall's mailbox. We had not seen them since our visit to the Michigan revival.

Though she did not understand Cal's sudden desire to begin preaching, Mother did agree to attend his first church service. Cal would preach a short installation sermon in which he would draw from the work of Puritan ministers he'd studied in graduate school, Edward Taylor, to be sure, but also Michael Wigglesworth and Cotton Mather. Of course, he said, he would also rely upon his own inspiration. I don't think I ever saw him quite so excited.

Friday morning we awoke to find snow falling heavily, huge flakes swirling in a soft breeze. Three or four inches had already fallen, had settled in balanced white shadows on the branches of trees, on the roof of the house, barn, and machine shed, on the sagging heads of dried sunflowers. In the early sunlight, angled low across the fields, the snow looked almost blue in color. Throughout the day, the skies darkened and the snow continued to fall. We sat at the kitchen table by lamplight, listening to Cal read aloud from his Bible. He searched the concordance for references to snow, found Psalm 147: "'He sends out His command to the earth; His word runs very swiftly. He gives snow like wool; He scatters the frost like ashes; He casts out His hail like morsels; Who can stand before his cold?'"

Late at night, as the snow continued to fall, JJ and I huddled shoulder to shoulder in our room beneath a blanket with a flashlight, with Cal's American literature anthology opened in front of me to John Greenleaf Whittier's "Snowbound." JJ rested on her stomach with her eyes closed while I read aloud from the poem, which was more than twenty pages long:

> So all night long the storm roared on:
> The morning broke without a sun;
> In tiny spherule traced with lines
> Of Nature's geometric signs,
> In starry flake and pellicle,
> All day the hoary meteor fell;
> And, when the second morning shone,
> We looked upon a world unknown,
> On nothing we could call our own.

Halfway through, JJ started crying.

"What's wrong?" I asked.

"I don't know," she said. "I don't know what's wrong with me." I leaned a shoulder into her. JJ swallowed and nodded. She wiped her face with her hands. "Read, Johnny," she said. I read until she fell asleep.

In the morning, the sun rose on a white shining world. We shielded our eyes as we stood at the picture window in the living room. Snow hung from the rooftop like hardened lava and, where it had drifted, left a shoulder-deep layer of frosting across the yard and fields. Only the windows of our truck were visible above the driveway.

At least two feet of snow had piled on the roof and inside the box, and the rest of the truck was buried. It dripped like candle wax from the sagging blue spruces and rose like a top hat from the roof of the bird feeder, where black-capped chickadees and a gloriously red cardinal busily pecked and dug sunflower seeds from the snow. We'd had plenty of snow during the winters we lived in West Allis. But nothing like this.

"There must be two feet of snow out there," Cal said.

"The radio said three," Mother said.

I said, "We need our snow blower back."

Cal smiled. "We have four of them in the shed," he said, "with wooden handles."

"We're going to shovel all this?" I asked.

"A little at a time, John," Cal answered. "It took some twenty-four hours for it to get down here. It will take us at least as long to move some of it out of the way."

"I wonder if they plow the roads up this far," Mother asked. She had been walking from window to window in her robe, parting the curtains and raising the shades to let through striking bars of light.

"Doesn't matter if they do or don't," Cal said. "We have everything we need here."

"But people won't be able to come to your service."

"Then we'll have a service without any other people," Cal said.

Later that morning, a heavy orange dump truck with a huge plow shaped like an arrowhead cleared a single wide lane up the gravel road, leaving snow five or six feet high piled along the sides. Cal smiled as if he'd known all along that the plow would come.

That Sunday, six people sat on hay bales wearing coats and hats and gloves when Cal walked up on the altar to begin his first church service: JJ, me, Mother, Bill and Eunice Hall, and an old Black man who walked with a cane. The first Black person we'd seen since we left West Allis, he came in wearing a thick parka, the hood lined in coyote fur, baggy brown wool pants, leather mittens, and a huge raccoon-skin hat. He shuffled slowly into the church a minute or two late, his back stooped, his legs bowed and wobbly. Once his eyes adjusted to the dim light, he walked to a hay bale right next to the hot wood stove and sat down.

"My friends," Cal said, "Welcome to New Eden Church of God with Signs Following in the Cathedral of David. Thank you for coming." He rubbed the palms of his hands together, nervously. "I hope you don't think it inappropriate if I start off with a little joke."

Bill and Eunice stared straight up at Cal, their faces expressionless. The old man sitting by the stove nodded his head. "I like a good joke!" he said, his voice raspy. He had sharp, bird-like features. Water dripped from his pointed nose and his face was coated in white stubble. His glasses looked as thick as the heels of a dress shoe, which magnified his eyes.

"All right," said Cal. "Thank you." He stepped forward to the edge of the altar. "You see, a minister showed up for services one Sunday morning, and there was just one man, an old farmer named Clarence, sitting in the back of the church, all alone. The minister waited for a couple minutes to see if anyone else from the congregation would arrive, but no one came. So he went ahead and started the service. He believed Clarence should get what he came for, so the minister took care to work his way through the whole service, beginning to end. He'd prepared a sermon, after all. He'd written it, revised it, practiced it, and by God, he would deliver it. And that's just what he did.

"An hour later, at the end of the service, Clarence got up to leave, but he came up and shook the minister's hand before he did so. 'Nice service,' Clarence said. 'Thank you,' said the minister. 'But I have to ask you something,' Clarence said. 'I've got fifty head of cattle back home, and once each day I haul out a wagon load of feed and dump it for them. Now, suppose one day I go out there, and only one cow shows up to eat? What do you suppose I should do?'

"The minister smiled, recognizing the analogy. He said, 'Well, that cow has to eat. You must feed him.' Clarence nodded in reply. 'That's right,' he said. 'I'm going to feed that one cow, because he needs to be fed. But I'll be damned if I'm going to give him the whole load!'"

Cal smiled, and the old man in the coonskin cap laughed. "That's a good one!" he said. Bill and Eunice smiled. Mother and I chuckled a bit, and JJ looked at me and rolled her eyes.

Cal sighed. "Yes, well, I thought it might be appropriate this morning." He looked at Mother and nodded. "We don't have any songbooks just yet," Cal said. "So I asked my wife to lead us in a song."

Mother stood up and started singing. She sang "Amazing Grace," just the opening verse, and people joined in as best they could. The old man by the stove swayed from side to side with the music.

When the song was over, Cal began the service. He told everyone the story of how we had come to live at New Eden, explained how David had died, talked about his own car accident, and the dream he had of a field with a single white oak tree in the middle of it. He told us how he'd been guided to this very spot, and how he had heard the voice of the Lord instructing him to build a small church here, out of logs. It was, he said, still a surprise to him, and a mystery as great as life and death.

"Right before my son John and I finished building this church," Cal said, "our barn burned down. You might have seen it, or what's left of it, buried outside under the snow. Now, I know it's not the first barn to burn down, and it won't be the last. As my friend Bill Hall here has taught me, wet hay in a dry barn is a bad combination. I won't soon forget it. But that barn fire reminded me of what Cotton Mather always said. He was the minister of Old North Church in Boston, back in the seventeenth century, and like all those preachers of old, he was certain of one thing, and that was wherever God appeared to do His work, the devil would appear there also. The devil is like a jealous child. He wants what God has, and he will do terrible things to try to get it.

"So when I think about that barn burning down, I know in my head that wet hay had something to do with it. But I know in my heart that maybe the devil was just leaving his calling card, letting us know he'd be watching us closely, looking for his chance."

Cal paused, took a step back, looked around the inside of the church. He smiled.

"I've been thinking about all this the last few days," Cal said. "I don't know how many people know this, but the ancient Celts believed that there were certain places on earth, what they called 'thin places,' where the distance between heaven and earth was so slight, that people could go there to get a glimpse of heaven. I believe we are living in just such a place. I feel as if I've been called here, and when the Lord calls, you best go see what he wants.

"I had to learn that, too, my friends. When the Lord calls, you going to put Him on hold? You going to say, 'Hang on a second, Lord, I'm busy doing my laundry'? Or, 'Hang on, Lord, I don't want to be late for work'? You going to say, 'Oh, I'm sorry, Lord, I don't take phone solicitations, please send me something in the mail.' You going to say that? Of course not! You could be in the middle of a shower, up on the top rung of a ladder, or eating a gourmet meal at a four-star French restaurant in Paris! You're going to stop what you're doing and go to him. You could be having a baby! You could be making love! You could be mourning the death of your youngest child! It doesn't matter, my friends. You're going to stop what you're doing and go to the Lord."

"Amen!" someone said. JJ and I looked at the old man. He smiled at us and nodded.

Cal looked up from his text and squinted. "Amen!" the old man said, again. "Preach it!"

"That's right!" Cal said. "Amen! The Lord is calling!"

"Amen!" shouted the old man.

"That's the Lord on the phone, calling collect! Answer the phone!"

"Amen!" he said.

"The Lord is saying, 'Follow me.'"

"Amen!"

"I'm not joking, now!" Cal said. "You could be in the middle of heart transplant surgery! You could be the lead car in the Indianapolis 500 with just one lap to go! It doesn't matter. If the Lord calls you, you've got to go. You have to say, 'Here I am, Lord. What do you need? You need me to pick up some extra groceries and drop them off at the homeless shelter on the way? Done! You want me to give up drinking? Done! You want me to build a church out of logs in the middle of northern Wisconsin and start preaching and reading signs of your presence?'" Cal paused to look up from his text. He looked out at us, then lifted his chin to stare straight up the hollow opening of the steeple above him. "Well Lord," he said. "That's about the craziest thing I've ever heard, but if that's what you want me to do, I'm going to do it."

"Amen," the old man said.

"That's right as rain," Cal said. "Amen. Amen."

At the close of the service, after I collected the offering inside an old cigar box—two dollars from the Halls, five from the old man—Cal shook hands with Bill and Eunice Hall.

"Quite a ruckus you raised at that revival," Eunice said.

Cal smiled and nodded. "Maybe I got a little carried away."

"We didn't appreciate the nudity," said Bill.

"But you made us think," Eunice added, touching Cal on the arm.

"That lightning fire burned a hundred acres before it was over." Bill smiled. He and Eunice left the church.

Cal introduced himself to the old Black man sitting by the fire. He had his hands out of his leather mitts and was warming them over the stove. "Name's Jeremiah Gibbons," the old man said. "I seen a sign in town, and I said, by God, that's just a couple miles down the ATV trail from my place, I'm going to get on my snowmobile and ride on over there, check it out."

"I'm pleased you did," Cal said.

"Sorry I was late," he said. "Couldn't get the damned snow machine started."

"You were right on time," said Cal.

Jeremiah raised a single finger and shook it at Cal. "You have the Holy Spirit," he said. "I hear it in your voice."

"You're kind," Cal said.

"I'm old enough I don't have to be kind," Jeremiah said. "I can get away with the truth."

"Well, thank you."

"Listen," said Jeremiah. "Can I ask you for something? Would you touch my knees?"

"Your knees?"

Jeremiah nodded. "Got arthritis so bad sometimes I can't even walk. Just bone grinding on bone now. Doctor wants to operate, give me new knees, but I told him forget it. I'm ninety-four years old. I got about five teeth left in my mouth, I'm legally blind, I shit once a week and it takes so much effort, I'm exhausted for days afterward. I don't want no operation."

Cal laughed.

"But I know if you touch my knees," Jeremiah said, "my arthritis will be healed."

Cal shook his head. "I don't think so."

"Why not? I'm not going to bite you."

Cal smiled at him. "Oh, I'll touch your knees," he said. "I'm happy to do that. I just don't want you to get your hopes up."

"I have faith in you," Jeremiah said, turning toward Cal. "I have faith in the Holy Spirit. Wait a minute." He stood up, using his cane for support, undid his belt, and pulled down the brown wool pants he wore on the outside. Beneath his pants, he wore red cotton long johns, pocked with holes. He sat back down. "Okay. I'm ready."

Cal stepped forward, crouched down on one knee, and put one of his hands softly on each of the old man's knees.

Jeremiah jumped as if he'd been shocked by electricity. "Your hands are cold!" he said.

"Sorry." Cal laughed. Cal cupped his hands to his mouth, blew on them, warmed them. He placed the palms back on Jeremiah Gibbons's knees. Jeremiah closed his eyes. After about five seconds, Cal removed his hands from Jeremiah's legs and stood back up. He looked embarrassed. Jeremiah stood up, too, pulled up his pants and tightened his belt. "Thank you," he said. He pulled on his gloves, adjusted his hat, gripped his cane in his right hand. Mother, JJ, and I watched intently as Jeremiah slowly turned and began to shuffle out of the church, his legs bowed as before. I was slightly disappointed to see him walk the same way he walked when he came in, hunched over his cane, shuffling his heavy boots forward, one at a time, carefully. But when he reached the door, he turned around and stood erect. He took a deep breath, looked up above him, and lifted the cane to a small branch that protruded from one of the logs in the wall. He hooked the crook of the cane over the branch, and he let it go. It dangled there like a candy cane on a Christmas tree.

Jeremiah walked outside and closed the door behind him.

JJ looked at me, her eyes wide. I held my breath. We heard the rumble of a snowmobile engine starting, then the whine and roar as it sped away.

PART III: ICE

And for the season it was winter, and they that know the winters of that country know them to be sharp and violent, and subject to cruel and fierce storms, dangerous to travel to known places, much more to search an unknown coast. Besides, what could they see but a hideous and desolate wilderness, full of wild beasts and wild men—and what multitudes there might be of them they knew not."

—William Bradford,
Of Plymouth Plantation

Chapter 11

December winds thundered against the house and windows, bringing cold so frigid I felt as if my eyes would freeze open if I stayed outside more than a few minutes. Our chickens and ducks all died. I found the chickens in the coop, hard as a pile of feathered rocks. A weasel or rat had already eaten the comb and wattles off the rooster and had started in on the smaller wattles of the hens. The ducks died under a spruce tree, frozen with their beaks tucked back under their wings. Cal thawed them out, one by one, behind one of the wood stoves, and plucked and cleaned them. Mother roasted the ducks for dinner, but because we had given each of the chickens names, they seemed more like pets, and we couldn't bring ourselves to eat them. Cal said in the future, no naming the chickens.

At night, we burned a kerosene heater in the machine shed to keep the cows from freezing, but even so, every morning we'd find their buckets of water frozen. Inside the house, we stacked wood up to the ceiling in the upstairs hall and we kept the wood stoves stoked through the night. If the stoves went out, we'd wake with ice in our eyelashes and frost on our blankets, and it would take hours for new fires to warm the house again. The air smelled perpetually of firewood and wood smoke. I longed for a gas furnace. We all did.

An arctic front moved through two weeks before Christmas, and the thermometer hanging outside the kitchen window bottomed out at 30 below zero. Maybe it was even colder and we couldn't tell. A half-inch of ice coated the inside of our windows. The walls grew a heavy fuzz of white frost. The drainpipe under the bathtub wouldn't empty, the water inside frozen solid. In the privy, the toilet seat felt refrigerated. Sitting down required great fortitude.

Field mice overran the house. They grew brazen, skittering across the kitchen floor to hide in the warmth beneath the wood stove, even while we sat eating dinner. Larger animals followed the mice. We'd look out the window to see a red fox staring at us from the yard, forlorn, its thick tail tipped in black and white. Some nights we could hear great horned owls hooting on the roof of the house, perched close to the warm chimney belching wood smoke. In the perfect still of early morning, we'd often discover a small herd of deer grazing in our garden, or picking cracked corn from the ground beneath the bird feeder. They seemed too cold and hungry to fear us. If we opened the kitchen door, they would simply stand and stare, unwilling to waste the energy required to run away. Out in the woods, aspen trees popped in the frigid air, and the mournful gurgling of ravens echoed through the cold.

For amusement, Mother mixed liquid soap with water and a bit of glycerin, bent paper clips into small circles, and for a few minutes we blew bubbles outside and watched them freeze. The round opalescent bubbles would float off gently, but before they reached the snow, they'd turn opaque and harden into crystalline spheres. The effect dazzled us. We could pick them up in our gloved hands, breathe on them to make them melt and disappear, or drop them so they shattered like delicate glass ornaments.

Cal told me if I pissed into the wind, my urine might freeze before it hit the ground.

"Don't smile outside after eating something warm," Cal said. "You're liable to crack your teeth." He rubbed his hands together over the stove. "Lord, it's cold."

"We should buy space heaters," Mother said.

"We couldn't run them even if we had them. We only have about 25 amps of electricity from that generator and the panels. The wood stoves do the job. We just have to keep them burning. I'll set an alarm every couple hours or so on the coldest nights, keep the fires going, and we'll get through."

"Did you know it got this cold up here?" Mother asked.

Cal smiled and winked. "I guess not," he said. "The radiator in the truck is froze up like a Popsicle, but the block isn't cracked. She blew her freeze plug, though. When it warms up some, I'll put the plug back in, give her fresh antifreeze."

At night, to keep warm, JJ and I began pushing our mattresses together, doubling down quilts over us, our bodies separated only by the long underwear and sweatshirts we wore as pajamas. Beneath the quilts, we read to one another or turned our ears toward JJ's palm-sized battery-operated radio, warmed by whatever voices we could hear through the static. Sometimes we'd pick up a Canadian station broadcasting a hockey game in French, and I would mimic the announcers to make JJ laugh. At other times we'd hear polka music, or call-in talk shows, men and women telling a radio psychologist stories of lost love and betrayal, and JJ would pretend to be the host. She'd listen to their problems and provide her own offbeat advice.

"He no longer kisses you to sleep at night?" JJ said. "Try some mouthwash, honey. If that doesn't work, smack him on the forehead with a flyswatter and shout, 'Hey, lover boy! Over here! Remember me?'"

Or, "Your dog died and you're so depressed you don't want to live any longer? *Hello!* There are children starving and dying of painful diseases all over the world. There are ten-year-old girls sold into prostitution, people who have lost their whole families in earthquakes and floods. Repeat after me: *it's just a stinking dog!*"

Near the end of November, we had listened to a program about the loss of the Edmund Fitzgerald, an iron ore ship that had gone down in Lake Superior during a blizzard many years earlier. Twenty-nine men had died in the shipwreck, and the ship, now broken in two, remained at the bottom of the lake, along with their bodies. The radio played Gordon Lightfoot's song, "The Wreck of the Edmund Fitzgerald," and it filled me with a longing for David and for our old lives in West Allis. My heart ached again, and tears came to my eyes. Gordon Lightfoot talked for a while about how he came to write the song. Then they interviewed the wife of one of the men who had drowned in the shipwreck. She said she was outraged that people in submarines, with cameras, had been exploring the wreck and had seen some of the bodies. "That is a sacred grave," the woman said. "The human body is seventy-five percent water, and the remains of those men are at rest, returned to their natural state. They should be left in peace." She made drowning to death sound so peaceful, and JJ and I loved her for it.

Lying so close to JJ every night, something else started happening, too. Sometimes before we went to sleep, particularly after she'd taken a bath, JJ would ask me to brush out her hair. Always slightly curled, JJ's hair now reached nearly to her waist. After a windy day it might take her an hour to comb it free of snarls and knots. So she'd turn her back to me and sit cross-legged on the mattress, wearing only a T-shirt or camisole, and I'd run a comb and then a brush through her long, wet hair over and over, pulling out the tangles. JJ would close her eyes and tip her head back, complaining loudly if I wasn't gentle enough. To brace myself, sometimes I'd put my left hand on her shoulder or under her arm against her ribs.

One night I slid my hand down her side along her ribs until my fingertips touched her bare skin. Slowly, JJ lifted the bottom of her shirt, took my hand in her fingers, and slid it higher. I put down the brush. I raised my left hand slowly until I felt the bottom of her breast. JJ tensed. She remained still for a moment, then quickly leaned forward, pushing my hand away.

The following night, as I brushed her hair, my left hand on her side, fingers between her ribs, JJ suddenly crossed her arms in front of her, grabbed her T-shirt, and lifted it off over her head. I could see the white strip of skin where her swimming suit top had been tied across her back that summer. Her skin felt warm and soft against my hand. Her back was marked by a constellation of freckles. Neither of us said anything. Goose bumps formed on her arms and shoulders.

"The door's locked, right?" JJ asked, her back to me.

I got up, walked over to the door, closed it tight, and locked it. We didn't sleep with the door closed because the wood stove was in the hall. But we sometimes closed the door for privacy. I sat down and resumed brushing her hair. I put my left hand gently on JJ's warm rib-cage. She breathed deeply, lifter her elbow, turned slightly toward me. I slid my hand toward her chest, felt where her breast began against my fingertips. She closed her eyes, stayed perfectly still. I leaned forward until my chest touched her back. I lifted my hand, cupped it over her breast, felt the rubbery hardness of her nipple in the middle of my palm. As I touched her, JJ twitched and exhaled. She leaned back into me, put her head against my shoulder.

"I saw you like this the day David died," I whispered.

"I know," JJ said.

I ran my hand softly across her breast, felt her nipple with my fingertips. JJ inhaled sharply, arched her back.

"This isn't right," I said, pulling my hand back. "You're my sister."

"Stepsister," she said.

"Still," I said.

JJ reached for her T-shirt and pulled it over her head. She quickly blew out the lamp, opened our bedroom door.

For a long time, we lay silently in the dark. I thought about what Cal had said in a sermon, how the devil casts his seed in places where the Lord has taken root.

I said, "Do you want me to move our mattresses apart?"

JJ didn't answer right away. "It's too cold," she said, finally.

I began thinking that only a playful, cruel God would fill people with a desire, like hunger, and plant the tree of knowledge close enough to touch. Isn't that one meaning of Eve's behavior in the garden that no one ever talks about? Why blame her? Why send a starving child into a candy store with no money and say, "No stealing"? Why not just create people capable of always doing the right thing?

JJ just laughed when I asked her this.

"Because God would be bored out of his skull with people like that," she said. "Think about it. He put Adam and Eve in the garden because he *knew* they would mess up. Perfect people would be boring."

Early the next morning, still in darkness, while she thought I was sleeping, JJ rolled toward me and slowly slid her hand down the front of my long underwear, encircling my penis with her cool fingers until it hardened. I froze when I felt her and breathed carefully, pretending to sleep. She squeezed me between her thumb and fingers, held me softly for several minutes, then let me go.

I didn't say anything about it. JJ didn't acknowledge it, either. But the following night I found our mattresses on opposite sides of the room, with a rope tied across the middle, and a sheet thrown over that. JJ had taken the first step across some strange bridge that had been growing between us, connecting us, then had gone back to the shoreline to reconsider the danger.

Each week, in spite of the brutally cold weather, a few more shivering souls would shuffle into Cal's church. Jeremiah continued to come, walking more confidently now, without his cane. Bill and Eunice Hall attended every week. A few others started to show up regularly. Mother would sing, Cal would preach, and at the end of the service I would pass a cigar box to take up a collection. Some weeks, we collected sixty or seventy dollars. Each week, Cal's preaching grew bolder and more inspired. His gift for ranting and railing against the hypocrisies of the world now came in handy. Even when he went a little crazy, it no longer embarrassed me.

The week before Christmas, we struggled through thigh-deep snow to go to the woods, cut a ten-foot spruce, and hauled it into the church. Cal nailed a cross of two-by-fours to the bottom of the trunk so it would stand, and JJ, Mother, and I decorated it with whatever we could find. We cut out paper snowflakes, hung carrots, feathers, pine cones, fishing lures, old jewelry. We made a star out of cardboard and tin foil and tied it to the top. We pulled Boston ivy from the silo and used it for garland.

We celebrated Christmas Eve with a midnight service in the Cathedral of David, reading aloud from the Gospel according to Luke, passing the Bible from reader to reader after every few verses. Even though it was nineteen below zero, twenty-three people came for the service. We sat on bales pushed close to the wood stove, a bunch of ragtag country people in winter coats and hats, the men taking turns stoking the fire. The cast-iron stove glowed and seemed to whistle with heat, and many of the people felt warm enough to pull off their coats and hats. When it was twenty below outside, sixty degrees felt like a sauna.

The Christmas story, Cal said, had been written most beautifully in Luke, and he lectured a bit on the translator's elegant choices in diction and syntax. Cal had intended for us all to read only the first and second chapters of Luke, but people liked reading aloud so much they kept on going even beyond the return of the shepherds to their flocks, so Cal skipped ahead to the last three chapters, which told of Jesus's death, resurrection, and ascension, and we read through those as well.

Bill and Eunice Hall read together, evenly and methodically, holding a candle for light. Jeremiah Gibbons read slowly with his glasses off, his nose pressed about two inches from the page. Even JJ and I read. Mother did, too. A few people declined to read, for one reason or another, including a tiny elderly woman who had arrived with Jeremiah. The service closed with everyone singing the first two verses of "Silent Night," a cappella.

After the service, Cal wished everyone a happy holiday, and the people filed out into the cold, started their cars, trucks, and snowmobiles, and drove away. As always, Jeremiah waited to be last. He stood patiently, his pointed nose dripping. He introduced us to the tiny woman he'd brought to church with him.

"This is my lady friend, Agnes Jurasko," Jeremiah said. "She's a Slovak."

"Born in Slovakia," she said, nodding. "Pecovska Nova Ves."

Jeremiah said, "We met two weeks ago at the Senior Center in Herbster." He put his arm around her shoulders. "I was playing Sheepshead, and she came in with her friend Mary."

"We go on Thursdays," Agnes said, "for the chicken dumpling soup."

"Hello, Agnes," Cal said. He shook her hand and she smiled. "It's a pleasure."

Tiny and thin, her face a mask of wrinkles, Agnes had a bright smile and a puff of gray hair on top of her head that looked almost white. Little snowmen earrings hung from her ears. She wore a bright orange coat that reached to her waist, black snow pants, and white boots. She held a snowmobile helmet pinned to one side under an arm.

"This is the preacher healed my arthritis," Jeremiah said to Agnes.

Agnes nodded. "It's so nice to finally meet you!" she said. "Jerry talks about you all the time."

"She's going blind," Jeremiah said.

"Macular degeneration. My father had it, too, before he died. I had to give up driving a car six months ago. I can't hardly see the television or play cards anymore."

"They want to teach her Braille."

"I tell them you can't teach an old dog new tricks."

"She's only eighty-one," Jeremiah said. "People say I'm a cradle-robber!"

Agnes laughed. "I tell them, by the time I learn Braille I'll be six feet under."

"Would you touch her eyes with your fingers?" Jeremiah said to Cal. "She really wants to see again."

"Gosh, Jeremiah," Cal said. "I don't know."

"You got the Holy Spirit, Reverend," Jeremiah answered. "You shouldn't be so reluctant."

"Don't keep your flashlight under a bushel basket," Agnes said. "Let it shine."

"I can dance again because of you," Jeremiah said.

"People say me and Jerry look like Astaire and Rogers waltzing on the dance floor at the VFW."

"Rogers and Gregory Hines," Jeremiah said, smiling.

"That's right," Agnes said. "Gregory Hines."

"You're a healer," Jeremiah said to Cal. "You shouldn't hide that. Would you touch her eyes? Please?"

Cal sighed. "All right," he said. "All right." Agnes stepped forward. Cal raised his hands and placed them lightly on Agnes's forehead, his fingertips sinking into the white of her hair. She closed her eyes and tipped her head up to him, and Cal gently rubbed his thumbs in tiny circles over her eyelids.

"Your hands smell like oak trees," she said softly.

"That's firewood," Cal said.

Cal pulled his hands away and Agnes opened her eyes again.

"Anything?" Jeremiah said to her.

Agnes turned her head to look across the church. She squinted and shrugged.

"Give it some time," Jeremiah said to her. He shook Cal's hand. "Thank you, Reverend," he said. "Thank you for everything."

"Merry Christmas," Cal said, smiling.

"Yes," Jeremiah said. "Merry Christmas and Happy New Year."

We exchanged family gifts after the service. Mother had knit sweaters for Cal, JJ, and I. We gave Mother and Cal an assortment of flavored coffees and some coffee-making equipment that didn't require electricity. You placed ground beans into a funnel-shaped filter, then poured boiling water into the filter and waited for the coffee to drip out the bottom. Cal gave Mother and JJ silk long underwear and deer-hide gloves. He gave me a rifle. He had purchased a gun for himself as well.

"A gun?" I said, as he handed it to me with a red bow tied around the barrel.

"A rifle," he said. "Mine's a shotgun. I bought them used from Bill Hall, but they're in beautiful condition. I don't think he ever even fired yours."

"What do we need guns for?" Mother asked.

"From what I can tell, everyone seems to hunt deer up here," Cal said. "Even Agnes has a blaze-orange coat, which you have to wear, apparently. We could use the meat. One deer would feed us for a month or two."

"But deer are so beautiful," Mother said.

"We won't shoot the pretty ones," said Cal. He looked at me. "What do you say, John? You want to learn?"

"Sure," I said, holding the gun carefully. The stock had been cut from black walnut and polished to a smooth brown sheen. I liked the way it felt in my hands, the heft of the barrel, the feel of the stock against my cheek as I took aim.

Six days later, for his New Year's Eve service, which he called the Millennium Service, Cal intended to preach a sermon on covetousness. When I left the house Sunday morning around eight thirty to feed and water our cows, he had already been hard at work for several hours, he said, revising his text. He sat with a lantern at the kitchen table, the short stub of a pencil in his right hand, a cup of coffee in his left. Mother and JJ were still sleeping.

I didn't disturb him when I entered the kitchen, and he didn't look up from his work. I pulled on a warm coat, my boots, my hat and gloves, and I opened the kitchen door to go outside. I had opened the door only halfway when I saw the cars. Two rows were already parked in our driveway, their exhaust billowing into the cold air. Even more cars were stopped alongside the road, the line stretching maybe a quarter mile to the south. I closed the door.

"Cal," I said.

He smiled. "I know."

Agnes, I thought. "Do you think—"

Cal interrupted. "I don't know."

"But what if she can? Then what?"

"That would be quite a trick, wouldn't it?" He shook his head and then looked up at me and smiled. "I don't know what to think, John."

I didn't know then how much things were about to change for all of us and for Cal most of all. Before that Sunday, he didn't realize the effect he was having on people. He didn't really know what he was doing. Perhaps God was speaking to him, perhaps that is what inspiration and hope feel like, but until that morning, I don't think Cal actually believed he could heal the blind and sick or manipulate the weather. And maybe he didn't really fully believe even then—not yet, not until later in the spring. But Cal had placed his thumbs against Agnes Jurasko's eyelids, and whatever happened had now made Cal's church very popular.

That Sunday, we had to bring in six or seven more hay bales for people to sit on, and every seat was taken by someone who had seen Agnes Jurasko walk into the Herbster Senior Center on Thursday night with her glasses on, her collapsible red-tipped cane nowhere in sight. People sat bundled together, shoulder to shoulder, the way they did at football games, with the same nervous, expectant energy. I counted fifty-one, none of them younger than sixty or seventy, most of them much older. One elderly woman slumped in a wheelchair in front with heavy blankets thrown over their shoulders. Agnes and Jeremiah sat near the wood stove in Jeremiah's usual place. She and Jeremiah held hands.

"Well, my goodness!" Cal said, opening the service. "Welcome. Welcome everyone, to New Eden Church of God with Signs Following, in the Cathedral of David." He looked around the church. "So many people here this morning! Is someone giving away free Super Bowl tickets?" Everyone laughed. "It's 1999," Cal said. "We've reached the end of the millennium. The end of a thousand years of human goodness and folly. We may not see another thousand years. If Y2K is as bad as some folks believe, come midnight tonight, we may not see tomorrow. Computers might just go crazy and launch the cruise missiles, cancel the bank accounts, destroy the world. But I'm not worried. If Y2K ushers in the second coming of the Lord, my friends, there will be a rapture as sure as I'm standing here! And if the rapture comes, people, this time tomorrow, we'll be on our way to heaven."

"Amen!" said Jeremiah.

"In the first epistle of John," Cal said, "we're told, 'Do not love the world or the things in the world. For all that is in the world—the lust of the flesh, the lust of the eyes, and the pride of life—is not of the Father but is of the world.' And if we go back to the Ten Commandments, my friends, we find the admonition, thou shall not covet thy neighbor's stuff. What does that mean, to covet something? It's an unusual verb, isn't it: to covet. The *Oxford English Dictionary* tells us it comes from the Old French, *covetier*, which means to desire, especially to desire eagerly, to long for. We Americans know a lot, don't we, about desiring things? We are the kings and queens of covetousness.

"Last week was Christmas, and all over America, people opened presents—thousands of presents, millions of them. I mean, if you took all the presents exchanged in this country last week and stacked them end to end, they'd probably reach all the way to the moon and back. We live in the richest country in the history of human civilization. We own more stuff than any other people in all of human history, and yet we spent the month of December buying more stuff for one another. It's crazy, isn't it? We racked our brains, didn't we, at times, trying to think of things to buy for friends or family members who have everything? Kids made long lists for Santa Claus, and parents went out and melted their charge cards buying whatever their children wanted.

"And we sent out Christmas cards, too, right? Bragging about our kids, the stuff we've acquired over the year. You ever get those photocopied Christmas letters from braggy friends? 'Last year was another great year for the Smith family,' they usually start out. 'Bob made partner at his law firm suing people, so we bought a new house to celebrate, eight-thousand square feet, with a view of the ocean. Our son Bob Jr., who graduated valedictorian at his high school, took a semester off from Harvard because he's been working on a cure for cancer while also serving as an advisor at the UN. Buffy turned 12 this year, and she was a member of the team of mathematicians who recently discovered the largest prime number. We're so proud of her! Bob Jr. has a girlfriend now, too, a supermodel from Australia. We

traded our sailboat for a larger boat so that they'd have a bit of privacy last summer, when we took that sailing trip around the world we'd always dreamed about.'"

People laughed as Cal read this imaginary letter, and he laughed with them. "I see we're not the only ones who used to get that kind of letter in the mail on Christmas. But you know what? I think it's time for a change! Oh, Christmas is over, now. We can't go back and undo that. It's over and done with. We've read the braggy letters. We've given away the new blenders and the fruit cakes and the pasta makers and who knows what all else, and we've received the new neckties and the golf balls and the perfume. But I want you to think about something for a minute. It's something big so you best take a minute to make room in your brain to hold it. God's word is coming down the tracks like a mighty engine, and we better make some room at the station, because if we join behind Him, that train's going to be so long, we'll never see the end of it!"

"The Lord is coming!" Jeremiah said.

"Blow the horn and fall behind Him or get the hell out the way!" Agnes shouted.

"That's right!" Cal said, laughing. "That's right. His word is going to transform the world! Think about this, now. Just think about this. Unless we all die tonight at midnight, we've got a whole year to prepare for the change. And that change is this: next Christmas, instead of buying another sweater for your Aunt Hazel, who already has fifteen sweaters, why not buy it for someone poor and cold, someone who really needs it, and give it away? Instead of sending fruitcakes or a box of cheese and sausage to your in-laws, send food somewhere where it'll actually be eaten and appreciated, somewhere people are hungry every day of their lives!"

"Amen!" said Eunice Hall.

"That's right, amen!" Cal said. "Are you ready to transform the world?"

"Amen!"

"Just think about that! We have too much already. Our houses are full of stuff! Our closets are bursting. And you know why? Because the devil makes us do it!" Cal paused to glance around the church. "Yes," he continued, "you heard me right. We covet. We desire what we do not have. We long for things we do not need. We see our neighbor's goods, and we want them. A new car. New shoes. New golf clubs. Who teaches us to want so much, to consume without rhyme or reason?"

"Satan!" Bill Hall shouted.

"That's right!" Cal said. "The devil works in advertising, my friends. He has an office on Fifth Avenue. He works on new car lots, in department stores and jewelry stores. He haunts every single Wal-Mart in the United States of America, whispering in children's ears, 'Tell your mother you want that toy! If she says no, scream and stomp your feet until she buys it for you!'"

Everyone laughed and Cal smiled.

"Yeah, it sounds familiar, doesn't it? But we can change that, friends. Next Christmas, if every single American buys just one gift for a stranger who has nothing, and gives it away without expecting to be on a talk show afterward to be feted for his generosity, just think about what will happen! The naked shall be clothed. The hungry will eat. The poor in spirit will be comforted. But why wait until Christmas? What if we started right now? What if we went home today and emptied our closets of our superfluities—that's a big fancy word that means all our extra junk—and gave it away to folks who needed it? I'll start right now! Think about how much money you planned on putting in the collection plate today—a dollar, twenty-five dollars, a hundred dollars. Whatever the number, don't give it to this church. We can eat tomorrow. We can eat all month. In the future, in fact, we're going to resume taking up collections, but we're going to give that money away, friends. We're going to meet our expenses, which are minimal, and then we're going to give the rest away to folks who need it. So today, for practice, I want you to take that money, and you go out into the world, and you give it away yourselves. Do it anonymously. Just find someone needy and give it away. Will you do that?"

"Amen, I will," said Eunice Hall.

"Amen," said some of the others. Everybody nodded their heads.

"Damn right," Jeremiah said. "Give that shit away."

"And now what if we were walking somewhere in our nice winter coats, and we passed a bum lying on the sidewalk, shivering, and we just took off our coat and covered him? What would happen then? What if you gave him your shoes, too?"

"We'd have cold feet!" Jeremiah shouted.

"That's right," Cal laughed. "You'd have cold feet. But you'd have a warm heart. And the Lord would provide you with new shoes. You know he would."

"The Lord provides!" said Jeremiah.

"Yes he does," Cal said. "And what if you opened your wallet and poured the money out to someone in need? What if everyone who had the means did that?" Cal took a deep breath and sighed. "My friends, I'll tell you what would happen. We would have peace on earth, good will toward men. It would feel like Christmas in our hearts every day of the year.

"You know," Cal continued, "back in 1630, a bunch of Englishmen and women came across the Atlantic Ocean and settled in Massachusetts. They sailed on a ship called the Arabella, and along the way, a wealthy man named John Winthrop preached a sermon similar to this one. As those people crossed the ocean, preparing to begin new lives in the New World, Winthrop said, 'we must be knit together, in this work, as one man. We must entertain each other in brotherly affection. We must be willing to abridge ourselves of our superfluities, for the supply of others' necessities. We must uphold a familiar commerce together in all meekness, gentleness, patience, and liberality. We must delight in each other; make others' conditions our own; rejoice together, mourn together, labor and suffer together, always having before our eyes our commission and community in the work, as members of the same body.' But you know what happened? It was all just talk. Beautiful words. They didn't get it done. But we're going to change that. We're going to start over right here at New Eden Church of God with Signs Following, and we're going to get it right." Cal closed his eyes and took a deep breath. He smiled and nodded, asked Mother to begin a song.

"While my wife sings," Cal said, "if there's anyone here who is sick, anyone who is hurting or injured in any way, please ask for God's holy and healing grace to descend upon us now, and then come forward so that I can meet you. Make a line right down the middle here. Right down the middle."

One by one, many of the older people in the church got to their feet and shuffled through the hay bales toward the front. Agnes and Jeremiah were first in line. Jeremiah shook Cal's hand, and Agnes pulled him down and kissed him on the cheek. They returned to their seats. In all, thirty or forty people wandered up to Cal. Mother sang "We Three Kings" and then began "O Little Town of Bethlehem." All that time, Cal spoke to people quietly. He touched their heads, their arms, their backs. He put his finger into their mouths. He knelt and touched their feet. He bent over the woman in her wheelchair, touching his forehead to hers as he spoke. And then one by one, and two by two, the people pulled on their coats and left the church. Agnes backed down our driveway in her car, a huge Lincoln Town Car, with Jeremiah sitting in the passenger seat, his coonskin hat on his lap. After the last person had left the church, Cal sat alone on a straw bale, his feet touching the ground, and stared straight ahead. He put his head into his hands. He looked exhausted.

Mother and JJ had already gone back to the house. I went from candle to candle, blowing them out, until only those on a table by Cal remained glowing.

"Are you coming back to the house?" I asked.

"In a minute," he said. "You go on ahead."

"Agnes can see."

Cal nodded. "Sure looks like it."

"She was driving a car, Cal."

Cal smiled. "Well, I'm glad I'm not out on the road."

That night we slept through the change in the century. In the morning, the first of the year 2000, our world still looked white and cold. There were no assault helicopters on the horizon, no cruise missiles passing overhead. Computers hummed on in the civilized world, while the frozen world outside our windows remained shrouded in snow and in ice.

Chapter 12

The crowd at Cal's next church service grew even larger. People again arrived an hour early, most of them elderly, but a few younger families came, too, families with children. Someone started the fire in the wood stove, and they packed themselves shoulder to shoulder on the hay bales and stood with their backs along the walls. Some children sat on the ground on blankets at their parents' feet. Everyone's eyes wandered curiously about the building, examining the log construction, the peg joinery, the pair of canes—Jeremiah's and Agnes's—that now dangled above the back door. Someone had also hoisted a wheelchair into the rafters and tied it securely into place.

Cal seemed shocked by the size of the crowd, and he stared a long time at the wheelchair above him. He looked tired and frightened. His hands trembled slightly as he gripped the table. He preached a short sermon on miracles, and at one point had the audience in such a frenzy of "Amens" I could hardly hear him.

He said the word *miracle* was derived from the Latin word *miraculum*, which means object of wonder. The *Oxford English Dictionary*, he noted, defines miracle as "a marvelous event not ascribable to human or natural agency, and therefore attributed to the intervention of a supernatural agent, especially, in Christian belief, God." In this sermon, he sought to distance himself from the attention being heaped upon him, sought to turn the people away from him and toward the God who was responsible for their lives, their bodies, their spirits, but it had the opposite effect. The people surged toward the altar, reaching for him, and he had to stop preaching. Cal turned to Mother, and she began singing "Our God, Our Help in Ages Past," but instead of joining in the people kept coming. They pushed toward him, reached out their hands. One man carried a small boy in his arms. I could see metal braces shining on the boy's heels and protruding against his pants. The man carried the boy to Cal, extended his arms, the skinny boy dangling there like a blanket. Cal hesitantly touched the boy's legs and people around him shouted and cheered. The man had tears in his eyes.

I watched it all, enthralled. The people came to Cal and sought the touch of his hands, and he reached out to them. In the gospels, the apostle John seems able to describe the miracles Jesus performs with objectivity, even detachment. Water is changed to wine. A nobleman's son is healed in Galilee. Five thousand people are fed with a few loaves of bread and a couple of fish. John relates it all as if he's describing the weather.

When I watched Cal stand in front of that church and touch people, I was so filled with excitement, awe, and anxiety, I could not stand still. JJ and I walked to the front of the church to listen, to see with our own eyes. Like Mother, JJ remained more skeptical, but I think I began to believe. People who approached Cal on crutches lifted them over their head and waved them in the air, joyfully, as they turned away. Those who looked distraught, their faces hardened in pain, relaxed and softened, their mouths blooming with smiles of joy.

As the line of people seeking Cal's help shortened, I passed around the cigar box to take up the offering. It filled up, and I emptied it into a milk crate in front of the church. It filled a second time, then a third.

At the end of the service, Cal sat alone, counting the money. He shook his head. "There's nearly seventeen hundred dollars here," he said.

"Wow," I said.

"Yeah wow. Next week, we'll ask who is in need, and we'll give most of this away."

Mother sat quietly, watching Cal count the money. "Is this what you want?" she asked. "These people think you can heal them."

"Maybe he can," I said.

Mother frowned.

"What about Jeremiah and Agnes?" I said.

"We don't know he had arthritis," Mother answered. "And we don't know Agnes was blind. We don't know anything about those people, John."

After that Sunday, though, people began arriving at our door at all hours of the day and night, and no longer just on Sundays. Most were from the immediate area, as word of mouth passed from person to person, but others drove in from Minnesota, from Michigan and Illinois, one from as far away as Missouri. Most of the people came for the same reason: they were sick, and they wanted to be healed. A few others had heard that Cal was giving money away, which was true. Each week, he'd announce how much money had been collected at the previous service, and he'd ask for suggestions about where to give it away. On occasion, a few bold people would ask for the money for themselves. Sometimes, Cal gave it to them.

At first, Cal tried to speak to everyone who came to him to be healed, but he could rarely eat a meal or read for an hour alone without being interrupted. Some people wanted to drive him to the hospital where their young son or daughter lay critically ill. He became overwhelmed by all the attention and expectations. He started having trouble falling asleep, went nights without sleeping altogether. He brooded. He grew agitated. He began to avoid the attention. Cars would pull up the driveway and he would run down into the root cellar to hide while Mother turned the people away. Sunday mornings would come, and there would be so many cars in the yard, and so many people pushing and shoving trying to get into the little church, that Cal couldn't even get inside.

A television news crew from Duluth came to the house, took footage of the outside of Cal's log church, asked to tape during the church service. They also wanted to do an interview. Cal declined both requests.

Some of the people Mother turned away returned to their cars but parked down the road, waiting, often for days. Someone even pitched a tent in the snow in the far corner of our alfalfa field. Encouraged, others followed, until a small group of pilgrims had gathered there, their colorful tents dotting the landscape, their campfires smoking.

"This can't go on," Mother said.

Reluctantly, Cal agreed. In mid-February, he erected a wooden gate completely across the end of our driveway and nailed a No Trespassing sign to it. Beside that, he posted a sign announcing that the New Eden Church of God with Signs Following would be temporarily closed for the rest of the winter.

The food supply in our freezer began to dwindle. Canned vegetables slowly disappeared from the shelves. Some of the baking potatoes Mother kept in the root cellar began to sprout and soften. Cal and I carried our guns out into the woods to look for deer, for rabbits, even squirrels. "Hell," Cal said, "I'd take a chipmunk if I saw it." But we saw no game at all. We didn't even see any birds. We put up paper plates as targets and shot at those, for practice, and then we returned home.

He proposed that we go out in the truck with our guns, late at night, to hunt in the dark. We'd use a powerful flashlight to locate the deer. Shining, people called it, and it was illegal.

"If feeding your family is illegal," Cal said, "the law has to change."

We got into the truck just after midnight, put the headlights on high beam, and slowly cruised the ice-covered gravel roads north of New Eden. Our windows remained cracked open to keep the glass clear. Icy, bone-chilling lake air blew through the truck and clouded our breath. I didn't have a driver's license, but Cal let me drive. He sat next to me, my Winchester on his lap, the barrel pointed out his window. The night was so clear and black I could see the swirl of stars in the Milky Way, like a splash of flour across the sky. We drove on like this, beneath the beautiful, cold, dark silence of space, for nearly fifteen minutes. I could see Polaris, the Pleiades, Ursa Minor and Ursa Major, Orion, Gemini, Eridanus.

Cal began reciting Genesis almost in a whisper.

"'In the beginning, God created the heavens and the earth. . . .'" Three deer, all does, came into view in the deep snow on our right. They'd been nibbling on the tips of aspen saplings. Cal and I saw them at the same time.

I looked at the deer but then beyond them. We'd driven further north than we ever had, and I could see Lake Superior in the distance, pockets of ice and water reflecting the moonlight through the trees. The deer froze and raised their heads, cupped their ears toward us, their bodies ghostly in our headlights. A white fire burned in their reflective eyes. I stopped the truck, plugged my ears with my fingertips, and opened my mouth.

As he raised the rifle to his shoulder, Cal whispered, "'The earth was without form, and void; and darkness was on the face of the deep. And the Spirit of God was hovering over the face of the waters.'" Cal closed his left eye and aimed down the barrel. "'Then God said, "Let there be light.'"' The air inside the truck convulsed against my chest and an orange and yellow flame burst from the barrel with the explosion. The three whitetails leaped straight up and bounded across our headlights, one lagging behind the others, pumping blood from her heart, until she collapsed dead thirty yards from the road.

Cal gutted the deer quickly. The foul-smelling offal—tangles of thick gray intestines, the smooth vein-marked stomach, the shocking purple-blue of the liver—steamed in the cold air, and her hot blood melted into the snow. While I held the flashlight, Cal cut through the diaphragm and plunged an arm into the deer nearly to his shoulder to pull the pink rubbery lungs and bloodied heart free. He dropped them in the snow by the gut pile. We loaded the hollowed-out carcass into the back of the truck, covered it with a tarp, and hurried home.

We dragged the deer into the machine shed and closed the doors behind us. Cal lit a lamp, and in the glow of the light, I could already see feral cats in the shadows, slinking toward the blood trail. They lapped at it with pink, sandpapery tongues. Smelling blood, the cows shifted nervously in their stalls.

Pleased with our success, Cal spread the deer's hind legs and tied a rope to each one, preparing to winch her still liquid body up off the floor, for butchering. He recited the rest of the opening of Genesis: "'Then God said, 'Let Us make man in Our image, according to Our likeness; let them have dominion over the fish of the sea, over the birds of the air, and over the cattle, over all the earth and over every creeping thing that creeps on the earth.'"

I nearly threw up watching Cal butcher that deer. I helped him tug on yellow nylon ropes and the deer's body rose off the floor of the barn, rear legs first, until it hung spinning slowly with its nose just off the ground, its gray tongue hanging from its mouth.

After Cal cut off the head and front legs with a saw, he skinned the deer, working the hide slowly down the body, tugging on it, sometimes using a knife to cut the silver skin—which looked a bit like plastic wrap but more iridescent—that connected the smooth, blue-gray inside of the hide to the flesh. As the hide drooped down, inside out, like a sock slowly pulled from a foot, steam rose from the deer's body.

A deer's raw flesh is darker than beef. The flesh of the doe was maroon, almost brown, and covered across the back with yellowish fat an inch thick in places. With the hide removed, Cal cut the deer in half with a meat saw, from tail to neck. When he finished, the deer swung into two pieces, and in each half a row of split white vertebrae glowed like the two sides of a zipper. He pinched and peeled the back straps from the inside, which is like peeling one slice of an orange from the rest of the fruit. With bloody hands, he carved the shoulders into roasts, cut and butterflied the tenderloins and sirloins, separated rump roasts, and then cut ten- or twelve-inch-thick slices across the grain of each hind leg with the saw, the small round femur glowing in each oval steak like a white eyeball.

"The muscles of a deer are a work of art," Cal said. "Such beauty! 'All flesh is grass, and all its loveliness is like the flower of a field.'" He raised his eyebrows at me.

"Isaiah."

Cal nodded. "Very good!"

"The hardest part to watch," I said, "is when you saw the legs off."

"Don't watch then."

The head, legs, and fleshy skeleton of the dead deer—which, stripped of its meat, looked like a prehistoric fossil—would be thrown out in the field in the snow, along with the hide. Over the next several days, all the remaining flesh would be picked from the bones, and many of the bones themselves would be carried away, the snow around those that remained pocked by the tracks of barn cats, weasels, mice, and coyotes.

"John, let me ask you something," Cal said, as he cleaned the knife and saw in a bucket of water. "How's your sister doing, you think?"

I became nervous. "Okay, I guess," I said.

"You two getting along?"

I swallowed. "Yes."

"Your mother thinks she's depressed."

"She is," I said.

"I thought you said she was all right."

"She cries sometimes," I said.

"So does your mother." He shrugged. "What about you? Do you like living up here?"

"I don't hate it."

"Not much of an endorsement," he said. "Your mother wants to go back to West Allis. I think she just wants to be able to visit David's grave." He took a deep breath, sighed noisily. His eyes teared. "When the weather warms, John, all of this will be redeemed. I promise you." He wiped his eyes with his fingertips. "We just have to hang on," he said. "Spring is coming. Spring can't be too far away."

Chapter 13

By mid-March, at last, spring occasionally put her leg through the door, giving us a vision of more beauty to come. There were days when the temperature reached into the upper 40s, and the driveway and parts of the yard devoid of snow would soften into a muddy mess. The sunny days broke the monotony, helped to offset our increasingly fractured lives, but the tension between Mother and Cal had grown so great that at times they seemed unable to even speak to one another. One evening, Mother publicly raised the subject of our return to West Allis, and that tension boiled over.

"I've already told you," Cal said. "There's nothing there for us."

"David is there," Mother said, near tears, her mouth quivering.

"But our lives are here now."

"Look at us!" she said. "Look at our children! They're thin as scarecrows, Cal. You and John haven't had haircuts for almost a year. We haven't been to the dentist. The kids haven't been to school. What are we doing? Can you tell me that? What are we waiting for?"

"We have to be patient," Cal answered.

"I'm done being patient," Mother said. "Sometimes I am so lonely out here I want to scream."

"It's peaceful here," Cal interjected. "It's beautiful."

"Lonely is not the same as peaceful," JJ said.

Cal said, "The Lord works at his own pace."

Mother sighed. "Well it's not fast enough," she said. "I know that's not what you want to hear, but it's true. We're waiting. For what? I don't know what to think anymore."

"If I understood everything that's happening," Cal said, "I'd certainly tell you. But I don't."

Mother said, "I sit here day after day, no machine to wash our clothes in, no lights at night, my hands so cold I can't even button a shirt. All I can do is think. I've got all the time in the world for that.

I start thinking about David, and I start missing him so badly I can't even breathe. He's so far away. I can't visit him. I can't bring flowers." She started crying, dropping her forehead into her hand.

"It's our time to mourn," Cal said, reaching for her hand. "A time for every purpose under heaven."

"I miss him so much," Mother said through tears.

"I do too, darling. The Lord says, 'Be not afraid, I go before you always.'"

JJ slapped her hand against the table. "Will you cool it with all the Bible crap, Daddy! I am so fucking sick of it! Speak like a goddamn human being!"

This outburst shocked Cal. It shocked all of us.

"Watch your mouth, darling," Cal said. Veins bulged in his forehead.

"I'm through watching my mouth!" JJ sneered. "Anna's upset. She is trying to talk to you. And the best you can do is quote from the Bible like a fucking parrot."

"Jennifer!"

JJ looked at her. "It's the truth, Anna. I'm sick of it. He's out of his freaking mind and we're all just sitting in the boat watching him paddle us over the waterfall."

Cal nodded slowly. "I see." He stood up, put his hands to his belt, and pulled the tail of the belt free of the buckle.

"Don't you dare," Mother said.

Cal's belt was thick brown cowhide, two inches wide. The buckle was a large silver square the size of a deck of cards. He grabbed it with his right hand and slid the belt slowly from his pants without taking his eyes from JJ. He had never hit either of us, had never even threatened. So this was new. It frightened me. "Do you know Ephesians six, verses one through three?"

"Fuck Ephesians and the horse they rode in on," JJ said defiantly.

"Jennifer, stop it right now!"

"I'll tell you what it says, darling," Cal said calmly. "'Children, obey your parents in the Lord, for this is right. Honor your father and mother, which is the first commandment with promise: that it may be well with you and you may live long on the earth.'"

"Cal!" Mother yelled. "Sit back down!"

"JJ," I said.

"Shut up, Johnny," she said to me, without taking her eyes from her father.

"That's an easy one, love," Cal said to her. "We'll just do the opening verse: 'Children, obey your parents in the Lord.' Easy as pie."

"Talk to me like my daddy," JJ said. "Use your own words. I want my fucking life back. I want my daddy back. God damn you."

Cal shook his head and took a step around the table, closer to JJ, an arm's length away. "'Children, obey your parents in the Lord,'" he said.

A north wind howled against the house, rattling the windows. JJ glanced at me once, fearfully, then looked back up at Cal.

"Jennifer, for me," Mother said. "Please."

JJ shook her head no.

Cal said again, "'Children, obey your parents in the Lord.'" He looped the end of his belt back against the buckle, which shortened the belt by half, and doubled it. In his right hand, it dangled at his side to his knee. He stood behind JJ's chair.

"'Children,'" Cal said, "'obey your parents in the Lord.'" He gathered JJ's long hair in his left hand and pulled down softly. JJ's head tilted back, the white of her throat exposed to the ceiling.

"Cal, what are you doing?" I said.

JJ reached her hands back to try to pull her hair free, but Cal held on and leaned over her. "Just say that, please, darling," Cal said. "'Children, obey your parents in the Lord.'" Tears spilled from JJ's eyes.

"Fuck you," she said through gritted teeth.

Mother ran around the table and grabbed Cal by the arm, but he wouldn't let go of JJ's hair.

"I'm sorry, honey," Cal said.

I slowly reached one foot beneath the table. I had wool socks on, and I reached until I found JJ's knee. I put my foot against her leg, ran it up her thigh. She strained to turn her head toward me, looked at me through the corners of her eyes.

"'Children'" I said, beginning the verse for her.

JJ bit her lower lip. Tears spilled from the outside corners of her eyes.

127

"Cal, please stop," I said.

Mother walked to the sink, and when she appeared again, she held a carving knife in her hand. She walked over to Cal and placed the tip of the knife against his ribs. Her voice was hoarse with rage: "I said let her go."

"I'm not hurting her."

"You let that child go right now."

JJ looked at Mother. "Anna," she said. "What the hell?"

"'Children,'" Cal said softly, his eyes locked on Mother, "'obey your parents in the Lord.'"

"Oh for Christ's sake," JJ said. "Children," she intoned, flatly, "obey your crazy parents in the Lord."

Cal released her. No one spoke. We all looked at each other. It felt as if we were surveying the damage of a terrible windstorm. JJ pushed her plate away. She buried her face in her arms and began sobbing.

Mother glared at Cal, who watched her intently. Slowly, she put the knife on the table and sat back down. Cal turned and walked back to his chair, threading his belt through the loops of his dirty blue jeans.

"Thank you, sweetheart," Cal said.

Mother sneered at Cal. "What the hell has happened to you?"

Cal raised his eyebrows. "'Wives, submit to your own husbands, as to the Lord,'" he said. "'Therefore, just as the church is subject to Christ, so let the wives be to their own husbands in everything.'"

Mother's hands began to tremble. She stood up from her chair, raised her plate over Cal, and threw it to the floor at his feet. The glass exploded, the pieces scattering across the floor. Mother walked around the table to JJ, gently tugged on her arm to get her to stand, wrapped an arm over her shoulders, and led her up the stairs, slamming the bedroom door behind her.

Cal and I finished our dinner together awkwardly, scraping our plates and trying not to look at one another.

"That could have gone better," Cal said, trying to get me to laugh.

I wouldn't look at him.

"I wasn't going to hurt her, John."

"You did," I said. "You did hurt her."

He nodded. "I'll apologize. Your mother will have me begging for mercy over this, when all is said and done."

"If we don't go back to West Allis," I said, "then we should start going to school here."

Cal glanced at me. "I thought we'd already talked about this."

"I want to go to college, Cal! I have to graduate from high school to go to college."

"Not necessarily. You're learning so much here, John. I've been reading the Bible, and you've been listening. That education will take you anywhere."

"The Bible?"

Cal nodded. "God's encyclopedia."

"What about trigonometry?" I asked. "What about art? History? Spanish?"

Cal shrugged. "That's all probably in the Bible somewhere."

"Spanish is in the Bible? Come on, Cal! Listen to yourself!" I sighed and shook my head, exasperated.

"Listen to me now."

I stared at the table angrily and refused to look at him.

"John, please," he said. "Just listen. Next week is Easter week, and I'm going to open up the church again. I'm going to put signs up in all the little towns around here, and I am going to put on a Good Friday service people will be talking about for the rest of their lives. I'm going to need your help with it, with one small part of it." He put a hand on my shoulder. "You know, when I met your mother, you were a little boy, two years old. She thought I wouldn't be interested in a woman who bore a child out of wedlock. Those days, that was somewhat scandalous. But none of that mattered. I loved your mother more than my own life, and from the first time I took you up in my arms, I loved you, too. You have been a son to me, John, in every way. You know that." He smiled, slapped my shoulder twice, and stood up from the table. He stood at the sink and looked out the window.

"John," Cal said, "I want you to take the chain saw out into the woods, and I want you to find a nice, straight oak tree about as big around as your thigh. Take the tractor. When you find the right tree, take it down, trim off all the branches flush at the trunk, and then cut the tree into two pieces, one about twelve feet long, and the other about five feet long. Then drag the pieces to the cathedral and leave them right outside the door. Okay, can you do that?"

I nodded. "Why?" I asked.

Cal smiled. "You're going to play the role of a Roman carpenter today. You're going to build me a cross the size that Jesus was crucified on."

I didn't mind doing the work. I loved driving the tractor, and I was pleased Cal trusted me alone with the chain saw.

I took down the tree, then dragged the best fifteen feet of it through the muddy field and unchained it in front of the church. I cut the five-foot section away from the longer pole. Cal showed me where to notch each piece, and then I took out the two notches with an axe and a chisel and attached the cross piece with four-inch pole barn spikes so it was almost flush with the longer section.

Inside the church, near the front, Cal had augered a hole about three feet deep. At the base of the cross, he measured up five feet and then nailed a small platform about a foot long.

"Okay," he said. "Let's drag her inside."

We muscled the cross into the church and then carefully slid the base into the hole Cal had made. The cross dropped into place.

"Perfect," Cal said.

"Once it dries out," I said, "we could strip off the bark and it would look even better."

Cal shook his head. "No," he said. "I know people wear pretty crosses as jewelry, but they miss the point. Roman crucifixion was ugly. Horrific. They flayed the flesh from your bones with whips, then drove nails through your heels and hands and left you up there to suffer. Sometimes days passed before you died. Imagine the agony."

I nodded.

"Human beings are the only creatures on the planet to inflict suffering and death for its own sake. And we're particularly good at it. I wonder why in the hell that is."

Cal's Good Friday service was scheduled for three o'clock in the afternoon. People started arriving at two-thirty, parking their cars along the road, walking solemnly up the muddy driveway. Jeremiah and Agnes were among the first to arrive, and many others from the Herbster Senior Center pulled up not long afterward. Cal greeted everyone at the door of the church, and they seated themselves on straw bales. Even though it was probably fifty degrees outside, Cal had fired up the wood stove inside the church at one-thirty, so the temperature inside was well above 70.

"Put up a new cross, I see, Reverend," Jeremiah said, nodding his approval. "Left the ladder up there so we can all try it on for size?" He chuckled. Cal's wooden ladder was still leaning against the cross-piece. That morning, Cal had nailed a small wooden sign with the letters INRI to the top of the cross. Pontius Pilate had ordered the Latin phrase *Iesus Nazarenus Rex Iudaeorum*—Jesus of Nazareth, King of the Jews—be added to the cross Jesus was to hang on, and Cal had now included it.

"Should I move the ladder?" I asked Cal.

He shook his head. "No, John. Let's just leave it be."

"There is no resurrection without the cross," said Jeremiah.

"That's right," Cal said, smiling.

At ten minutes after three o'clock, with about sixty people in attendance, Cal closed the church doors and began the service. Mother stood and began the opening hymn, "Were You There?" and everyone sang along through all the verses, then looked up at Cal expectantly, where he stood with his papers at the lectern.

"I want to thank you all for coming, and I want to apologize for canceling services through the worst of the winter. This is a chapel, not a mega-church. I don't want to be a televangelist shilling God's mercy to the highest bidder. To be honest, I don't really know why I've been called to this. I don't even know if I'm doing right by all of you folks.

"But my friends, I'm here to tell you, I have heard the voice of God calling me. I have heeded that voice to the best of my ability, though I know I have fallen short. Without God's grace, we are nothing. With that grace we can move a mountain with a little hand shovel. With his grace we can soak up the oceans with a sponge!"

"Amen!" cried Jeremiah.

"That's right, amen!" Cal said, his voice growing stronger. "Be not afraid, God says, I go before you always. You know what that means, don't you? It means you don't need a map when God is leading you! You just get in the car and drive! You just start walking! You just get on the bike and pedal away! If you follow Him no matter where he takes you, you will never be lost."

"That's right," Jeremiah said.

"You might not recognize where you are," Cal said. He looked over at Mother and smiled. "You might look around and say, 'Lord, where the heck have you taken me? What is this place? What am I doing here?' But if we put our faith in God, we have to trust Him. We might not recognize the bed he provides, but it will be restful. We might not recognize the food he gives, but it will nourish us. And we may not even recognize the person we have become, but it is his grace and love that has shaped us and given us new life." He put his hands on his chest, moved his hands to the top of his head. "The body is an empty shell, the husk of an ear of corn, without God's grace. The brain is an unholy temple without God's love."

Cal nodded and looked around. "We talk about love all the time, don't we?" he said softly. "Rock stars sing love songs. Valentine's Day cards are filled with little love notes, roses are red, you know, that sort of thing. I used to be an English teacher, friends, and I can tell you that there may be no more beautiful love poems than Elizabeth Barrett Browning's *Sonnets from the Portuguese*. In Sonnet 43, and you might recognize this, she writes, 'I love thee to the depth and breadth and height / My soul can reach.' That's beautiful, isn't it? Human love for one another brings our souls to the heights of the angels." He pointed to the cross. "Great as it is, though, that love is nothing, friends. That love is nothing at all compared to the love it took to be tortured and nailed on that cross to die."

At this point, Cal paused and took a deep breath. He looked up at the top of the cross, and then back down at his lectern. His hands appeared to be quivering. From behind the lectern, he pulled out a small wooden handle—a short piece of broomstick—to which he'd attached five or six pieces of eighth-inch braided rope, each about twenty inches long. Something knotty and heavy attached to each end caused the ropes to dangle toward the ground. "I made this a few days ago," Cal said. "This is a model of the whip the Romans used to scourge prisoners prior to crucifixion." He fingered the ends of the ropes. "I've got a few jacks tied in here at each end—you know the game you played as a kid, bounce the ball, pick up the little metal jacks? But the Romans would have used sharp pieces of goat or sheep bone, and tiny lead balls with holes bored through the middle."

When Cal removed his shirt, everyone in the church went still. A collective hush settled over the room. His chest and arms were covered in dark curly hair, and his skin looked pale after a long winter of never seeing the sun. He lifted the whip again in his right hand. "The prisoner's arms would have been tied together"—he put his wrists together to demonstrate—"and then attached to a post of some kind, probably six or seven feet high to expose the full back and buttocks of the prisoner, who would have been naked." He shrugged. "Naked because the Romans weren't satisfied with agony. They wanted humiliation, too. The crucifixion team consisted of four Roman soldiers, called a *quaterno*, supervised by a centurion, someone called the *exactor mortis* who was responsible for verifying the death of the prisoner. There were no rules, with one exception: the goal of scourging was to make the victim suffer excruciating pain, but never to the point of death."

Cal bent over and lifted a piece of barn board, grayed and weathered with age, maybe six feet long, a foot wide. He leaned it against the cross on an angle. "Imagine our savior enduring this," he said quietly. He swung his arm forward, violently. The first time the ropes raked against the wood, someone in the church cried out. The whip whistled through the air with each stroke, and tiny pieces of wood exploded in strips. Each time the metal spikes struck the wood sounded like a rifle shot. Cal struck the board ten, eleven, twelve times. When he finished, he raised the board high so everyone could see the damage, then he passed it to someone in the congregation so people could all examine it more closely.

Long ugly gouges penetrated the surface, exposing the bright, fragrant, unweathered pine beneath. Some of the wounds looked to be a half-inch deep.

Cal dropped the whip at the base of the cross, then reached behind it again and produced a large hammer and two pole barn spikes, four inches long. He explained the various ways the Romans might have nailed a prisoner to a cross, noting that depictions of Christ in some medieval paintings seemed to have been more historically accurate than others. "The feet," he noted, "were most likely depicted wrongly.

Archaeologists have discovered many heel bones of crucified corpses with nails driven through from the side, so it appears often each foot would have been nailed to the side of the tree with separate nails.

"As for the hands, we don't know." He held the point of a nail to his palm. "Nails through the palms would have been sufficient if the feet were nailed well or if the arms were also tied with ropes, as they often were. If not, those nails would have been unable to support the full weight of a dying man without pulling through. So it is possible," here he moved the nail to a point in the center of his wrist, "that nails were driven through here, in the hollow between the ulna and the radius, or in the gap of the wrist where seven bones crowd together."

He put the hammer and nails on the lectern and then lifted the whip again. "Friends," he said. "As human beings, we have all known pain. Physical pain, emotional pain, spiritual pain, we might say that it is our ability to endure this range of difficulties that makes us human. But no matter how bad it gets, none of that approaches the pain of Jesus Christ." Cal looked at me. "John?" he said softly. He raised the whip in one hand. "John's going to play the part of a Roman soldier today. John, would you come up here, please?"

I swallowed. I shook my head and stayed sitting beside JJ.

"You're not going to scourge me, John," he said. "All I want," he paused, spoke softly. "What I'd like is to show these people a single example, a single stroke, of what Jesus endured probably by the hundreds. So—once, John. Once. Is all I ask."

I looked at Mother and she shook her head. I didn't move.

He nodded and sighed. "JJ?" he asked, his gaze shifting to her.

She almost laughed, her voice choked with terror, but she remained seated. Cal looked at Mother. She crossed her arms and looked down at the ground.

Cal looked out into the crowd of people, who stared at him, silently. He raised the whip as if to give it to someone in the congregation. All sat still. A couple of the older women began to weep.

"I understand your reticence," Cal said. "I do. But please. Someone."

A silent stand-off ensued for twenty seconds, thirty, a minute. Then Jeremiah raised his hand and got to his feet. Slowly, he removed his hat, adjusted his pants at the waist, and shuffled forward toward Cal.

"Thank you, Jeremiah."

At ninety-one years old, and frail, Jeremiah didn't have a lot of strength. I think everyone inside that church felt some relief when he stood up. But I still found myself holding my breath. I think everybody did.

Cal held the whip out to Jeremiah, and he took it in his right hand. He lifted it to his face, inspected each of the ropes carefully, felt the metal jacks with his fingertips. Cal walked to the cross and leaned forward, placing both hands against it, one on each side.

Jeremiah shuffled up beside him with the whip, but he stopped short. He dug into the pocket of his pants. "Reverend," Jeremiah said. "I will do this for you, for all of us, but on my terms."

Cal released the post and waited.

From his pocket, Jeremiah produced a small red pocketknife. "Reverend, the jacks on the end of these ropes will slice you open like razor blades. I can't have that. Can't have it." One by one, he cut the string of metal jacks from the end of each rope and let them fall to the ground. He closed the knife, put it back into his pocket. "Okay, now," he said. "That's more like it."

Cal gripped the post again. For a moment, Jeremiah looked out at the congregation. He took a deep breath and exhaled. "Well," he said. "Let's get it over with. You ready?"

"Ready," Cal said.

"My lord," Jeremiah said. "My lord." With a short grunt, and a little hop, Jeremiah swung the whip. The ropes met the flesh of Cal's back with a bright, loud snap, and Cal screamed and fell to his knees, and then to his side. He writhed on the ground, arching his back, kicking both legs, sliding his heels in the dirt. Then he went still. Jeremiah leaned over him and shook his head.

Mother rushed to the front of the church. She put her face down against Cal's. Some of the people stood to try and see. Cal stayed still for at least a minute. Then his legs stirred. He slowly sat up, eyes closed. Then he opened his eyes and stood up, and everybody started clapping. When he turned his back to us, the applause faded. On an angle across his back were five long, bright red welts, each raised to the thickness of a man's finger, all of them weeping blood. Cal whispered something to Mother, and she returned to her seat.

He shook Jeremiah's hand, then raised one of Jeremiah's arms as if he were a boxer who had just knocked out an opponent. People clapped for Jeremiah, too.

"Friends," Cal said softly. He chuckled. "I am never doing that again! Seriously, never felt pain like that. Every nerve lit up, like I'd been electrocuted, the force of it exploding in my brain. Everything just went black. Now my back feels like it's on fire. It's really throbbing, kind of like a burn. Wow." He raised his arms and grimaced. He took a deep breath and then glanced up at the cross.

Slowly, wearing only his blue jeans, Cal painfully pulled himself up on the tiny platform he'd attached to the front of the cross and then raised his arms as if in crucifixion. "This is where our redemption was fully delivered," he said. "This is where our Lord wrote the check that all of us cash every day. For at least three hours, according to the gospels, Jesus suffered here, his bloody body nailed to this Roman tree." He looked down at Jeremiah and smiled. "Jeremiah, you'll find the nails and the hammer there on the rostrum. I've got some three-inch common nails there."

Jeremiah looked up at Cal. He jerked his head. "Reverend, no."

Cal put out his hands, showed his palms. "Just the hands," he said. "There's a place here in the middle, Jeremiah. I've marked it with a small dot of ink. The nail will pass through flesh only. You'll find a bottle of bleach on the ground there. Just dip each nail in the bleach, and then climb up on the ladder. Two or three swings of the hammer on each side, you'll be done."

Jeremiah took a deep breath, let his cheeks puff up, then blew it out. He looked back at Agnes. Her eyes were wide, staring. Some of the people inside the church fell forward off of their straw bales to be on their knees. Seeing this, others followed.

"Reverend," Jeremiah said, sniffling. "You know I was a carpenter, right? You know that was my living, making stick-built houses."

"I didn't know that."

"Well, you putting me back to work today. Calling me out of retirement."

"Be careful," Agnes said to Jeremiah. She turned to the elderly woman next to her. "He has dizzy spells."

"I can climb a ladder four, five foot, sugar," he said.

Jeremiah took the hammer and one nail and shuffled to Cal's left side first. He put the nail between his lips and slowly climbed the ladder. He removed his glasses, folded and slid them into his shirt pocket, then pressed his hooked nose up against Cal's hand until he found the dot of ink.

"Right here?" he said, looking at Cal. Cal nodded and inhaled deeply, closing his eyes.

"Reverend, I really don't want to do this." Cal didn't respond. Jeremiah shook his head once, mumbled something softly, put the point of the nail against Cal's hand and swung the hammer hard.

Cal grimaced but did not cry out. Jeremiah took his fingers from the nail, and it held. The point had found purchase in the tree. A small bulb of blood, red as a rose hip, swelled where the nail penetrated flesh, and then it overflowed its drop and ran down Cal's hand.

"You all right, Reverend?" Jeremiah asked, his face just two feet from Cal's. Cal managed a small nod.

I moved the ladder over to the other side of the cross, and I held the base of it steady as Jeremiah climbed. He swung the hammer, but he needed a second strike to bury the nail through Cal's other hand and into the wood. Eyes closed, Cal gritted his teeth. Blood now dripped steadily from both of his hands. He moaned.

JJ leaped to her feet and left the church.

Still on the ladder, Jeremiah leaned his head over toward Cal's face. "How long you going to stay up here, Reverend?" he asked. "Because I'm fixing to yank these nails out right now."

"Awhile longer," Cal said. "Please."

Never had Cal's church been a more haunting, mysterious place than the three or four minutes he spent nailed to that cross.

Cal cried when Jeremiah removed the nails, and five or six of the men rushed forward and brought him down. I don't know why he cried. The pain of it, maybe, or relief. Or something else. He never said. After that afternoon, he never spoke of it. Mother went into the house and returned with a bottle of alcohol and an old dishtowel, and they tore the towel into narrow strips, washed the wounds in his hands, and wrapped them. Mother gently pulled his sweatshirt back down over his shoulders.

Before everyone went home, I passed around the cigar box, which filled with cash, and Cal sat hunched on a straw bale in front and put his bloodied, bandaged hands on anyone who wanted him to do so. Several elderly people came forward, including an old woman so crooked with osteoporosis her neck and shoulders curled like a fish-hook, and she had to tip her head to the side and look up through the corners of her eyes to see. She wore a gray sweater over a black dress. Her silver hair had been curled into a tight bun, and the knuckles of her hands bulged with arthritis. She moved slowly, with an aluminum walker.

"Reverend," she said softly, when she finally reached Cal. "I believe."

Cal gently took this woman into his arms, and he rubbed his bandaged hands along her neck and down her spine. "What's your name, darling?" he asked.

"Eleanor."

"That's a beautiful name," Cal said.

"Your hands feel warm," she said. "It is the heat of the Holy Spirit." She looked at Cal and began weeping. "I was sterile, so I never had any children."

Cal smiled. "There's still time. Sarah was ninety years old when she gave birth to Isaac, and Abraham was a hundred!"

"Oh no. That's not what I mean. I mean when I pass on, Reverend, I am willing everything to you."

"That's not necessary," Cal said.

"This has been the most beautiful day of my life," Eleanor said.

Cal kissed her gently on the forehead. She wiped the tears from her face with a handkerchief pulled from inside the sleeve of her sweater, then she turned around and slowly began to make her way back toward the doors. Halfway down the aisle, she paused to put on her coat and hat and gloves. She leaned forward and lifted the walker, but then, taken with a change of heart, she instead tipped the walker over on the ground and left it there. Placing one foot carefully in front of the other, her small arms outstretched for balance, she straightened as best she could and walked confidently from the church.

The following week, after Cal's church service ended, we were counting the money in the cigar box—Eleanor had left a check for $500—and a man we'd never seen before entered the church. He wore a tan uniform with a badge pinned to one pocket, and a dark brown cowboy hat, which he removed as he came in.

"Can I help you with something?" Cal asked.

"Morning, folks," the man said. He adjusted his pants and walked to the front of the church. He was short, rather heavy, maybe in his 50s, with a paunch of belly hanging over his belt, the sort of man who has to hitch up his pants every time he gets up out of a chair. He had a thick neck and double chin that hid the knot of his dark brown tie. "So you're the folks bought old Mr. Hinton's place out here," he said, nodding. "Looks like you've done a lot of beautiful work out there already." He shook Cal's hand. "Are you the minister here?"

"Yes I am," Cal said.

He nodded. "Gary Kalupa," he said. "I'm a deputy sheriff, Bayfield County." He smiled. "I've been hearing a lot about this church. Heard you're the guy who cured Agnes Jurasko of her blindness."

"You know Agnes?" Cal asked.

"My mother does," he said. "She lives over in Herbster. She's been out here a couple times, comes with her boyfriend from the nursing home. I got to tell you, you've got a lot of the old folks all stirred up."

"Preaching isn't against the law, is it?" Cal asked.

Sheriff Kalupa shook his head. "No, sir," he said. "It certainly is not." He seemed like a friendly man, a talker, the kind of person Cal usually seemed to like. He pulled a small notebook and pen from his shirt pocket, flipped the notebook open. "Someone called our office last week, though, a lawyer from Superior—you know those big city types—and said there might be an illegal business operating on the premises."

Cal frowned and shook his head. "An illegal business? What on earth are you talking about?" I'm not operating a business. This is a church."

The sheriff nodded, looked up at the huge cross in front. "Certainly looks like a church," he said. "The lawyer, though, he said his aunt was here, and that you treated her arthritis. Said you also brainwashed the woman. Eleanor Fisher, her name was. Older woman, real short, sway back."

"Eleanor," Cal said, nodding. "Yes."

"So you remember her?"

"I do."

"Apparently she contacted him because she wanted to make a change to her will? And it probably won't surprise you that he wasn't too excited about being disinherited. So he called the sheriff's office, made a complaint. And my boss said to follow up."

Cal laughed. "There's obviously some confusion," Cal said. "I'm a preacher, and this is the New Eden Church of God with Signs Following. It isn't a business, and it isn't a clinic."

Sheriff Kalupa nodded. He looked up in the church rafters and frowned at the wheelchair. Cal shrugged. "Someone put that up there."

"And people pay you," the sheriff said. He nodded at the stacks of money resting on the straw bale.

"It's a free will offering," Cal said. "We give most of the money away."

"So it's your contention that this is not a clinic or a business."

"It's a church!" Cal said. "That's my contention."

Sheriff Kalupa nodded. "You seem like a good man," the sheriff said. "Old people, you know, some of them can be like children. They don't make the best decisions. They can be taken advantage of. The word that lawyer kept throwing around was 'fraud.'"

"No one is being taken advantage of here," Cal said, growing agitated.

The sheriff raised his hands gently. "Please," he said. "I don't want any trouble." He kicked at the dirt, and I noticed his shoes were scuffed and unpolished. His pants were frayed in the back where they dragged when he walked. "I'm just doing my job."

"Doing your job," Cal said angrily. "Well, you can just march your fat ass right out of here, because this is a church, and I will not have it defiled by reckless accusations."

Mother walked toward the sheriff, close enough to lean in toward his shoulder. He didn't look at her, though. Not right away.

Sheriff Kalupa's face flushed. He looked at his hat, ran a hand over his short crew cut. He noticed Mother standing beside him.

Mother put a hand on his shoulder. "I'm sorry," she said. "We moved here last September after our youngest boy—" She looked at Cal. "Our son, David, drowned in the city pool. He was six years old."

Sheriff Kalupa nodded. The anger seemed to melt from his face.

"Ma'am," Sheriff Kalupa said, "I'm so sorry. I'm deeply sorry for your loss. The death of a child is an awfully difficult thing."

"Get off our property!" Cal shouted.

The sheriff breathed in deeply and nodded. He looked intently at Cal. "I'm sorry for your loss."

Sheriff Kalupa put the notebook in his pocket and left the church, walked to his patrol car. He started the car and waved before slowly backing down the driveway. He drove off toward the south.

"You didn't have to antagonize him," Mother said. "He seemed like a decent man."

Cal shook his head. "I didn't like his tone, and I didn't like his accusations."

In the morning, Cal walked into the kitchen with a manic energy unusual, even, for him. I sat alone at the table. JJ and Mother were upstairs, still asleep. He'd been up most of the night, he said. He'd had a vision.

"A dream?"

"A vision, John," he said. "I woke from a sound sleep at midnight. I had to walk. I went outside and wandered our fields. Then I walked all the way to Bill Hall's place, saw the light on in his kitchen, went in and had breakfast with him at five in the morning. I couldn't contain it. I told him what I'd seen. We talked about it. He drove me back."

"What is it?"

"I'll tell you in a few days. I'm talking about something bigger than anything we'd allow ourselves to imagine. I may need your help."

I shrugged.

"Promise me you can stare awe and wonder in the face."

When the time came, early one afternoon, just after lunch, Cal told Mother and JJ that he and I needed to take a trip in the truck, that we'd be gone all day and night and would return the following morning. He wouldn't say where we were going, or why, but he promised everyone would be happy when we got back home.

"Are we getting a flush toilet?" JJ asked.

"No," Cal said, and smiled.

We left the house, stopping off in Iron River, where Cal filled the truck with gas and made a telephone call from a pay phone. While he was on the telephone, I got out and looked in the back of the truck. Under a tarp I found a winch, a long length of chain, several coils of thick rope, two shovels, and a pickax.

An hour out of town, heading south on Highway 13, I again asked where we were going.

"You don't want to be surprised?" Cal asked.

"No," I said, "I don't."

"You sure?"

I nodded.

"We're going to get your brother," Cal said.

"David?"

"You have another brother I don't know about?"

I felt so shocked I didn't know what to say. I felt sick to my stomach. "What do you mean? I don't understand."

"We're going to bring him here, to New Eden."

"Ourselves? Cal, isn't that against the law?"

"If it is, it shouldn't be," Cal said. "He's my son."

I took a deep breath and looked out the windshield. I blinked my eyes and kept swallowing.

"John," Cal said quietly. "There's more. When we get your little brother home, I'm going to pray over him. I'm going to sit by David's side and pray. For days, if need be. I'm going to pray over his body until—I don't even want to speak it. But I know now what we've been waiting for. I know what I'm supposed to do."

I could no longer keep from crying. I can't really say why. Tears erupted from my eyes. I covered my face with my hands.

Cal reached a hand across the seat and put it on my leg. "That's it, John," he said. "Let it go. Let it all out. Believe me, I know. The Spirit's presence is overwhelming."

PART IV: EARTH

But, to conclude, Adam and Eve did first begin this innocent work, to plant the earth to remain to posterity, but not without labor, trouble, and industry. Noah and his family began again the second plantation, and their seed as it still increased hath still planted new countries, and one country another, and so the world to that estate is, but not without much hazard, travel, discontents, and many disasters.

—John Smith,
A Description of New England (1616)

Chapter 14

It was after one o'clock in the morning when we left the freeway and drove into West Allis, passing a series of traffic lights that slowed our progress through the city's west side. I'd fallen asleep, but the lights of the city flickered against my eyelids and I awoke, excited to see so many familiar things: billboards, a local park, businesses along Greenfield Avenue. I felt as if I'd been living in a foreign country and had returned home.

Cal turned into an alley and got out of the truck with a socket wrench in his hand.

"Wait here a minute," he said. When he got back inside he handed me the license plates from our truck. "Put these on the floor under the seat for now," he said.

We drove to the cemetery and slowly made our way to where David lay buried. We followed a winding gravel road, turned left along a hedgerow, under a line of trees, then pulled off the gravel into the grass between the marble markers next to David's headstone. Piled beside the headstone were square pieces of muddy sod, which had been cut neatly from the grave.

I was surprised to see another truck waiting for us, the engine idling. Two men inside got out to shake hands with Cal and me. One of the men was Bill Hall. I must have looked shocked, because he smiled as he shook my hand.

"Hello, neighbor," he said. "This is Harlan," Bill said to Cal. "He's a friend."

Harlan shook Cal's hand.

"Thanks for your help," Cal said. A short, stocky bull of a man, Harlan nodded and smiled. A thick white scar glowed on his chin, as if a fat grub had burrowed there. His boots were coated with mud.

"We're down to the vault," Harlan said.

"Ground was softer than expected," said Bill. "Didn't take no time at all."

Harlan said, "Should be no problem winching that vault lid off."

"I appreciate this," Cal said. "You don't know how much."

"Government got no right to keep a father from his son," Harlan said.

In the darkness, the cemetery looked nothing like I remembered from the day of the funeral. Remnants of melted snow and ice covered the grass. Trees stood skeletal and leafless. The vapor of my breath drifted in small white clouds. The flesh on my chest quivered with cold and anxiety.

Cal wrapped the chain around the thick limb of an oak tree that reached over David's grave. He locked the winch in place. Bill and Harlan stepped into the hole they had dug, their boots thumping against the cover of the vault. Cal handed them two lengths of rusty chain from the back of our truck, and they fastened these to the iron grips molded into the concrete. They connected these chains to a hook on the end of a silver cable that ran to the winch.

"Go ahead," one of them said. Cal turned the handle and the winch clicked rhythmically. The chains and cable tightened and stretched, and slowly, the concrete vault cover rose, scraping clay from one side of the grave. Cal paused to rest his arm, then continued. With each turn of the handle the lid of David's vault rose. Finally, when it was suspended above the open hole, the men pushed it to the side. Cal reversed direction on the winch and lowered the cover to the ground.

I peered into the darkness and could see small shining patches of David's silver-and-gold casket, surrounded by the concrete walls of the vault. The hole smelled like dirt and worms, like dampness and the decay of leaves. Bill and Harlan lowered themselves into the hole with coils of thick rope slung across their shoulders. They dropped to their knees, reached inside. They tied one end of the ropes to the handles on each side of the casket, then attached the other ends to the hook on the winch cable. Cal turned the handle again and smiled as the casket containing the body of his son slowly emerged from the earth.

"Come on, John," Cal said to me. "You can help."

My arms shook. I fought back tears. The four of us untied the ropes and grabbed the handles on the small coffin, two on each side. We carried it to the back of our truck and slid it all the way in, then closed the tailgate and tied the tarp tightly over the top.

Working more quickly now, Cal and his friends hooked the cable back to the chains on the concrete cover, winched it just high enough to be swung over the hole, then lowered it back down on the empty vault. When this work was completed, Cal put the winch, ropes, and chain on the floor of the cab at my feet.

"You go on home," Bill told him.

"You sure?" Cal asked.

Harlan said, "We'll fill it back in, lay the sod out, bring in some clean snow. Couple days, it'll look just like it was. No one will ever know the difference."

"Let me know if there's trouble," Cal said.

"Won't be any trouble," Harlan said.

"I appreciate this." The men shook hands with Cal, waved at me through the windshield, then quickly started shoveling dirt back into the hole. We pulled away with our lights off, gravel crunching beneath our tires. I felt like I couldn't breathe. I thought I heard the wail of police sirens. I imagined a helicopter with a huge searchlight beneath it, aimed at us.

Cal sent me to open the cemetery gate, pulled the truck through. I closed the gate behind us. Lincoln Avenue looked deserted as we pulled away.

"Want to take a drive past the old house?" Cal asked.

"Not really."

"Me neither."

It was after two in the morning when we pulled back on the interstate. We drove north, with Polaris over our left shoulder. One corner of the tarp covering David's coffin flapped like the wing of a wounded bird in the back of our pickup.

"Well, that wasn't too hard."

I forced a smile. I felt sick to my stomach. What do you do when you love somebody and you are repulsed by what he has done?

"You know the story of Lazarus?"

I nodded. Cal smiled, and I knew what he was thinking. He had cured Jeremiah's arthritis, given Agnes her sight, healed countless others. He believed he had the power to bring my little brother back to life. I slouched in the seat and rested my knees on the dash. The warm air blowing from the heater, and the hum of the tires on pavement, lulled me into sleepiness. It struck me that after tonight perhaps I would no longer be shocked by anything Cal did. What struck me most forcefully, though, was that even though I knew better—David was not Lazarus; Cal was not Jesus—inside of me burned a small pitiful fire of hope.

"You go ahead and sleep, John," Cal said to me, running a hand over my hair. "We've got a long, dark drive ahead of us."

I nodded. I wanted to say something, but I couldn't.

"'In the beginning, God created the heavens and the earth,'" Cal began, reciting Genesis. I fell asleep sometime before the seventh day, as God himself was about to rest.

"Son of a bitch!"

I awoke, startled. I could see the glow of the truck's headlights on the dark highway in front of us. Cal stared into the rear-view mirror, his face a mask of fear. "John, wake up!" he yelled. The inside of our truck pulsed with an eerie red glow.

I sat up and turned around. A state patrol car was close behind us, lights flashing.

"Were you speeding?" I asked.

"I don't know. Probably."

I glanced at the speedometer. We had slowed to forty-five miles per hour. The police car was so close behind us the headlights were hidden by the tailgate of our pickup. We were still on I-94, heading north. It was five-thirty in the morning.

"It's just the one cop."

"Maybe he'll just give you a speeding ticket," I said.

"No!" Cal shouted. "No. He won't just give us a ticket. I took the plates off the truck, remember? We've got a casket in the back under a tarp."

A blinding light beamed into the cab of the truck. The police officer had turned on a spotlight mounted to the top of his car. It illuminated the whole inside of the truck.

"You have to stop."

Cal slowed to thirty-five miles per hour.

"John, listen to me. I'm going to stop and get out. When I do, I want you to slide over, slowly. Get behind the wheel if you can. I want you to shift into gear and go. I'll keep him occupied. Take the truck and head for home. Drive it into the machine shed and close the doors. Move whatever you have to and make room. I'll get back up there in time." Cal glanced at me. "Okay?" he asked.

"I don't know the way, Cal."

"Sure you do," he said. "Just keep heading north."

"But—"

"Listen!" he said angrily. "You just do what I tell you. Please, John."

"What are you going to do?" He didn't answer.

"Cal," I said. I swallowed.

"Whatever happens, you just drive, you hear me? You punch that gas pedal and you move forward. Don't even look back. Just go." He looked at me. "All right?"

I nodded.

Cal took his foot off the gas and we coasted. We slowed down to fifteen miles per hour, and Cal directed the truck to the shoulder of the highway. Cal shifted the truck into park.

The squad car stopped perhaps ten feet behind us. The spotlight was so bright I couldn't see the officer. All around us, the air pulsed red.

"All right," Cal said. He winked at me. "Let's get it right."

He opened his door, stepped from the truck, disappeared into the bright light behind us.

I was so frightened, my legs and hands shook. As slowly as I could, I eased myself over toward the middle of the seat. I reached my left foot toward the gas pedal. I put my left hand on the shift lever.

An amplified voice outside startled me. "Get out of the vehicle, now!" it said. I froze. I let my hand drop to my side. After a few seconds, the voice came again. "Get out of the vehicle and keep your hands in view!" I turned my head to look behind me. I shaded my eyes from the bright light. A pair of headlights approached from behind, and an eighteen-wheeler blew by, its taillights disappearing as it slowly moved into the darkness.

"Cal!" I shouted.

"It's okay," I heard him say, "Come on out."

I slid under the steering wheel, opened the door, and climbed down out of the cab. I walked away from the truck, out from the glare of the spotlight. Cal stood calmly on the highway near the squad car with his hands raised. The police officer had his door open, and he was standing next to the car holding his radio in his right hand.

"That's it," he said. His voice came from a speaker mounted on top of the car. "Keep your hands in sight and step away."

"Come over here, by me," Cal said.

I stood beside Cal. He looked calm. His hands were held about shoulder high, his elbows touching his body. His flannel shirt was untucked and hung loosely over his belt.

The cop left his car door open and approached us. "Step over to the back of your vehicle, please, and stand with your legs apart. Keep your hands high and apart. Grab the tailgate."

Cal and I walked slowly to the back of our truck. My heart raced, and my hands still shook.

"I told the boy to put those plates on his truck," Cal said. "I told him they weren't doing any good inside on the floor. But you know how kids are." The officer didn't respond.

Cal and I stood behind our truck with our hands raised. A light wind blew our long hair forward, over our shoulders and across our faces. I glanced back and saw the police officer approach us from the side. He looked young, still in his 20s, maybe. He was thin, and not very tall. He wasn't wearing a hat.

"May I see your license and registration, please," he said.

"That's all in the glove box," Cal said, then turned to me. "Why don't you go ahead and get them."

"Stay where you are," the officer said.

"They're in the glove box," Cal said again. "The boy knows where they are."

I looked over my shoulder at the officer. He eyed Cal cautiously for a moment, then nodded at me. "Go ahead," he said.

I walked around Cal and moved toward the passenger door. I knew that all we had in the glove box were some tools and a can of Fix-A-Flat. The officer followed me.

As I neared the door, I saw a flash of movement in the corner of my eye. The officer fell forward to his stomach, Cal on top of him. He groaned and cried out once. "Go!" Cal yelled. But I panicked. Instead of getting into the truck, I ran into the tall grass off the highway and turned around. By that time, the cop had worked an arm free. I heard the crack of his nightstick against Cal's body, the sound of a struggle.

"Run!" Cal yelled. I didn't see what happened next. I heard a gunshot and I ducked, expecting to feel the sharp heat of a bullet cutting through my back. But nothing happened. When I turned around, I saw Cal on top of the police officer. Cal sat on his back, and he had a rock he must have found in the field grass raised over his head in his right hand. Cal brought the rock down against the cop's arm, and the officer screamed and kicked his legs. Cal dropped the rock. He got up to his knees with one knee driven into the officer's back. He leaned over the cop's head and lifted his revolver from the grass.

"Cal?" I said. He was breathing heavily. The police officer moaned beneath him. "Cal, you all right?"

"Get his handcuffs!" Cal yelled at me. I did as I was told. I crawled through the grass beside them and found the handcuffs attached to the officer's belt.

"Please," the officer said. "I have a family. I have a little baby at home. Oh—" he moaned again.

"Stop," Cal said. "I'm not going to hurt you." I gave Cal the officer's handcuffs, and he put them on the cop, locked his hands and arms behind his back. Then Cal stood, his left arm hanging loosely against his side, wet blood shining on his shirt.

"Open the trunk," Cal said to me, softly.

"Please. My wife just had a baby."

I pulled the keys from the ignition and opened the trunk.

"Get up." Cal held the gun on the cop, who struggled to stand. Blood shone on the sleeve of his uniform, just above the elbow. Through the blood and a tear in the fabric, I could see bright, white bone. The cop dropped his head and vomited on his shoes.

"I'm sorry about your arm," Cal said. I walked over to the officer and he leaned against my shoulder with one arm as he walked to the back of his car. His nose was bleeding and there was a cut on his forehead as well. "Son, get those guns out of there." Two shotguns were mounted in a rack inside the trunk. I lifted them out, put them in the car's back seat.

"Get in."

"Please!" the officer begged, but he did as he was told. Cal slammed the trunk closed.

"Give me the squad car keys," he said. "And then follow me."

The sleeve of Cal's shirt was soaked in blood. It ran down his arm and dripped like water off of his fingers. I felt strange, as if I were just waking from a dream, and didn't know where I was or whether or not the dream had actually happened. My mouth and lips went dry. I could not find spit to swallow.

Cal slammed the door of the police car closed and started the engine. The spotlight went off, and then the flashing red lights went dark.

I followed him for about three miles on the interstate. He exited in Black River Falls. He turned off the headlights and drove in the dark along a country road pocked with potholes, and then he turned off that road into thick woodland bordering a farmer's freshly tilled field. He followed an overgrown dirt road into a crowded stand of evergreens, stopping when he reached too many trees to continue. Then he returned to the truck and got in on the passenger side.

"Get us home," he said. "Just drive north on 94, and then take 53. I'll guide you in when you get closer." He gritted his teeth and leaned his head back against the rear window.

"He shot you."

His face looked pale. "Bullet went through. Flesh wound. Hurts like hell but it's not all that bad. I feel a little dizzy, though." He dropped the gun on the seat between us. "Up ahead, we'll cross the Black River. Throw this pistol into the river."

"Should I take you to a hospital?"

"No. Just get us home." I didn't know what to do. My heart and head raced. Cal's breathing seemed labored. His left arm rested on his lap. The blood made his shirtsleeve stick to his skin. He wrapped one sleeve of his sweatshirt around the wound and pulled it tight.

I floored the accelerator and headed for the freeway again. Cal's head lolled from side to side against the window. His eyes remained closed.

I stopped on the bridge, threw the pistol into the river, then drove home into the morning, the sun rising over the horizon in a dull glow behind us as I left the freeway. I nervously watched the rear-view mirror for signs of trouble.

I expected to see a police car waiting for us in the driveway. But that didn't happen. I stopped the truck and looked at Cal, at the jellied blood on his shirt and on the seat beside him. His face was pale. But he was still breathing. When Mother saw us, she ran to the truck. When she saw the blood on Cal's body, she screamed.

Chapter 15

"**H**old still, Cal!"

Sprawled on an old blanket on the floor of our sun-filled kitchen, Cal was a bloody mess. Mother knelt over his mangled arm with her face close to the wound, pulling bloody blades of grass and dirt and gravel from it with the tips of her fingernails.

"What the hell have you done now?" Mother said.

Each time Mother touched him, Cal writhed in pain. Saliva thick as Karo syrup oozed from his mouth. When he screamed, Mother yelled at him to hold still. The bullet had passed through his bicep, leaving an ugly wound about the size of a marble on each side, the flesh surrounding the oozing holes wet and pulpy like a cotton ball soaked in cherry juice.

Mother shook her head. "What have you done?" She passed her hand across the back of his head, softly rubbing the hair down to his neck.

Cal smiled at her but didn't answer.

"We should disinfect this." Mother turned on the water, reached beneath the sink for her gallon jug of chlorine bleach.

"Did he shoot himself?" JJ asked me.

"No."

"John, wait," Mother said to me. "Just wait until we're through here, so you don't have to tell it twice."

"A police officer shot him," I said.

Mother turned and stared at me. JJ's jaw dropped open.

"State patrol," I said. "Cal broke the cop's arm with a rock. We left him in the woods in the trunk of his squad car."

Mother ran a hand through her hair. She closed her eyes and shook her head.

"What did you guys do?" JJ asked.

"John, wait," Mother said. "Please. Let me finish cleaning him up first. Then you can tell us everything."

Mother carried the bleach and knelt down beside Cal. "Close your eyes," she said to him. She poured bleach directly from the bottle into the wound in his arm. Cal roared in pain. The bleach trickled through his arm and puddled in a slippery red mess on the blanket. Cal's body went slack and stopped twitching. When he regained consciousness he screamed, his face pressed into the floor.

"It's all I have to stop infection," Mother said. "I'm sorry." She shook her head vigorously. "What were you thinking, hitting a police officer!" She swabbed the wound with a yellow sponge, wiping the blood and bleach from his skin, then wrapped his arm in a towel.

She wiped the blood from his face and hair. Cal winced when she passed over a lump on his scalp, torn open by a laceration nearly an inch long where the police officer had hit him with his nightstick.

"Okay," said Mother. "Let's get him up to bed." I stood behind Cal, wrapped my arms around his chest, and lifted him to his feet. His wounded arm swung loosely from his shoulder like a stick of salami, but he could hold his weight steady on his legs. His skin smelled sour and a bit salty, like deer blood. It took the three of us, but we managed to help him stagger up the stairs into the bedroom.

Mother untied Cal's boots and pulled them from his feet, slid his belt from his pants, then tucked him beneath the blankets in bed, still in his bloodied blue jeans. Already, a round red spot had begun to bleed through the towel on both sides of his arm.

When Cal fell asleep, JJ, Mother, and I went downstairs and sat around the kitchen table. I told them everything, saving the detail of exactly what we'd gone south to recover until the end. We put on our shoes and I asked them to follow me outside.

The three of us went together into the machine shed where I'd parked the truck and closed the doors, as Cal had instructed me. I untied the tarp and threw it back.

"Oh my God," Mother said.

JJ sucked in her breath as if someone had socked her in the stomach. She ran for the house. She went in and slammed the kitchen door behind her.

Mother put one hand to her mouth and began crying. She stepped forward, leaned over the truck, and put her hands on the small casket, as if testing its temperature, running her fingers across the cool metal. Leaning over the side, standing on tiptoes, she put her cheek to David's coffin and closed her eyes. Tears streamed down her face.

"How in the world?" she asked. "This can't be, John. Oh, I can't believe it." Mother put her hands on my shoulders and looked warmly into my face.

With Mother on one side and me on the other, we grabbed the handles and slid the casket from the bed of the truck. We carried it to the back corner of the shed, where we left it suspended three feet above the ground on a set of wooden sawhorses, hidden from view behind a wall of hay bales. Though it was stained by dirt and clay in a few places, the casket looked new, no different than it had at the funeral eight months earlier. Buried inside its concrete vault, it probably would have lasted forever.

Mother took a chair from the kitchen and went back outside to sit in the shed beside David's casket, with a blanket thrown over her shoulders.

JJ locked herself in our room and refused to let me in. When I knocked, she yelled at me to go away, and said that I was as crazy as her father.

"Come on, JJ!" I said. "Let me in." My head buzzed with fatigue. I went downstairs to lie down on the sofa in the living room.

That evening, finally, well after dark, JJ let me into our room. She had refused to come out for supper, and consented to unlock the door only when Mother threatened to pry it open with a crowbar.

JJ sat on her mattress looking out our bedroom window toward the shed, her hair a greasy nest of tangles. Thick black smudges creased her face beneath her eyes. Drops of Cal's blood had dried in her hair and on one of her arms. She had not washed it off.

"Why did you bring him here?" she asked.

"It was your dad's idea," I said.

Cal made it through the night and the following day. He slept most of the time. Before dawn the next morning, however, while the sky was still dark, we were awakened by loud noises coming from Mother and Cal's bedroom. Cal's voice sounded like the eerie howling of a pack of wolves, a loud and pitiful wailing. Outside our bedroom door, I heard Mother's strained whispers, then the sound of footsteps, the pine boards creaking on the floor. Our bedroom door opened. Mother passed a flashlight beam across my face.

"John and JJ," she said aloud. "Wake up."

"What's wrong?" JJ asked.

"Your father has a fever," Mother said. "Please go down and fill the bathtub with cold water. The bucket's under the sink." She put the flashlight beam on my chest. "John, you'll have to get him down the stairs."

JJ looked frightened. She brushed past me and disappeared into the hall. I followed Mother across the hall into their bedroom. The room smelled of sweat and blood. Cal looked as if he had been swimming. His hair was drenched, the sheets clammy and streaked with blood and vomit. Cal's wounded arm flopped against his side, and he kicked his legs sporadically, as if he were fending off attackers.

"Help me get this belt on him," Mother said. I held Cal's thrashing legs while she looped a belt around his waist. She secured the buckle behind him, pulled the belt tight.

"How are we going to do this?"

"You'll have to take him down on your back. Hold his good arm over your shoulder. I'll follow behind you down the stairs holding onto his belt." I stared at her. "You have to try," she said. "I can't carry him."

When I lifted Cal from his bed, he yelled out in pain and swung an elbow into my head, just above my ear. The blow opened a cascade of stars behind my eyes, but I held on. I lifted his good arm over my head and tugged his body up against my back. His skin stuck to me like a hot, wet towel. He felt impossibly heavy.

"Ready to go?"

"I don't know," I said.

"Come on," Mother said. "You can do it, John."

I leaned forward and lifted, raising Cal up higher, over my hips, floating his ribcage up between my shoulder blades. He screamed in my ear as his bloodied arm flopped down across my face. I staggered briefly, then carried him out into the hallway. With one hand, Mother held the belt she'd tightened around Cal's stomach. With the other, she pointed the flashlight at the wooden stairwell between my legs.

"Be careful," she said. "One step at a time." Cal moaned and shook. I could feel the sweat from his face against my hair. His breath smelled like vomit.

Downstairs, I could see the flicker of an oil lamp on the kitchen table. I could hear JJ pouring buckets of ice-cold well water into the cast-iron bathtub, then running back into the kitchen for more. I struggled down the first step and held onto the banister with my free hand. My bare feet felt for the smooth, cool wood of the stairs.

"That's the boy," Mother said.

I brought my other foot down. The muscles in my thighs quivered and burned. I took the next step, and the next. Cal had stopped moaning.

A few steps further and I could see JJ in her T-shirt and underwear at the kitchen sink, her bare legs and feet shining in the uneven light. She turned over her shoulder to look at me, then looked back into the bucket of water she was filling.

"Easy," Mother said to me, softly. "That's it. Halfway there."

I took the next two steps too quickly and almost fell. I gripped the banister and stopped. My hand was slick with sweat. I could feel Cal's blood against my cheek each time his arm swung into my face.

"Careful!" Mother said.

"I have to rest."

I waited a minute, stood with my chest heaving, my legs quivering under Cal's weight. I leaned forward and kept going. Sweat stung my eyes.

When I stepped down off the final step to the kitchen floor, JJ grabbed the smoking oil lamp from the kitchen table and carried it on ahead of us, a bucket of water hanging from her other arm. She set the lamp on the floor next to the tub and then poured the last bucketful of water in. The water filled the tub halfway.

"Let's put him in," Mother said.

"The water's really cold," JJ said.

"That's good," said Mother. I turned my back to the tub and with Mother holding Cal's belt, we carefully lowered him until he sat on the side of the bathtub. Heat radiated from his body. His head hung with his chin against his chest, and his wounded arm fell backward up to the wrist in the water.

"JJ, grab him under his good arm. John, go across the tub and help me pull him over."

Cal's legs jerked and kicked.

I reached across the tub and grabbed Cal by the belt, and with Mother and JJ's help, we tugged Cal backward into the water. He fell in and water surged over the sides. Cold water splattered off the floor and wet our legs. Cal's eyes opened. He choked and thrashed, soaking all of us.

"Anna!" Cal cried, hoarsely. He rarely used Mother's first name, and the word seemed strange. He clawed madly at the air with his good arm and kicked at the water. Water hissed against the hot glass globe of the oil lamp.

"Easy!" Mother said, "I'm right here, Cal. Take it easy." She sat down on the edge of the tub and swung her feet and legs into the water. She rubbed one hand across Cal's forehead and smoothed his long wet hair out of his eyes. She held his wounded arm gently. "You're in the bathtub, Cal. You have a fever."

Cal fell backward. His head thumped against the back of the tub, and he stayed there. The tip of his beard rested in the water. Cal closed his eyes, and his mouth fell open. His lips quivered. Slowly, the water began turning pink.

Cal reached his good arm up out of the water and grasped Mother's hand. Mother brought his hand to her lips and kissed it.

JJ stood with her shoulders against the wall and her arms crossed over her chest. Her hair had fallen across her face, but I could see her eyes, watching me. Her wet T-shirt clung to her breasts and the sharp ripples of her ribs and clavicles.

"We don't have to decide anything right now," Mother said. "Let's see how the night goes." She looked at JJ and me. "Why don't you two get into some dry clothes and go back to sleep. I'll stay here with him."

On the way up the stairs, JJ grabbed my hand. Inside our bedroom, JJ turned her back to me and changed out of her T-shirt, then sat down on her mattress and started to cry. Already, the dull light of dawn was beginning to creep over the horizon and wash the world in gray light.

"What if he dies?" JJ asked.

"He won't die."

"How do you know?" she asked. I didn't know. I wondered, though. I wondered if he could heal others, why couldn't he simply heal himself? But I remembered Jesus, who had raised Lazarus, who had healed the sick and lame. Dying on the cross, one of the other prisoners executed beside Jesus taunted him, said if you are who they say you are, save yourself and us also. But he didn't. Maybe he couldn't.

JJ crawled across the floor and lay with her head on my shoulder. She threw her blanket over both of us. I closed my eyes and felt her breathing, smelled her breath against my face. I covered my eyes with a pillow and counted backward from a thousand, and somewhere in the three hundreds, as birds outside began to sing, I managed to fall asleep.

When I awoke, JJ was already gone. I sat up quickly, pulled on my clothes. Cal was still in the bathtub. The water was a pale rusty brown. Mother had removed his belt and had slid it under his armpits, fastening it around the leg of a chair she'd backed against the tub. This kept Cal's face out of the water.

Mother and JJ sat at the kitchen table. Mother had the keys to the truck in her hand. She looked exhausted.

"JJ and I are going into town to try to get some antibiotics."

JJ said, "I'm inventing a wild sexual history for myself. Standing up, doggy style in a changing room at Wal-Mart. That could give you a killer UTI, I would imagine."

Mother frowned at her. "Jennifer, please," she said. "I don't know where the clinics are, so it may take us awhile. Give him aspirin. If he's awake and won't bite the thermometer in half, check his temperature. He was at one hundred and two this morning, but that was while sitting in seventy-five-degree water. Tell him we've gone to get some medicine."

I nodded. "What if you can't find any?"

"We won't come back until we do," Mother said.

Cal slept with his head back and his mouth open, his bad arm dangling over the side of the tub. Mother had tied the wrist to one of the chair legs, to keep the wound dry. In the daylight, I could see where blood had coagulated in the hairs of Cal's beard and hardened even in his eyebrows. He looked feeble here, tied in a bathtub with just his jeans on.

I pulled a few strands of long hair off of his face. Cal stirred awake, floated to one side and winced in pain as his wounded arm pulled against the rope holding it in place. He opened his eyes and looked at me.

"Morning, Cal."

He blinked and swallowed. "John," he whispered.

"You have a fever," I told him. "An infection."

"The flames of hell." He smiled. "A little preview."

I went to the kitchen and came back with a glass full of water and two aspirin. "Take these," I said. He opened his mouth. I dropped in the aspirin and then held the glass to his lips and poured. He opened his mouth, but most of the water spilled down his beard and trickled into the tub.

"Mom and JJ went into town to get antibiotics."

He winced as he chewed the bitter aspirin. He closed his eyes. "David's here," he said.

"Yes he is."

He smiled. "Read to me, John," he said, his eyes still closed.

"All right." His Bible was on the chair. I picked it up. "What do you want to hear?"

I waited a long time for an answer. I thought he'd fallen asleep again.

"Something exciting," he whispered. "Revelation."

"Revelation. Okay." The pages of Cal's Bible were well worn, even soiled in places. All the way through, various passages were under-lined in pencil, with notes written beside them, in Cal's tiny printed script. I paged all the way through to the very end.

"'The Revelation of Jesus Christ,'" I began slowly, "'which God gave Him to show His servants—things which must shortly take place. And He sent and signified it by His angel to His servant John.'"

Cal raised his good hand from the water, opened his eyes, and pointed at me.

I nodded. "I'm John," I said. I held the Bible up. "But not this John."

He closed his eyes, and I began to read again. I read through the first eight books of Revelation, through all seven seals on the scroll and the first four of the seven trumpets, ending with, "'And I looked, and I heard an angel flying through the midst of heaven, saying with a loud voice, "Woe, woe, woe to the inhabitants of the earth, because of the remaining blasts of the trumpet of the three angels who are about to sound!"'" My throat was dry. A half hour had passed. Cal breathed the deep, slow breaths of sleep.

All of our bloody clothes soaked in a washtub of cold soapy water on the floor in the kitchen. Mother had also scrubbed Cal's blood from the blanket, and it hung heavily from the clothesline outside in the yard, its bottom brushing the ground. A large stain with uneven edges marked its center where the bleach had discolored the blanket. I sat by the washtub and scrubbed Cal's dried blood from the lines in my fingertips, from the creases in my hands, from my face.

I went into the machine shed and looked at David's casket. A bar of sunlight came through the window and cut across it. One of the barn cats, a gray-and-black-striped female, slept on top. When she saw me, she leaped off and scurried away. I still felt uncomfortable sitting alone with David's casket, but not the way I felt at the funeral home that horrible day, with the casket propped open, surrounded by long spikes of flowers, David tilted inside wearing a little suit and tie, his hands folded and holding a little white angel. I had wanted to pull off the tie and put him in a T-shirt with chocolate stains on it, pluck the angel from his hands and replace it with a Power Rangers figurine.

I spent the remaining hours of the morning outside, walking the fields, smelling the air of early spring. We were not far from May. Most of our snow had melted. I wandered along the fence line that bordered the road, walked through the woods to the far corner of our property to watch the swollen creek flow north, the shorelines still bordered by snow and a silver lace of ice.

When I went back into the house, I nearly fell over Cal. He slumped on his knees in a puddle of water on the kitchen floor, hacking at his wounded arm with the blade of a butter knife. Bright blood dripped from his arm to the floor. Wet hair sagged over his face. Water dripped from his arms, from his beard. He pressed the blade of the knife awkwardly against his arm, denting the flesh.

I grabbed his hand and pulled the knife away, knocking him to the ground in the process. I threw the knife into the kitchen sink. "'Cut it off and cast it from you,'" Cal said.

His wounded arm looked gruesome, bloodied and pulpy, with thick pus oozing from the edges. When I gently squeezed the flesh around the wound, pus and blood puckered out. I took a clean cotton dishtowel from the drawer, wrapped it around Cal's arm twice, and tied it.

"No more water," Cal said softly. "Please! I'll need gills. Help me up to bed."

It took us awhile, but I got him upstairs and into his bed. I pulled off his wet pants, and he curled beneath the bedsheet and fell asleep.

I cleaned the water and mess from the floor and sat in the kitchen waiting for JJ and Mother to return home. The knot in my stomach had grown to a whole coil of rope.

They returned in the early afternoon, JJ triumphantly waving a small bag with a brown plastic bottle of antibiotics inside. They ran from the truck into the house.

"We got it!" Mother said. "How is he?"

"He's upstairs sleeping, now."

"Ciprofloxacin," JJ said, shaking the bottle. "I told the doctor it burned when I peed. I told him my boyfriend was huge and liked it from behind. He frowned at me. 'You probably have a urinary tract infection,' he said. He wanted to give me a pregnancy test. He asked me to pee in a cup, but I said I couldn't."

For two days, while Cal suffered in bed, hallucinating, crying out in his sleep, mumbling, speaking in tongues, we waited fearfully for a knock on the door. But none came.

Sometimes, when his fever spiked, Cal would talk of angels and devils and judgment day, screaming that the devil had him by the arm and that Satan's claws were burning into his flesh. Mother remained with him, reading aloud quietly when he asked. When she became tired, she slept on a quilt on the floor next to the bed. Cal urinated in an empty milk bottle, and defecated in a frying pan Mother had converted into a bed pan. Each time, Mother emptied the contents and cleaned Cal with warm water.

In the morning, while Cal slept, Mother would go out to the shed and sit by David's casket with the door slightly open. Mother's hair was a wild tangle of vines falling from her head to her shoulders. She sat in blue jeans and a heavy tan wool coat with her knees together. Her leather boots, caked with mud, remained untied. Sometimes she took Cal's Bible out with her and read softly aloud from it. A shaft of sunlight cut through the back window and across the casket, and one morning I sat outside in the sun and listened as Mother read.

Her voice sounded calm and assured. Some of this language was so beautiful it sounded like music. In the seventeenth century, Cal had taught us, King James had ordered the Bible translated into English, and many men had spent years sitting in the Jerusalem Room at Westminster Abbey, in London, scribbling with quill pens on unbleached paper, translating from Hebrew, from Greek, from Latin, line by line, chapter by chapter, book by book. Outside the abbey, thousands of Londoners were dying of bubonic plague. Inside, with ink black as tar, learned men were scratching out the words Mother now read to David: "And now abide faith, hope, love, these three; but the greatest of these is love.'" There was no more beautiful English in the world, Cal said, than the English of the King James Bible.

After an hour or more with David, Mother would return to Cal's side, drawn back and forth by the force of both the living and the dead.

Without Cal's manic energy hovering over us and ricocheting throughout the house, there seemed to be more room for the rest of us. Mother, especially, seemed to grow stronger. Her renewed industry and energy seemed wondrous to me. She cooked, she cleaned, she darned socks, hung wash on the line, visited with David, tended to Cal. When she did the dishes with JJ or me beside her at the wash tub, to dry them, she hummed songs to herself. With David there, and with the sun and warmth of spring now with us, she seemed to be emerging from the cocoon of sadness that the cold and isolation had spun around her.

And Cal came back to us. On that third morning, as Mother, JJ, and I sat at the kitchen table together eating breakfast, we heard a thumping coming down the stairs, and Cal wandered unsteadily into the kitchen. His cheeks and eyes were sunken, and behind the curls of graying hair on his chest I could see each of his ribs clearly outlined beneath the skin.

He smiled at us. The spark of life had returned to his eyes.

"I've been dancing with angels," he said to Mother. His voice sounded hoarse, gruff. "They're partial to jazz. In heaven, apparently, it don't mean a thing if it ain't got that swing."

Mother hugged him, then led him to a chair. He kissed the top of JJ's head, sat down, winked at me. He reached out and took Mother's hand in his good hand. He didn't let go. His wounded arm looked decayed, the skin sagging on bone.

"What day is it?" he asked.

"Saturday," Mother said.

"Church service tomorrow."

"No," Mother said. "I put up signs. Canceled. Said you were ill."

Cal nodded. He looked at me. "Any sign of trouble?"

"No," I said.

He smiled. "We're all right, then."

"How's the arm?" Mother asked.

He slowly lifted his wounded arm at the shoulder, then raised his hand, wincing as he did so. "Sore," he said. He reached around Mother's waist, pulled her to him. "But not too sore to dance with you."

Chapter 16

With David's casket in our machine shed, and Cal well again, both Mother and Cal seemed to have been transfused with joy—not only for life, but for one another. JJ and I heard them whispering and laughing, rolling around on their bed. This was a sound we had never heard in our new farmhouse.

Though it was still somewhat cold in the evenings, we slept with our windows cracked open. Spring air blew through, and with it the smell of clean water and wet earth. Even with our bedroom door closed and locked, we could hear Cal reciting passages from the Song of Solomon, the fabulous Song of Songs: "'O my love, you are as beautiful as Tirzah, lovely as Jerusalem, awesome as an army with banners! Your hair is like a flock of goats going down from Gilead.'" We heard the muffled smack of kissing.

"What are they doing?" I said.

"Duh!" JJ answered, from her mattress across the room. "What do you think?"

Mother laughed and moaned softly. The room went quiet for a while, and suddenly the headboard of their bed began to thump against the wall separating their bedroom from ours. The wooden cross hanging on our wall jumped around like a fish pulled from the water. Cal said, more loudly, "'My dove, my perfect one.'"

Their lovemaking grew louder and more passionate. Mother's muffled cries and laughter brought more recitation from Cal.

"He must have memorized the whole damn thing," JJ said.

"'How beautiful are your feet in sandals!'" Cal shouted. The words gushed from his mouth between heaving breaths. He paused between sentences to concentrate on the task at hand. "'Your navel is a rounded goblet; it lacks no blended beverage. Your waist is a heap of wheat, set about with lilies. Your two breasts are like two fawns, twins of a gazelle.'"

In the darkness, I heard JJ get off of her mattress. I saw her silhouette in the window and heard her breathing as she came closer. She crawled across the floor between us until her face was inches from mine.

"Move over," she said.

I moved aside to make room. Warmth flooded my body as JJ moved closer. She pulled back the blankets and crawled into bed with me. We lay beside one another on our backs, breathing soft, shallow breaths, saying nothing. We allowed our bare feet to touch and mingle beneath the blankets. I could feel JJ's body rise and fall as she breathed.

With the fingers of my right hand, I found JJ's hand, and grasped it. Her fingers locked into mine. I could hear my heart beating in my ears. My penis swelled, rising against the heavy covers, a pleasant, hard ache.

Across the hall, Cal and Mother moaned in delight.

I rolled toward JJ. Slowly, I slid one hand under her shirt, ran my palm up the gentle ripples of her ribcage, cupped my hand around one warm, smooth breast. JJ turned toward me. I could hear her breathing. With her face pressed into my shoulder, she put her hand on my stomach, then slid her fingers beneath the elastic band of my shorts. Her fingers found my penis and she squeezed.

"John," she whispered, fearfully.

"It's all right," I whispered.

"It doesn't seem right." She slid her hand around me. The rush of heat and pressure came quickly. I could not stop it. The sudden pulsing of muscles was so pleasurable I felt as if I might faint. JJ's muffled laughter made me remember where I was.

"Pretty quick on the draw, cowboy," JJ said. She lifted the blankets playfully, then dropped them.

Across the hall, Cal shouted Mother's name, then wailed long and loudly, a winter's worth of sap iced-in at the roots now spreading up the trunk to limbs and branches and soft, fuzzy buds, an explosion of color. JJ started to laugh. I covered her mouth with my hand, and she licked it with her tongue, then took two of my fingers into her mouth. I felt the warm wetness of her tongue, the sharpness of teeth against my knuckles. She pulled my wet fingers from her mouth, then guided my hand down under the blankets.

She looked at me. "'Oh, that you were like my brother, who nursed at my mother's breasts! If I should find you outside, I would kiss you; I would not be despised.'" She smiled.

"I *am* your brother," I said.

"*Step*," she said. "Step. Step. Step. Step. Step."

If the devil was guiding us, he was clever and assured, because I did not feel evil lying with my stepsister beside me. I felt JJ's hot wetness on my fingertips as she writhed beneath my awkward probing. I moved my fingers gently in small circles on the outside, then slid one finger partly inside her, stopping when her body tensed. She held my arm in both hands and moved her hips from side to side, breathing loudly, gasping and smiling, her eyes closed. I moved my fingers as I had moved them against JJ's tongue, and her whole body jerked against me. Her fingernails cut into my arm. Then she stopped, relaxed. She pulled my hand back out from under her clothes, and rested her head on my shoulder. We didn't say anything for a long time, not until Mother and Cal seemed to be starting up again.

"Oh my love!" Cal said, in a full voice, "you are as beautiful as Tirzah!"

At breakfast, Cal told us he planned to spend the night alone inside our church with David's casket.

"Don't take him out," Mother said. "Please."

"I have to lay my hands on him."

"Please don't," she said.

"What's he talking about?" JJ asked.

"Drop it, JJ," said Mother. "Please."

Cal shook his head. "This is no secret," he said. "I'm not ashamed." He looked at JJ. "Jennifer, I'm going to try to bring your little brother back to life."

JJ stared at Cal. She started to speak, but Mother stopped her.

"JJ, don't say anything," Mother said, "please." She looked as if she were about to cry. JJ looked up at Mother, her mouth open in protest. "Please."

"We can add a small bedroom onto the house this summer," Cal said. "John and David can share that one. Jennifer, you can have a room to yourself. How does that sound?"

JJ got up from the table and ran upstairs. She closed the door and locked it.

Cal shrugged. "I think she'll like that," he said. "A room to herself."

Mother shook her head. Her eyes pooled with tears. Cal winked at me, put on his coat, and walked out the door.

"Mom?"

She didn't answer me. Like JJ, she went upstairs to her bedroom and closed the door.

I didn't sleep at all that night. I imagined Cal on his knees beside David's casket, or hovering over its open lid, his hands touching my little brother's body. His shadow would rise behind him in the candlelight, and he would pray, from Psalms, most likely, but it was impossible to know what he'd say. He would ask that David's spirit return to his body, reawaken his brain, and reanimate his beautiful, young flesh.

JJ found the whole thing monstrous and repulsive, and she refused to speak about it. I'm not sure what Mother thought. She objected to Cal's intentions, but not as strenuously as she might have. I am ashamed to admit that even though I found Cal's behavior irredeemably sad, even pathetic, there burned within my heart that small ridiculous ember of hope. I wanted David back again so badly I would believe in anything to make that happen, even the reversibility of death. Too much hope, Mother said once, can make you crazy. And what about too much faith? I asked. Faith and hope are twins, she replied. But she was wrong, Cal said. Faith and hope are triplets, he said. You're missing love.

When JJ's breathing grew shallow, I crawled to our bedroom window. I got on my knees and looked out at our log cathedral, at the dull, flickering candlelight dancing against the windows. I put my head on the glass and looked up at the night sky, at the splash of stars across the heavens.

Cal did not return to the house that day or the next. Mother, JJ, and I ate breakfast, lunch, and supper, tried to fill our days as we normally did, but of course that was impossible.

"He's not even eating?" JJ asked.

Mother shook her head. "He took a gallon of water with him. He has the church door blocked from the inside."

JJ shook her head. "What a loon," she said.

Mother's eyes flashed with anger. She reached a hand across the table and grabbed JJ by the wrist. Mother opened her mouth but seemed too distraught to speak.

"I'm sorry," JJ said. Mother released her.

Late the evening of the second day, after JJ and Mother went upstairs to bed, I sat alone at the table and read the eleventh chapter of the Gospel according to John. The death and resurrection of Lazarus: "'Then they took away the stone from the place where the dead man was lying. And Jesus lifted up His eyes and said, 'Father, I think that You have heard Me. And I know that You always hear Me, but because of the people who are standing by I said this, that they may believe that You sent Me.' Now when he had said these things, He cried with a loud voice, 'Lazarus, come forth!' And he who had died came out bound hand and foot with grave clothes, and his face was wrapped with a cloth. Jesus said to them, 'Loose him, and let him go.'"

Early the following morning, I looked out my bedroom window and found the cathedral door ajar. Slowly, I snuck downstairs. I wanted to run outside, but I couldn't. I opened the door but changed my mind, fell back.

I pulled a chair away from the kitchen table and sat down. I stared at the open door expectantly. I did not really believe Cal could raise David from the dead, and yet my heart pounded as I sat in that chair. I sat waiting, wondering if my little brother was about to run inside and jump into my arms.

Chapter 17

Cal wandered into the house alone, his eyes red. He looked devastated, defeated, exhausted. He walked stiffly, bent forward at the waist, his shoulders sagging. He shook his head at me once and slowly climbed the stairs to his bedroom. He closed the door behind him.

Cal and I dug David's grave that afternoon, inside the church, directly beneath the steeple, and we buried him in the evening. Kings and queens, Cal said, are buried in all of the great cathedrals of Europe. You can't move a foot without stepping on somebody, he said. He stabbed at dead sod with the point of his shovel and peeled it back, exposing white hairy tendrils of roots. He cut the sod away in large oval pieces that I rolled back, exposing earthworms and bright white grubs. Beneath the sod was loose, damp sand.

We hit rocks as we went deeper, and I had to use a crowbar and sometimes even a sledgehammer to get them out. The muscles in my arms burned and quivered. We finally stopped digging when the hole was about three feet deep. The sand on our hands and clothes dried and fell from us like salt.

Near midnight, with a new moon high overhead, Cal, Mother, JJ, and I carried David's small casket over to the hole we'd dug, with JJ and Cal on one side, and Mother and me on the other. Cal had the Bible squeezed between his injured arm and ribcage. Mother cried softly as we walked together.

We set David's casket down on the smaller pile of sand next to the grave, which we'd leveled off in a shallow angle toward the hole. Cal and I went to the other side of the grave and reached across, and with us pulling and Mother pushing, the coffin slid easily down into the hole and rested there.

Each of us took hands full of sand, and we stood on the four sides of the grave. "David," Cal said, "there's more love in my heart for you than I can ever show. Everything I've done wrong or unholy, I've done out of my love and inconsolable grief for you." He tossed sand on the center of the coffin, and it splattered and settled. He wiped tears from the corners of his eyes. Then he opened the Bible and held a small flashlight on the pages so he could see them. He read from Psalms 90 and 91, about the immeasurable power of God and the frailty of men. When he finished, he closed the Bible and nodded at Mother.

"I love you, baby," Mother said, and sprinkled her sand over the head of the coffin.

We all looked at JJ.

"JJ?" Cal asked. She just stared down at the ground and let the sand fall from her hands. Cal looked at me, and nodded.

"I'm sorry, David," I said, and let the sand fall at his feet.

JJ ran out of the church and headed for the house.

I started to go after her, but Cal grabbed my arm. "Let her go," he said.

I stood back and watched as Mother and Cal used the shovels to cover the casket with sand.

I sat down on a bale of straw and watched. They filled the grave to the top and over the top, and Cal walked across it until the sand was almost level with the ground around it.

"It will settle some," he said. He reached his arm around Mother and squeezed her next to him.

"I've failed you," Cal said, shaking his head.

"You haven't failed me," said Mother.

"I have. I've failed all of us. I'm closing the church," said Cal. "I'm no preacher, no healer. This is a tomb now, a sepulcher. It belongs to David."

A few days afterward, as I wandered the southeastern fence line of our farm with a hammer and nails, putting up "No Trespassing" signs at Cal's instruction, I saw a county sheriff's car coming up the road. It slowed down when it reached me, then pulled over and stopped. The door opened, and Sheriff Kalupa got out and waved.

"Hey," he said, "how you doing?"

I waved and nodded at him. He stepped off the road and into the muddy ditch. I walked to the corner of our property where we shook hands, separated by the barbed-wire fence. His hand was strong and warm. His chin and neck bulged over his tight shirt collar, and he smelled like cigarette smoke.

He waved his fingers at the back of his head. "I can recommend a good barber in town," he said, and smiled.

I shrugged. "I'm used to it being long, now."

"Oh, I'm just playing with you," he said. "Do the same thing to my own boy. He's got longish hair, too. Says the girls like it."

I smiled and nodded.

"I never did get your name."

"John."

"John," he said, nodding, "I'm Gary. What's your sister's name?"

"JJ."

"Unusual."

"Her full name's Jennifer Joy," I said, "but she hates it, so she goes by initials."

"Sounds logical," he said. "And your dad's name?"

"Stepdad, actually. Calvin, but he goes by Cal. My mom is Anna."

He nodded. "And how are you all doing? Make it through the winter okay? It was a rough one, even by our standards."

"Pretty much," I said. I tried to respond briefly. I worried that Cal might see me talking and get angry. The land here was slightly higher, and we could clearly see the house from where we stood.

"Shouldn't you be in school today?" Sheriff Kalupa asked.

I shook my head. "We're being homeschooled," I said.

"Ah," he said, nodding. "And how do you like that?"

"I like it okay," I said.

"What about your sister," he asked, "is she all right?"

"She's doing all right."

"Good," Sheriff Kalupa said, "that's good. You're both here of your own free will, then, you'd say. What I mean by that is, your mom and dad aren't making you or your sister do anything you don't want to do, staying here."

"No," I said. "Of course not."

He raised his hands. "Sorry," he said. "No offense. Losing a son, you a little brother, must have been awful hard on all of you."

"He drowned," I said.

Sheriff Kalupa shook his head and groaned. "Awful," he said. "I'm so sorry."

"Right in front of us. Of me and my sister." I felt obliged to tell him the truth. I don't know why. "We were at the pool and we were supposed to be watching him. And he drowned."

"Sweet Jesus," Sheriff Kalupa said. "You poor kids."

An awkward silence followed. I started to walk away, tried to think of something to say that would separate us, but he held up a hand.

"Listen," he said suddenly. "The main reason I've come all the way up here is I wanted to ask you a question."

I nodded and swallowed. I felt a rush of anxiety inside and tried to hide it by putting my hands in my pockets.

"John," he said, "let me ask you something. Now, I'm sure there's nothing to this. In fact, I'm so sure there's probably nothing to this I almost didn't even bother driving all the way up here this afternoon. But I figured, what the hell, it's a pretty drive, you know, and I wanted to check to make sure everything was okay with you folks, anyway."

"We're all fine," I said.

He nodded. "Good," he said. "That's good to hear. But here's the thing, now. A while ago downstate there was a little incident. I won't go into all the details because we don't know exactly what went on or why. But what happened was, a young state patrol officer pulled somebody over for speeding on the interstate, no plates on their truck, and in the course of the traffic stop, they assaulted him, busted him up pretty badly."

Both of my ears started ringing, and my face got hot. Inside my pockets, I pinched my legs and looked past the sheriff across the road into the woods, trying to distract myself.

"They dumped the officer in the trunk of his own squad car, then parked the car someplace and took off. Now, they could have killed the man, but they didn't. That's in their favor. They weren't the kind of people to kill someone, that's what it tells me. By the time someone found that officer, though, he was in rough shape."

"Is he okay?" I asked.

"He's fine," he said, "but he's going to lose some of the use of one of his arms."

"That's terrible," I said. I felt I had to say something.

"Yes, it is terrible," Sheriff Kalupa said. "A young man with a family. It's a rough job, sometimes. Anyway, in police work, when something like that happens, they send the information out over the wire to every county in the state. That's how we catch the bad guys when they're on the run."

The sheriff paused and looked at our house, then looked at me again. "The reason I'm here, John, is that the officer said that the truck he pulled over was an older red model without any license plates. He said there were two people in the truck, one young, and one older, probably a father and a son, and they both had long hair. He thought the father's name was Al. He thought he heard the name of the son was John. John and Al. And your father's name is Cal."

"He's my stepdad, actually."

"Oh, right. But isn't that a crazy coincidence?" He forced himself to chuckle, but he looked me in the eyes. "I know this sounds stupid, and I apologize, but I couldn't help thinking of you and your dad, you know?"

I smiled and looked at his shoes. I even laughed a little.

"Wasn't us," I said.

"Oh, I figured that," the sheriff said. "I mean, what would you and your dad—your stepdad—be doing driving around downstate sometime before dawn? But you do have a red truck, don't you? The officer reported a red truck, a red Ford, he thought. He couldn't tell, exactly, because they had a tarp or something tied over the bed and it hung down over the tailgate. You do have a red truck, don't you?"

I nodded.

"But if I remember right, yours is a Chevrolet. Isn't that right?"

"I think that's right," I said.

"Well okay," Sheriff Kalupa said. He nodded. "That's what I thought. I knew it was probably nothing. But I wanted to see how you all were doing, anyway. If any more information becomes available, I'll probably come back out to talk to your dad at some point."

"Sure," I said.

"Well, take care of yourself."

"Thanks, I will."

"Good," he said. "We got some pretty weather coming up. Three months of summer to make us forget about nine months of winter is what some folks say. Taking a long time for spring to come this year, I'll give 'em that." He took a deep breath and pulled up on the belt in his pants. "Well, I best get back to my business." He put out his hand, and I shook it. "Nice to see you, John."

"Thanks," I said. "Good to see you, too."

He smiled. "One more thing, I almost forgot. What is it your dad calls you most of the time? Is it John, Johnny, Jonathan?"

"Johnny," I lied. "Always Johnny. Like in Johnny Appleseed."

Sheriff Kalupa nodded and smiled. "Thank you," he said. "All I needed to hear." I breathed deeply and turned to walk away. "Wait," he said, "please."

He reached into his shirt pocket and pulled out a card. "Here. I've got my name and number on here. I want you to take this."

"We don't have a phone," I said.

He held the card out between his thick fingers. "Take it anyway," he said. "Keep it someplace. You might need someone to talk to, or if there's some kind of trouble, you'll have someone to call." I took the card. "Use a pay phone. That's me there," he said. "Gary Kalupa. Work and home phone numbers. I live over in Ashland. My kid's there on the weekends. Got a boy about your age, maybe a little older."

"I'm sixteen," I said.

"He's almost eighteen," he said. "Maybe, you know, if you need to talk to someone your own age. He's there. Most of the time he's at his mother's house—I'm divorced, you see—but Saturdays he's with me. And she don't live that far away, anyway. Just a few miles."

I shook my head. "I don't need to talk to anyone."

"Keep the card, anyway," he said.

I put it into my pocket and nodded.

"That's the boy," he said. "You need anything at all, now. You hear? Remember, you call, for anything. No saying the sins of the father have to be visited on the son." He smiled. "Nice talking to you."

He did a U-turn in the road and slowly drove away. I watched him until the car disappeared over the hill then hurried home. Before I went into the house, I ran into the machine shed to look at the back of our truck. Splashed across the back, in white, was the word "Chevrolet."

I found Mother and Cal in the house. "I just saw the sheriff," I said. "I was out in the field and he stopped to talk to me."

"What did he want?" Cal asked.

"Everybody knows what happened! The police know two guys with long hair hurt that police officer. One of them young, like me, the other one older. The guy thought our names were Al and John. They know we were in a red truck without license plates. The sheriff said it made him think of us."

Mother put her hand to her mouth.

I said, "But he said the truck they're looking for is probably a Ford. We have a Chevy."

Cal said, "What did you tell him?"

"I told him we didn't do it."

Mother asked, "Did he believe you?"

"I don't know," I answered. "At first I thought he did. But then he asked what you usually call me. I lied and said Johnny. And then he said the sins of the father are not the sins of the son, or something like that."

"Maybe he wants to help us," Mother said.

"He's just fishing," Cal said. "If we sell the truck now it will look suspicious. If someone comes around asking where John and I were that night, we'll just tell them we were home, that we never left. There are a lot of red trucks in the world."

For weeks afterward, through the rest of April and May, we worried and watched for signs of trouble. But the only thing that arrived was spring. The last drifts of snow slowly melted, leaving shrinking, dirty, dripping piles where they had been deepest, turning the barnyard into one large sloppy quagmire of mud. Huge flocks of Canada geese winged their way north again, pulled by some mysterious force toward their nesting grounds near Hudson's Bay. Spring winds blew across the waters, across the wet earth, and forgotten smells—the odor of dirt and water, grass and bark, wet manure—returned to us. The sun regained its heat, and almost overnight the farmland was green again. Thick green buds formed on the branches of trees. Mornings were noisy with the songs of birds, and the once silent white world was filled with color, beauty, and music.

"'He has made everything beautiful in its time,'" Cal said, lifting the shades to let the warm sun stream into the kitchen, as we sat for breakfast on the first day of June. "'Truly the light is sweet, and it is pleasant for the eyes to behold the sun.' Ecclesiastes, chapter eleven, verse seven."

I looked at JJ. "'In them He has set a tabernacle for the sun,'" I said, "'which is like a bridegroom coming out of his chamber.... There is nothing hidden from its heat.' Psalm nineteen."

JJ smiled at me. We looked at her expectantly. Then she shrugged and said, "'Here comes the sun!' George Harrison."

"Secular poetry," Cal said, "but divinely inspired."

Chapter 18

In June, Cal began to work the fields, the old greasy John Deere tractor belching smoke and straining against the plow. He looked as happy as I'd ever seen him sitting on that tractor, a thick cloud of blue smoke swirling around him. He'd never plowed a field before, and at first his rows were not straight. They curved and wiggled like a surf washing against an uneven beach. Mother stood along the fence line, watching him. Each time he passed her, he waved his good arm and smiled, and Mother waved back. Soon enough, he got the hang of it. He learned to keep his eyes on distant trees, the way you learn not to look at a cup of coffee poured to the rim as you walk, to prevent spilling. His rows straightened. He planned to plant a small cash crop of soybeans and of corn, and he did not intend to spray the fields with insecticides or herbicides. "We're going totally organic," he said. "No chemicals, no pesticides, nothing. We may not end up with much to sell after feeding the animals and all the bugs and insects, but what's left won't be covered with poison."

A freshly plowed field smells like night crawlers and dirt and rain, like life and death all mixed together.

JJ and I sat in the pasture and watched as the shining silver blades of Cal's plow curled the earth over cleanly, like someone taking the first scoop of chocolate ice cream from a frozen gallon. Hundreds of Lake Superior seagulls, shifting clouds of white and gray, trailed behind the tractor, shrieking and fighting for the red worms, night crawlers, and grubs exposed by the plow. Even our elderly cows watched as the screeching flock followed along behind the tractor.

From the air above, our land must have looked like a colorful puzzle, with squares and rectangles divided by fences and hedgerows, the pastures and woods various colors of green, the freshly plowed field a dark, wet brown, and then a lighter sand color where it had dried. Two separate, smaller parcels were pastureland, one just behind the barn, and one on the far northwestern corner of our property, where a small spring-fed creek passed through. During the spring thaw, particularly during April rains, muddy water rushed through the creek, sweeping branches and ice and caramel-colored foam through deeply cut earthen banks. Now the water ran clear and cold, two or three feet deep in most places, plunging into deeper pools beneath undercut banks, where I could often find small trout finning on the bottom against the current. Most of the fish were brown trout, with white bellies and golden sides dotted with spots of red and black, surrounded by white halos. Sometimes I could see the silver slivers of fingerling salmon and steelhead. Our creek flowed into the East Fork Cranberry River, and the Cranberry River flowed into Lake Superior, where thick muscular salmon and steelhead swam by the hundreds of thousands. Some of them fought their way upriver to spawn before they died. In early May I found some of their crimson-splashed bodies washed ashore, drying in the sun and covered with flies.

When I discovered the East Fork Cranberry River that day in May, there were still small piles of snow melting on the shady northern slopes in the woods. I'd been following the bed of our little creek through the woods, looking for springs where the icy water bubbled up out of the earth through the sand. I liked to plunge my bare feet into these springs, to feel the sand and water bubble around them until my feet went numb. I would drink that water, too—cold and pure, filtered through clay and sand. I'd seen a pileated woodpecker that morning, seemingly too large a bird to fly in woods so crowded with trees. It swooped away from me behind the trees, and my heart pounded as it disappeared. And then up ahead I heard the sound of running water, and I found myself on the banks of a wild, meandering river, the shorelines crowded with willow and alder and birch, carpets of white trillium, and scattered beds of Jack-in-the-pulpit, just sprouting, the spears of their green stalks sharp, like daggers. And where the riverbanks opened into wildflower meadows and marsh, I found skunk cabbage and cattails, wild irises, and pretty butter-colored flowers. Later, looking at a county map Cal kept above the sun visor in the truck, I learned this was the Cranberry River. But at the time, I thought it was an unnamed tributary of some larger stream, and I imagined myself the one who had discovered it.

I walked downstream along the shore for a while, following the curving path of the water. I found the dead salmon, which had beached themselves on a sandbar or had been washed or dragged ashore by gulls or raccoons, whose tracks crisscrossed everywhere in the sand. Just beyond the fish, in the woods along the shore, tangled in wild blackberries and turned up partially on its side against a poplar tree, I found a wooden rowboat, a flat-bottom skiff, a ten-footer. At one time, it had been painted green. Flakes of paint the size of corn-flakes still clung to the bow. It had two seats, one in front and one in back, with the wide expanse of middle open. The oars had once been painted white, but now only a section in the middle remained that color. The blades and handles were a weathered, unpainted gray, the color of the boat. The oars were still in the rusted oarlocks. I wondered how the boat had gotten there, wedged in the middle of the woods along a tiny stream. I pulled the boat away from the tree and climbed inside for just a moment. I imagined myself floating down the river, staring up at the clouds as I drifted.

Eventually the path along the shoreline grew too muddy and too overgrown for walking, and I turned back to go home.

It took JJ, Mother, and me more than a week to till and plant our huge vegetable garden. Cal used the tractor and plow to turn over and then disc the soil, and the rest of the work was done by hand, with shovels and pointed hoes. Our hands grew blistered and calloused. We planted a bit of everything—root crops such as carrots and beets; a large section of potatoes in the sandiest part of the plot; storage onions, cucumbers, green and wax beans, zucchini, squash, tomatoes, pumpkins, radishes, lettuce, spinach, and peas. We planted turnips and sugar beets for the cows. We put in twenty rows of sweet corn, each of them thirty feet long. Cal and I erected a fence around the garden to keep the rabbits and deer from eating the sprouts. When a late frost killed all of the warm-weather seedlings, we replanted.

Cal ordered fifty white Leghorn chicks from a hatchery catalog, and they arrived in the mail in a large peeping box. JJ and I would sit in the yard and watch them, little puffs of bright yellow the size of baseballs. Sometimes we'd put cracked corn on our laps and watch as they scurried over us, peeping and pecking, waving their little feath-

erless wings to keep their balance. Cal had larger dreams for our farm,
too. He intended to purchase several sheep to raise for their wool.
He hoped that Mother would learn to spin wool into yarn and then
weave or knit into sweaters and mittens and hats and blankets. He
also wanted to buy llamas, alpacas, younger cows that would actually
give milk. He talked about getting horses and goats. Mother simply
smiled at him, pleased to see him happy and hopeful about something.

Nearly two months had passed since Sheriff Kalupa had first
come by asking questions. Though the mornings were still cold, all
of our faces and hands grew suntanned and leathery. Our fingernails
were rimmed with dirt, and our hair smelled like the wind. At night,
we slept long and hard, our bodies pleasantly exhausted from tangible,
meaningful work.

Even JJ seemed to be thriving and, if not happy, at least newly
alive. Sometimes she wore a red or yellow bandanna around her head,
tied behind her ears beneath her hair. She taught me how to braid her
hair, and sometimes she'd braid mine. She wore necklaces made from
small loops of flowers woven into strands of wild grapevines, and from
each of her pierced ears dangled a soft, blue tail feather from a blue
jay. She looked wild and beautiful. Because we were busy planting,
we spent little time together apart from Mother or Cal. I ached to be
alone with her, to touch her as I once had. When I hugged JJ, it felt as
if large geese were beating their wings desperately inside my ribcage.
At night sometimes, before sleep, she would run her lips against my
neck, breathe into my ear, and my body would swell and pulse with
yearning. But we resisted. Once, when JJ grabbed me on the thigh
before supper, I caught Cal looking at us, glancing at us through the
corners of his eyes. Perhaps it was my imagination. But after supper
that night he read about the fall of Sodom and Gomorrah and, it
seemed to me anyway, he spent a lot of time looking at me and at JJ
while he read.

Sometimes, on a warm afternoon away from work, JJ and I rested
on our backs in the far pasture in the sun—out of sight from the
house. If the sun was warm enough, and Cal was occupied far away
from us, she took her shirt off, as did I, and we sunned ourselves. We
lay on our backs with our hands behind our heads, sprigs of timothy
between our lips, the wind moving the hair under our arms, the sweet

smell of cow manure all around us. Red-winged and yellow-headed blackbirds sang in the marsh grass along the creek. Blue flies buzzed on the manure piles. Large dragonflies rattled their papery wings over us, looking like little flying dinosaurs with bulging eyes, and the smaller damsel flies, the ones with bodies like iridescent blue needles, landed on the tips of tall grasses and twirled like weather vanes in the breeze.

I'd look over at JJ, and my contentment would vanish. Her small breasts would be flattened against the outsides of her ribs, like twin balloons of water pulled by gravity. Her breasts and nipples darkened in the sun, and beneath them, her ribs rippled. I hardened inside my jeans, and it required all the restraint I could muster to keep from touching her. Sometimes we fell asleep this way, and would awaken in the shade of one of the cows, who stared down at us curiously as she chewed her cud.

At other times, JJ and I would go for long hikes in the woods, crossing the road to wander in the Chequamegon National Forest. We had discovered a beautiful pond full of painted turtles, teeming with tadpoles. Sometimes we caught the turtles in a fish net and flipped them over in the grass to admire the brilliant yellows and oranges of their plastrons, colorful Rorschach splotches, no two the same. The turtles' heads, legs, and tails were striped in yellow and green, and when we flipped them over, they arched their necks and strained, their clawed feet swimming in the air, to try to right themselves.

JJ wandered knee-deep into the water and laughed as the tadpoles wiggled in huge black swarms around her legs. Sometimes she scooped them from the water by the handful and carried them ashore, a mass of wiggling black jelly. We'd look at individuals more closely to identify the nubs of developing arms and legs, the shrinking tails. At times, JJ would wade far out into the pond and stand in the muck and weeds until the frogs and turtles trusted her. Turtles which had flopped into the water at her approach would circle back curiously, their heads reappearing at intervals on the surface, like little periscopes. One by one, they'd return to their warm logs, just feet from JJ, to resume sunning themselves. When she walked back ashore, JJ's legs would often trail a dozen or more horse leeches—squirming, rubbery brown ribbons which had attached themselves to her calves and thighs. Some of them were three or four inches long. She'd sit on a rock and pick them off, one by one, flinging them back into the water. If the leech had been attached too long, blood would bloom in a bright red circle where she'd pulled the leech from her skin.

Late one hot summer night, as the crickets sang outside our open windows, JJ and I tossed on our beds, trying to sleep.

"Johnny," JJ asked suddenly. "Do you ever think about sex?"

"Never," I said, and started laughing. JJ laughed too.

She looked at me. "How does it make you feel, thinking about it?"

"I don't know," I said. "It's like drinking six cans of Mountain Dew, or something. It makes me all jittery." I started feeling it right then, just talking about it, the light buzz inside my chest.

JJ looked at me and laughed.

"What?"

"Sex is like six cans of Mountain Dew? Really?"

"Like you can do better."

JJ crawled across the room and sat on my stomach, her thighs locked against my ribs. She took my wrists in her hands and pinned them over my head. Her hair fell across my face. I could have easily rolled her off of me. She was light and small, and I had grown stronger. JJ said, "Once at the state fair a few summers ago, a lady was leading this pretty chestnut mare outside to wash her down before showing her. The mare was in heat, and one of those Budweiser horses, a male Clydesdale, was in his paddock halfway across the barn, and he smelled that mare. His nostrils blew open, and he just exploded. He kicked open the door, splintered wood two inches thick, and then charged through the gate, yanking out three-inch screws that held the metal latch. I was standing right there. He looked like an elephant coming at me.

"I jumped back and that Clydesdale rushed past me, like a moving wall, his eyes wild, and I could see his cock hanging underneath him like a baseball bat. He went straight for that mare. Her owner started screaming. She grabbed a shovel and swung it at the Clydesdale, and the handle snapped right across his throat. Didn't even slow him down. The mare could see what was coming. She broke free and ran outside, and the Clydesdale followed her. He'd mount her or he'd die trying. You could see that.

"The mare got back into the barn and into her stall, and the Clydesdale tried to mount her there. But the mare sat down. The Clydesdale bit her in the back, frustrated. He was slick and covered with sweat. He smelled like something wild. Men and women came running with ropes, and in a minute they had so many ropes around that Clydesdale's neck he looked like a fat horsefly caught in a spider web. They finally had to get a small tractor in there to pull him away from that mare." JJ smiled. "Six cans of Mountain Dew is nothing," she said.

JJ let go of my hands and kissed me. We started awkwardly at first, but then her hands came to my face, and I felt her tongue on my lips, smelled the sweat on her face, felt the breath coming in soft bursts from her nose. I returned her kiss, let my tongue slide against her upper lip. I cupped my hand along the side of her neck, kept my eyes closed. JJ spread her legs and straddled me, pushed her small, light body against mine. Her hair fell across my face. I plunged my other hand under her shirt, ran my palm along the soft skin of her back, the smooth ball of each vertebra.

When she stopped, we both opened our eyes. I slid my hands toward her breasts, but she pinned my wrists to her ribcage with her elbows, and sat back. She stood up suddenly and tucked her shirt into her pants. "Let's go swimming."

Under a half moon, JJ and I snuck out of the house, crossed the road, and headed for the Chequamegon National Forest. We had bath towels slung over our shoulders. We followed a narrow footpath to the pond. It was a breezy night, too windy for mosquitoes to fly, at least on the high land. JJ walked ahead of me wearing one of my T-shirts, cut-off blue jeans, and untied leather boots without socks. Her hair flew freely behind her. She walked purposefully, putting one foot firmly in front of the other, her boot laces dragging against the tall grass and catching in the blueberry bushes that lined the path. On the hills in the open fields, the bright pointed stalks of pink lupine glowed like mottled cones of light.

We could hear the pond ahead of us before we saw it. The croaking of frogs, hundreds of them, guided us to the water's edge. The water was dark, shrouded in mist or fog. In this hollow, the pond was hidden from the wind, and almost still. It looked as glossy and black as obsidian.

"God, look at it!" JJ said, aloud. The frogs and crickets went silent. JJ stepped over to a large rock along the shoreline and kicked off her boots. She pulled her T-shirt off over her head, then unsnapped her shorts and shimmied them and her underpants down her legs and off over her bare feet. In the darkness, her nude body looked white and narrow, like a birch tree growing in a stand of oaks.

"Come on," she said. In three quick steps she was in the water up to her knees, and with a splash she disappeared beneath the surface, coming up in a stream of spray and bubbles thirty feet from shore.

I stuffed my socks in my shoes and finished undressing. It felt odd to be naked in the cool, open air. My testicles sucked themselves up against my body. I crossed my arms over my chest and shivered as I walked slowly into the lake, sinking into the mud. Tendrils of weeds, like soggy fingers, brushed against my legs. The water was warmer than the air. It was an unusual sensation, like expecting to drink cold water and tasting hot chocolate, instead, on your lips and tongue.

"Come on, get in here!" JJ called, sending a shower of spray toward me.

I took a breath, closed my eyes, and went under. The water covered me, rushed past my ears, along my ribs and legs. I stroked down toward cooler water on the bottom, feeling weeds like wet hair on my fingers. The increased pressure pushed against my ears. When I opened my eyes, I could see just more than nothing—a wavering, warm grayness, and tiny spots floating across my field of vision. I could hear only the thumping of my own heart and the occasional gurgle of water against my ears. I pushed off the soft, weedy bottom and arched my back, let bubbles of air rise from my nose, kicked for the surface.

I blew out lungs full of air and felt the cold on my head. I stood in dark water, neck-deep. I could hear again. JJ was next to me, her head like a willow stump, trailing suckers. She took my hand silently and pulled me toward her. She clung to me like someone rescued from drowning, wrapped her legs around me, encircled my neck with her arms. I felt her breasts flatten against my chest. Her hair floated like a cape on the surface of the water behind her.

"Dive, Johnny," she said, her lips warm against my ear.

I did. I pushed off in the muck and the warmth of the lake enveloped us. I wrapped my arms around her and we drifted this way in the quiet grayness. I rolled to my back, feeling milfoil and water cabbage on my back and bottom, behind my knees, and on my heels. I opened my eyes, and I could see through bubbles to the sky, the quivering, broken light of the moon. JJ let me go and floated to the surface, and I followed her.

We blew out our air, and she pulled herself against me. "Do you think," she asked, "it would ever be possible for us to get married?"

"To each other?" I asked.

She nodded.

"Cal would probably kill me."

"He wouldn't," JJ said. "I mean, we're not related. We don't share blood. If Daddy and Anna weren't married, you and I would be strangers, right?"

We went under. We swam together, our legs thrashing, and I felt the tubers of lily pads and globs of algae against me. We stood up on the opposite shore of the pond, knee-deep, the cold air a shock against our bodies, and we dove alone, one after the other, back to deeper water, and found one another again. Our bodies were slippery and cool like seals, skin to skin beneath dark water. My penis hardened, felt warm against the skin of JJ's stomach, back, or legs as she circled me.

"You feel wonderful," she said to me, as she pressed herself against me. We dove straight down into the mud and weeds, and I imagined clouds of black tadpoles all around us, as thick as moths around a lantern. My ears began to ring. My heart pounded. We spun slowly in the water. JJ's hair swirled around my face. My lungs swelled and tried to burst. When I turned to kick toward the surface, JJ gripped me tighter and pulled me down. I bent my knees and pushed, but JJ struggled to hold me under. I panicked. Pulling away from her, I kicked fiercely, swallowing water, choking, as the cold air hit my hair and face. I coughed up water, stood gasping for air.

JJ surfaced behind me, dove under, then resurfaced across the pond.

"What was that for?" I yelled at her. She didn't say anything, but went under again.

She surfaced next to me.

"Sorry," she said. She grabbed my penis in her hand, then let go. "Hope there are no snapping turtles in here." She went under, and I dove for her, found her in the water with my fingers. JJ circled me underwater, ran her hands all along my chest, cradled my testicles in the palm of one hand. We resurfaced in the middle, stood facing one another. I ran my hands across JJ's breasts. She pushed her face into my neck, kissed me hard. We dove under again.

I touched JJ everywhere, and she touched me. We had gone beyond holding back. Underwater, we seemed free of the arrangements that ordered life in the air. We dove again and again, desperately kicking for the bottom, suspended, grabbing at weeds to keep us under longer as our busy hands probed. She put her fingers, one by one, into my mouth, ran them across my teeth, pressed them gently against my tongue. I ran my hand down her back and over her bottom, against the slippery wetness between her legs.

And when our bodies ached for air we floated to the surface, where the singing of distant crickets and the hush of the wind in the trees, the crowded chattering of aspen leaves, were all that we could hear.

JJ's hands tugged against me, and I felt the swell of pressure building inside me. She let go and dove away, alone. Standing shoulder-deep in the water, I paused to gather breath. I looked up at the clean white edges of the moon and the powder work of stars glittering in the arch of blackness above us, and I felt as if my body could not contain me. It all felt too big to hold inside. Yearning and love and hopelessness all mingled together in the middle of nowhere in a life too complicated to ever understand. Why did she have to be my sister? I wondered. Why couldn't she be anyone else?

"Hey," JJ yelled at me, from across the pond. "You're not tired already, are you?" She dove toward the middle of the pond, and I dove to intercept her. We surfaced and I stood on tiptoes to keep my face above water. JJ reached a hand out to me, and we held one another tightly. "One more time," JJ said. "Dive again. Take a deep breath this time." And we went under once again, straight down, swam toward the depths. When I reached the bottom, I opened my eyes and JJ's face was against mine. Her hand felt for my penis between her legs. I could feel her heels against the back of my legs, pulling me toward her. I felt the heat gathering in me, the certainty of unstoppable force and pleasure, the swelling of an apple blossom about to burst into color. I lowered my hands to try to feel where I was in the water, but JJ pushed my hands away, then locked her arms against my neck and held me so tightly the back of my neck burned.

My body let go, then. I could delay no longer. I grabbed JJ as I came, curled her hair around each of my fists, like ropes, pulling her to me. I found JJ's lips and pressed mine to hers, awkwardly. I felt her breasts against my chest. I began to feel dizzy, lightheaded. Cramps tugged against my calves and feet. I let go of JJ's hair and looked up toward the surface.

The pressure in my lungs increased. Bubbles came from JJ's nose and mouth, but she held tightly to the back of my neck. I struggled to free myself, but she wouldn't let go. I broke away. I felt her feet slide away from the back of my legs. I reached for her and found her wrist. She pulled free. I could hold my breath no longer and I kicked madly and surfaced, crying out as I felt the cold air on my face.

I gulped a breath and dove again, straight down, and thumped into JJ. She struggled to stay down. I gripped her tightly, pulled her toward me. I pushed for the surface again. JJ fought against it, tried to jerk her arm free, but I wouldn't let her go.

JJ coughed and choked on the surface, wheezing as fresh, cold air poured into her lungs. I stood chest-deep and held her against me. She coughed and spat up water. She gagged as if she were about to vomit. Her breathing was panicked and fierce. She shivered now, too. She pushed her fists against my chest, trying to break free, but she was not strong enough. She began to cry, put her face against my chest, pushed with her forehead against me.

I reached an arm beneath her legs and lifted her. I carried my sister toward the shore in my arms, the cold air creeping down our bodies as we emerged dripping from the pond. I sat on the rock and held JJ next to me for a long while, shivering and crying, until a few frogs began to trust in the silence again and began to sing.

I lowered JJ to the ground. She sat naked on her towel on the grass, shivering, her arms wrapped around her knees. Her teeth chattered. The look in her eyes frightened me. She let me pull her T-shirt over her head and lift her hair through the hole from behind. Her hair was wet and cool. I slowly pulled her underpants on over her feet, and left them over her knees. She stood.

A dark spot had grown on the towel where she'd been sitting. Blood.

"You're bleeding," I said.

"It happens," she said. JJ took the towel and wiped between her legs. She bit at the edge of the towel, then ripped a long, clean piece that she folded over, again and again, before tucking it into the crotch of her underpants. She tied the rest of the bloody towel around a large rock and threw it into the middle of the pond, where it sank from view.

She pulled on her shorts and snapped them. Then she sat on the rock and watched while I dressed myself. She had stopped crying.

JJ pulled on her boots, one after the other, and left them untied. We held hands as we slowly walked the path back to the house, our hair wetting the back of our shirts. We did not speak. When we neared the edge of the woods, where they opened into brush and field, JJ gently let go of my hand and walked ahead of me.

As we neared the house, we saw candlelight burning in Mother and Cal's bedroom window. Through open windows we could hear Mother and Cal laughing and thrashing in their bed.

"They're like rabbits in heat," JJ said. "Every night it's the same thing: 'Your belly button is like a wine glass! Your nipples are like bottles of beer! Your butt is a sirloin steak!'"

We laughed. Then JJ grabbed my hand and held it. "I love you, Johnny," she said.

"I know. Me too."

But those warm, careless nights did not last. The storm we'd been waiting for, the one we thought had passed us by, drifted back into view. On the morning of July 2, Sheriff Kalupa pulled his squad car into our driveway and knocked on the door. We could see his face and brown hat through the window. My stomach lurched. Beneath the table, JJ reached over and grabbed my leg.

"Now what does he want?" Cal shouted, springing from the table.

"Take it easy," Mother said. She held her hand out and stopped him. "Please. Everyone. Just stay calm." She put a hand on Cal's shoulder. "Cal, please sit down."

Mother wiped her hands on her pants and opened the inside door, speaking to the sheriff through the screen door.

"Good morning," she said.

"Hello." Sheriff Kalupa didn't smile. His face looked serious.

"Can I help you with something?" Mother asked.

Sheriff Kalupa ran a hand over his mouth. "I'm afraid I have some news," he said. Under the table, JJ took my hand and squeezed it.

Mother opened the door. "Come in, please," she said. Sheriff Kalupa removed his hat and walked into our kitchen.

"Could I talk to your husband for a moment?"

Cal stood defiantly. "If there's something you need to say, we can all hear it together."

"Okay," Sheriff Kalupa said. "Okay." He took a deep breath and let it out. "Your little son, the one you lost downstate, his name was David, right? David Franklin? Same last name as yours?"

"That's right," Mother said.

Sheriff Kalupa nodded. "That's what I thought," he said. "Well, what's happened is a caretaker at the cemetery where you buried your son, he noticed the gravesite had been disturbed. This was some time ago. He didn't think much of it, really. Sometimes high school kids out late will drive their cars through, run off the road and into the grass and so forth.

"But every time it rained, that gravesite would fall in a little bit more. And it kept happening, for about a month or so, until there was a depression, a hole there, on one side, as long as the grave and a couple feet deep."

Sheriff Kalupa looked past Mother and stared directly at Cal. "They figured maybe a cracked vault lid. Happens once in a while. Never on a grave that new but, you know, that was what they thought it might be. So they went ahead and dug down to the vault to make things right."

Mother walked backward away from the door and reached behind herself blindly with her other hand to find her chair. She sat down without taking her eyes off of the sheriff. Her lower lip trembled.

"Go on," Cal said.

"I'm sorry," Sheriff Kalupa said. "But when they got to the vault, they discovered the cover wasn't on correctly. It was a bit sideways, out of kilter. And—" he paused "—well, this may not come as a surprise to anyone in this room, but your boy's casket was no longer inside. The casket was gone."

The silence that hung in the air then was as stifling as any I'd ever sat through. JJ gripped my hand under the table, and she kept rubbing the back of my thumb with hers.

"It was in the papers. I guess you didn't see that. I saw the name and it stuck in my head, and the age of the little guy, and I thought to myself, 'Why is that sticking in my head like that?' Then I thought of you folks and, well, it all came together."

No one said anything.

"You've brought your bad news," Cal said. "Now you can go."

Sheriff Kalupa raised his hand. "Cal, now wait a minute," he said. "I've been turning it over in my head, you know, and I think I understand what happened." He looked directly at me. Or maybe I just imagined it. "You should know that a pair of detectives are working on this, and they'll likely be up here in a couple of days. They might even want to arrest you, I don't know. They're going to take pictures of you and the boy. They're going to take a good look at that truck." Mother looked up from the table. Sheriff Kalupa nodded at her. "I thought you might want to know that. Might be a good time to call a lawyer. They'll have a cadaver dog with them, and someone will probably be poking around the property with a metal detector."

"They won't get anywhere near my property," Cal said. "I will not allow it."

The sheriff frowned. "Now, don't do anything stupid," he said. "I'm sorry," he said, nodding at me. "I guess that's all I have to share. You all take care of yourselves." He turned and walked out of our house. Cal closed the door and locked it.

No one said anything until the sheriff's car was out of sight. Cal stood at the window, watching to be certain. Mother spoke first.

"He's trying to help us," she said.

"Why?" Cal asked. "Why would he help me?"

"Not you!" Mother said. "Us! All of us!"

Cal looked at JJ and me. JJ quickly dropped my hand. "You two, would you please leave your mother and me alone? We need to talk."

Mother sighed. She nodded at us. JJ and I walked together around the silo, then headed along the fence line toward the pasture where the cows were grazing, their tails flipping from side to side to chase away flies.

"What's going to happen now?" JJ asked.

"I'm not sure," I said.

She took my hand.

"They can see," I said. "They can see us from the house."

JJ looked at me. "I don't care."

When we got back to the house, Mother and Cal were in separate rooms, and they weren't speaking to one another.

The next morning I awoke to find the house deathly quiet. JJ was not in her bed. When I went downstairs, I found JJ and Cal in the kitchen. Cal was pacing the floor. "What's going on?" I asked.

"Anna's gone," JJ said. She added, softly, "She took the truck."

"We have to remain calm," Cal said. "'Surely I have calmed and quieted my soul. Like a weaned child with his mother. Like a weaned child is my soul within me. Surely I have calmed and quieted my soul.'" Lines from Psalm 131. He repeated them over and over as he paced in the kitchen.

"I woke up cold at four in the morning," Cal said. "When I rolled over in the bed, she was gone."

"She's *gone*," JJ repeated. She waved a piece of paper at me.

I took it from her. Written upon the paper was a single word: Canada.

Cal said, "Did either of you hear anything or see anything suspicious?"

"No," we told him.

"Maybe Kalupa's men took her."

"Cal," I said, holding up the note. "She took the truck to Canada so they won't find it. She's trying to help."

He looked at me, puzzled. "We've probably been under surveillance for a long time," he said. He parted the curtains and looked out the window. "You kids stay here." He hurried outside.

JJ said, "Anna's trying to save him."

I nodded. I struck a match and burned the single-word note that Mother had left for us. It writhed like a living thing as it burned, leaving behind feathery, white ash.

"Without Anna here, Daddy's going to go crazy," JJ said.

This turned out to be an understatement.

Part V: Air

In Heaven soaring up, I dropt an Eare
On Earth: and oh! sweet Melody:
And listening, found it was the Saints who were
Encoacht for Heaven that sang for Joy.
For in Christs Coach they sweetly sing;
As they to Glory ride therein.

—Edward Taylor,
"The Joy of Church Fellowship Rightly Attended" (1680)

Chapter 19

The morning after Mother left, Cal walked the four miles to Bill
and Eunice Hall's farm. When he returned with Bill, several
hours later, they unloaded two large wooden boxes from the back
of Bill's truck and carried them down the stairs into our root cellar.
They worked deliberately, earnestly, silently, communicating only by
nodding their heads, pointing their fingers. Cal and Bill made two
more trips together in Bill's truck, each time returning to unload
additional wooden boxes, almost all of them marked in a language JJ
and I couldn't understand. "What are they doing?" JJ asked me, as we
watched them from the backyard.

I shook my head. "I don't know."

Before Bill and Cal went away for the last time, Cal came to us
and said we were not to go into the root cellar.

"I'm just preparing for the future," Cal said. "That's all you need
to know for now."

When Bill's truck disappeared down the road, JJ stood watch at
the kitchen door while I snuck downstairs with a flashlight. The cellar air smelled damp and pungent, a blend of dirt, dust, and mortar.
Spider webs heavy with dust hung from the joists. Rusted milk cans
lined one wall beside our shelves stacked with canned goods. Next
to them were the wooden crates where we stored our potatoes and
onions. Empty boxes once filled with rat poison littered the floor.
Mice and rats had not only eaten the poison but had also devoured
portions of the boxes.

In the far corner of the root cellar, where one of the rock and
mortar walls bulged inward, I found the wooden boxes Cal and Bill
had carried in. They were stacked on the dirt floor, covered by an old
canvas tarp. I slid the tarp off, propped the flashlight under my arm,
and tried to lift the covers. Some of them were nailed closed, but the
lids of other boxes were loose. Carefully, I removed the cover of the

smallest box, then pointed the light inside. Arranged in rows, like eggs in a carton, were what looked like small black pineapples with wire loops at the top. Grenades. With great care, I put my hand around one, slowly lifted it from the box. It felt dense, as heavy as a piece of lead. I returned it to its slot. I opened a second box, far larger than the first. It held two dangerous-looking rifles, black steel assault weapons with banana clips half as long as my arm. Beside that, the longest open box—the size of a narrow coffin—contained several thick metal tubes tipped with missiles. They looked like miniature rockets with red nose cones and steel fins. Each missile carried a tag wired to the narrow neck behind the fins, and the writing on the tag looked like it might be in Chinese or Korean. In the final box I could open I found a pile of camouflaged clothing, a brick of military MREs, and more than a dozen boxes of brass ammunition.

I hurried upstairs to JJ. "Weapons," I said.

"What kind?"

"All different kinds," I said. "Rifles, grenades. And some kind of missile launchers."

"Bill Hall had all that stuff," JJ said. "He's like one of those nuts we saw in Michigan." JJ shook her head fearfully. "I hope Anna gets back soon."

JJ and I traced Mother's imagined route into Canada in a weathered *Rand McNally Road Atlas*. We had no idea where she was, of course, but we imagined a wandering path for her that seemed possible. Her journey thus far might have followed the northern shoreline of Lake Superior in a northeastern arc over Thunder Bay. In Nipigon, she would have reached a fork in the road: she could have continued driving northeast on Highway 11, into the wilds of Ontario, toward James Bay, or she could have followed Highway 17 as it turned southeast along the Lake Superior shore. If she stayed on Highway 17, she could ditch the truck, get a different one, and return to the United States through upper Michigan. If she kept going deeper into Canada, she could drive northeast until she reached Hudson Bay, or turn west through Manitoba, into the Northwest Territories.

We suspected she intended to make sure our truck would never be found. We imagined her sending it off a cliff into some unnamed lake, or leaving it deep in the wilderness where it would be overtaken, in the course of decades, by trees and vines and rust. We thought she'd buy another vehicle and return home, and though we knew it was unlikely, we pictured her circling Lake Superior, a route that could take a full week, even longer, to complete. We charted her imaginary progress along the Canadian shoreline with little stars of red ink—through Nipigon Bay to Schreiber, Terrace Bay, Marathon, and White River, Ontario; across rivers named the Black Sturgeon, the Aguasabon, and the Magpie; and through the Rainbow Falls, Obatanga, and Batchawana Bay Provincial Parks. Even the word *Canada* became magical to us, our tongues clicking three times, softly, against the roof of our mouths as we said it.

Without Mother on the farm, Cal still read the Bible aloud after dinner, but without his customary zeal. Sometimes he forgot altogether, or stopped in the middle of a passage, looking lost. "Well," he'd say, "that's enough for now."

Each evening he walked along the edge of our property in the fading sunlight with a rifle hanging from a sling around one shoulder, often with the sleeves of one of Mother's shirts tied around his neck like a scarf. He walked the fence lines until well after dark, his eyes scanning the woods and fields. On clear nights sometimes he'd stop in the middle of the field and stare at the sky for minutes at a time, his head tipped back as if his neck were a hinge. If JJ and I were outside and the wind blew in our direction, we could hear bits and pieces of Cal's voice traveling back to us. We believed he was talking to God, which is not necessarily a problem, JJ said, unless you hear God talking back to you.

Cal claimed to see satellites moving across the night sky, convinced himself they were spy satellites, that our land had been put under surveillance. He tore all forty-two chapters of the Book of Job from his Bible and taped the loose pages to our refrigerator and to the wall beside it. Chapter seven was taped just to the right of the freezer door handle, with Job 7:4 underlined in thick black pencil: "When I lie down, I say, 'When shall I arise, And the night be ended?' For I have had my fill of tossing till dawn."

In the front yard Cal planted a straight wooden pole, cut from the trunk of a young aspen tree, fifteen feet high. Across it, near the top, he spiked a thick branch eight feet across. At the top of this cross, he hung a large white flag made from half a bed sheet picturing a coiled, angry-looking snake with its mouth open, its fangs bared to strike. Across the bottom of the flag, Cal had painted the words "DON'T TREAD ON ME," in large black letters.

"He's going crazy, Johnny," JJ said, as we watched him hang the flag.

"We have to help him."

"How?"

"I don't know," I said.

"Anna would know what to do."

"We could ask Sheriff Kalupa to help us."

JJ nodded. "Maybe," she said.

"We just have to keep him calm," I said.

In his sleeplessness, Cal's visions returned, too, vivid dreams that spoke to him, he said, in some holy language that warmed him like the breath of angels.

"The things I've been missing!" he announced to us at breakfast. "Listen to this: the least part of any human being is the part that is visible. The body—he touched his chest with his hand—is just a vessel, like a vase, really, full of water and flowers. The vase will crack and age. It can be repaired, but sooner or later, the rigors of time destroy it. Inside, though, the water evaporates, becomes air, mixes with the scent of the flowers, and it is that invisible part, that unseen presence, which stays forever."

JJ and I looked at each other.

"Don't you see?" he asked. "The vase *seems* like the permanent part, but it's just the opposite. The water is never really gone! It evaporates, rises in the air as hydrogen and oxygen, turns to water again, and falls as rain. It's forever. Do you understand what I'm saying? There is no death! Not in the way we supposed.

"And there's something else you children should know," Cal said. "Without my clothes, naked as I came into this world, I am invisible to those who would harm me."

I shook my head. "No, you're not, Cal."

"John," Cal said, smiling. "You doubt me?"

"I do."

JJ shook her head.

"You too, JJ?" Cal asked. He stood from the table and stepped away from his chair. He lifted his T-shirt from his belly, pulled it up over his left arm, then his right, then over his head. He pulled the bandanna from around his hair and it dropped over his forehead and past his shoulders. He raised his arms and stood smiling at us, his chest and arms covered with curly black hair, peppered with gray. The bullet scar on his arm looked like a cigar burn.

"Daddy, we can see you," JJ said.

I nodded at him. "We can."

He raised his eyebrows, undisturbed. "Of course *you* can," he said. "But anyone out there—he pointed to the window—who seeks to harm me, all they would see is a pair of pants and boots wandering around this kitchen. Naked, the water and spirit inside me merges with the air."

"Daddy," JJ said. "Listen to me. That's not true."

He laughed. "It upsets the paradigm, I understand that. Think about the sunrise. People all think the sunrise is orange and yellow, right? But who ever sees it? Who ever looks at the sunrise and *really* sees? You know what I'm talking about! Sometimes you look at the horizon just before sunup and my God, the colors! Layers like a rainbow flattened out by a big bulldozer, purple and blue and yellow and orange and red, right on up the ladder. If you tell someone that the sunrise is purple and red, blue and yellow, they'll think you're blind. But you'd be right."

JJ sighed. "Invisibility is different," she said. "Invisibility is impossible."

"Is it, now?" Cal asked. "What about your memories? Memory is invisible, isn't it? But isn't what you remember like a painting in your brain? You see it, don't you? It's invisible, but you see it clearly! I'm just saying that maybe the things we can't see are at least as real as the things we can—maybe more so." He shook his head and looked dreamily at the ceiling. "What if everything we've learned is all a big mistake? What if it's all just a shadow world?"

He looked at me and JJ. I shrugged and smiled. Cal winked at me.

Later that morning JJ and I went for a long walk in the sun. We walked south along our property line through the pasture to the open field, where the prairie grasses and wildflowers grew nearly to our shoulders. JJ stopped to braid several ox-eyed sunflowers into her hair, and I sat and watched as she wove the flowers into the thick braid that fell down the middle of her back.

Sheriff Kalupa's car appeared, moving fast, kicking up dust, and pulled off of the road and into the ditch beside us.

He got out of the car quickly and called us over to him. We climbed over our fence and walked down into the ditch to meet him.

"Hey kids," he said. "I'm so glad I found you out here. Listen now. They're fixing to come question your dad soon. Probably tomorrow. I'll be with them. They'll have a warrant. They're going to search the property and the truck, and they're going to get pictures of you, John, and your dad."

"Help us," I said. "Please."

"I've been helping you, John," he said. "But there's a limit to what I can do. I'm sworn to uphold the law and I haven't really been doing that, now have I? I got my reasons, but I don't think there's any more I can do, you understand?" He rubbed his hand across his mouth. "Maybe you can help your dad. Talk to him. Just tell him to come over to Washburn, to my office, to answer some questions. That would make things easier on everyone, and a hell of a lot safer."

I shook my head. "He won't come," I said.

"Anna left with the truck," JJ said. "They'll never find it."

Sheriff Kalupa frowned. "I see," he said.

"But Cal wouldn't come to town even if he could," I said.

"What about you kids?" he asked. "Why don't you come with me now?"

"Why?"

He sighed. "I don't want you getting hurt. You might be in danger if you stay out here."

"What do you mean?"

"I think you know what I mean, John," he said.

"Why can't they just leave him alone!" JJ said.

He shook his head. "I'm sorry. I hate this, I really do. Look." He glanced back at his squad car. He sighed deeply. "Listen to me. What I'm about to tell you opens me up to some pretty serious charges. But here's the thing. If your little brother is buried somewhere on this property, they're going to find him. That will tie you and your dad to a felony and some pretty serious business."

"And what if they don't find him?" JJ asked.

The sheriff smiled. "Smart girl," he said. "All I'm saying is your dad will be in significant trouble if they do. You understand?"

I nodded.

He smiled. "I'd get a haircut, too."

"Thank you," I said.

"You sure you two won't come with me now?" Sheriff Kalupa said.

"We can't," I said.

The sheriff held up his hands. "You take care of one another then," he said. "I mean it. Keep your eyes open." He took off his hat and wiped the sweat from his eyebrows with the back of one hand. "Supposed to storm tonight. We could be in for a wild one, hot and muggy as it is already. You kids take care of yourselves."

JJ and I hurried back toward the house. I looked over my shoulder to see Sheriff Kalupa sitting in his patrol car, watching us. Everything we needed to do was laid out clearly in my mind.

"Now what?" JJ said.

I took her hand. "I know what we can do."

The day dragged slowly, a humid morning followed by a stifling afternoon. The temperature soared into the 90s. I sat outside, sweating in a kitchen chair, while JJ cut my hair. She trimmed it short in back, and over my ears on the sides. Thinned it out on top. It felt as if five pounds had been removed from my head. When Cal saw me, he smiled. When JJ asked if he'd like his own hair cut, Cal agreed. So JJ cut his hair as well, her scissors flashing in the sun.

"Hot as the hinges of Hades today, isn't it?" Cal said, as JJ hovered over him. "Gets any more humid, we're going to need gills."

Evening came on and we ate supper together. As JJ and I washed the dishes, Cal cleaned his gun at the kitchen table.

"Don't let people fool you with that peace and brotherhood, meek-shall-inherit-the-earth crap," Cal said. "If Jesus were alive today in this country, he'd be cleaning house. He'd go to the New York Stock Exchange, and he'd turn that whole building upside down! It would be like his tantrum in the temple. He'd be flipping tables and tossing computer terminals. He'd have greedy traders diving under their desks for cover. He'd jump up and down in Hollywood until the whole state of California started sinking into the sea. He'd send a plague on Washington, DC, something politicians fear most: the truth. Can you imagine that! The poor would love him, and the rich and powerful would fear him. It wouldn't be long before the FBI would have his cell phone tapped, his house, his car, even the collar on his dog. The disciples would start packing sawed-off shotguns. Jesus, he'd carry something nicer, an Italian nine-millimeter, something classy that would fit under his robe. Feds come to bust up his last supper, probably in a McDonald's or a Kentucky Fried Chicken someplace, and I guarantee you all hell would break loose. The Big Mac attack!"

"I thought Jesus was a pacifist," JJ said.

"Mostly," Cal answered her. "Not when he was angry."

I wanted to ask about the guns and other weapons he and Bill Hall had carried into our basement, but he would know I disobeyed him if I said anything, so I decided against it. After he put his gun back together, Cal went for a walk outside. He returned home after dark, took off his boots, settled on the sofa with his Bible. Eventually he took the Bible and rifle and went upstairs to bed. JJ and I waited until nearly eleven o'clock before checking on him. He snored on his back on top of the covers, his rifle at his side, the Bible opened on his chest like a giant moth.

We went out into the Cathedral of David and stood with shovels in our hands. Above us, the log rafters we'd hewn from maple trees crisscrossed in a pattern of interlaced hexagons. We looked down at our feet, directly beneath the center of the steeple. The air felt humid and still. Night crawlers, wet and shining, some glued together in mating, slipped quickly back underground when JJ's flashlight beam touched them. Crickets sang all around us. Far out over the fields, fireflies glowed and dimmed like sparks rising from a fire.

The dull swish of our shovels temporarily hushed the crickets, made them listen for danger, but gradually they lost interest in our noise and began singing again. Without light, our eyes adjusted to night vision. Outside, the three-quarters moon was bright. I could hear JJ's labored breathing. We were both too frightened and anxious to speak.

Because the casket was just a foot beneath the surface, we reached it quickly. First JJ's shovel, then mine, knocked against it. We scraped sand from the cover, then cleared most of the remaining dirt away with our hands. It took all of our strength, but we slowly pulled David's casket from the ground. Then we filled in the hole. I had to haul in another wheelbarrow load of dirt from the garden to make up for the loss of the casket.

"We'll use the wheelbarrow to get David as close to the river as we can. Then we'll have to carry him together."

JJ helped me lift the coffin across the wheelbarrow, where I tied it securely while she returned our shovels to the machine shed. We headed for the woods, David, JJ, and me, alone together. We walked on a path along the fencerow toward the far corner of our property. When we reached the far pasture, where our two cows slept, they snorted and stared at us but stayed put, resting like giant, mottled rocks in the grass. I rolled David through the grass in front of me. Though he'd weighed forty-eight pounds when alive, he probably weighed less than thirty pounds now, plus the weight of the small casket. Still, the muscles in my arms burned, and I had to stop at times to rest.

Behind me, JJ carried a spool of wire, maybe ten or fifteen pounds of it, wrapped around itself in a thick coil about the size of a basketball, and stuffed into a gunnysack along with two rusted steel leaf springs we'd found in the shed, which weighed maybe ten pounds each. These long, narrow pieces of rusted steel and the wire would be heavy enough, we hoped, to guarantee that David's body would sink in the water.

When we reached the creek, we pulled the casket off the wheelbarrow and walked down into the water in our boots. Because it was late July, the creek ran shallow, though still five or six feet wide in places. In the corners and bends, the water gathered in deeper pools. We floated the casket along the creek, walking along beside it. From thick brush along the water, a ruffed grouse exploded from its perch on the limb of a poplar tree. JJ screamed.

"Partridge," I said. Aloud, my voice sounded foreign in the woods.

We followed the twists and turns of the creek bed. In darkness, without snow cover to reflect the light, with leaves shading out the moon, the woods seemed sinister. I feared that coyotes, wolves, or black bears would smell what we carried and would be drawn to us, though I didn't say anything about that to JJ. In daylight, we wouldn't have needed to follow the creek bed. I could have found my way through the open woods to the river.

Occasionally, thunder rumbled quietly in the distance, far to the west. The air hung heavy, humid and still all around us. Sweat poured into my eyes, and my T-shirt stuck to my back. Mosquitoes buzzed annoyingly in our ears. Finally, up ahead, we heard running water. The East Fork Cranberry River, flowing north toward Lake Superior.

"There it is," I said.

We hurried to the water's edge and slogged and slipped single-file along a muddy deer trail through the thicket of willows and alder growing along the shore. A hundred yards or so beyond the banks where I'd seen dead salmon in the springtime, we found the small wooden skiff I'd discovered, the oars, with blades worn and splintered, still in the rusty oarlocks, the bottom spotted with lichens and moss. In the darkness, the boat looked more decrepit than it really was. But there were no holes in the bottom, and the wood was still solid. Thick cobwebs stretched across the bow. Five or six inches of old rainwater and decayed leaves and branches rested in the bottom.

"This is it?" JJ said. "This thing is ancient."

"There aren't any holes in it," I told her. "We'll be fine."

We flipped the boat over to empty the water from the bottom. We picked out the sticks and leaves that stuck to the wood. Then JJ helped me slide the boat down the bank toward the river. The bow was tangled in vines and brambles, and we had to tug it free. The boat slid more easily in the wet clay of the riverbank, and we stopped just as the bow nudged into the current. In this spot, the Cranberry was nearly fifteen feet wide, running slow and straight. On the map it turned toward the west before joining the main branch, which flowed northwest to Herbster, under Highway 13, and into Lake Superior. I had only walked about a mile downstream from here, and I did not know how it looked beyond that. I was relatively certain the first mile would go smoothly. After that, we would be in unexplored territory.

JJ dropped the coil of wire and leaf springs in the bottom of the boat. We put David's casket in the bottom between us. The steel oar pins squealed in the rusted oarlocks, so I removed them and spit into the holes. I slid the boat halfway into the river and jumped in. With one push of the oar, we were free of the shoreline. The river grabbed us.

Chapter 20

The current was slow as rivers go, but the tangle of trees along the shoreline seemed to pass quickly. Out on the water the air felt cooler, and we could see more clearly. I wiped the sweat from my eyes and adjusted myself on the seat. JJ turned and looked ahead, her hair falling down over her shoulders.

The Cranberry is really more of a creek than a river, and I worried about running out of navigable water. We had only five or six hours of darkness left, and eight or nine miles of river to cover. If the river went dry or rocks punched a hole in the boat, we could be stranded in the dark with the body of our dead brother in the middle of someplace we'd never been. And even if we ran the river quickly, we still had to row into Lake Superior and return to shore before anyone saw what we were doing. Then we had to hitch a ride in Herbster that would take us back to the farm before Cal woke up.

I managed to hold the boat straight in the current, and we ran the first section of river fairly quickly. The moon seemed to be following us through the trees. Polaris was directly overhead, and the Big Dipper was west of it, the handle hidden in the clouds but the bucket exposed and tipped, pouring its blackness on us. Sometimes we could hear an owl or a whip-poor-will, but mostly we heard the gurgling of the water, the whining of mosquitoes, the almost continuous scraping of the boat against branches or trees that grew along the banks, and rocks thumping the bottom, under our feet.

The wind shifted as storm clouds rolled in from the west. Sometimes the river narrowed and grew shallow, and the keel of the boat dug in and we ground to a stop. JJ and I got out then and pulled the boat through the shallows, the icy water running over our ankles and up our calves. When the river deepened, we got back in and floated to the next obstacle.

It began to rain.

At first a few isolated drops pocked the river and thunked against the boat. Then the rain increased until it hissed in the leaves and splattered in the river ahead of us. JJ turned her face up and stuck out her tongue.

My wet T-shirt stuck to my skin. The rain fell lightly for a while, but then the thunder grew louder, and flashes of lightning lit the clouds. We watched a wall of blackness roll over us, broken only by streaks of lightning, and an eerie darkness settled in. Wind roared across the fields, whipping the treetops into a furious dance of leaves, and the rain increased to a steady, relentless pounding.

"Should we stop?" JJ shouted at me. She squinted against the wind and rain.

"We can't," I said. "We don't have time."

A flash of lightning blinded us, followed by a deafening crack of thunder. JJ screamed. All around us, trees bobbed in the wind. Branches and leaves broke off and drifted in the current. The skies opened, and the rain came like a waterfall, pouring into the boat and over the casket, stinging our backs. I huddled forward and strained to see the shoreline.

Another bolt of lightning struck just behind us. Rain blew in torrents across the current, stinging our arms and faces. The trees bent more sharply, now, nearly doubled over in the wind, and the water of the river rippled across the grain. Brief lulls would come, and we'd relax, hopeful that the worst had passed, but then the wind would stir again and the rains would fall even harder.

Then the rhythm of the downpour changed. The rains let up slightly, and after just a moment, something that sounded like sparks began to strike the boat and sting against our arms and our backs. Tiny spheres of ice the size of corn kernels. Hail.

It was now so black I could hardly see. I turned the bow toward an opening in the trees along the shoreline, and pushed against the oars. The hail pummeled our bodies, and like a white curtain it shrouded everything before our eyes and thundered against the boat and coffin. It hissed as it shredded the leaves in the woods. The bow of the boat shuddered as it struck muddy shoreline.

"Get out!" I screamed at JJ. She leaped over the bow and grabbed the gunwale as the stern swung downstream. I jumped out into water knee-deep, holding the boat with one hand. The current tugged the boat away from us. JJ held on to the bow, and it dragged her into deeper water. I leaned back with all my strength, but I couldn't hold it. I lost my grip on the gunwale.

"Let it go!" I yelled at JJ. She was thigh-deep and then waist-deep in the water. I went in behind her. "Let go!" I grabbed her arm. The hail was steady static in my ears as it pounded against my head and back. JJ released the boat. It swung into the current and drifted backward downstream. I took JJ by the hand and pulled her from the river. We crouched in a small opening beneath a tangle of willows on the shoreline. The boat spun around a bend and disappeared from view.

JJ slumped beside me and cried. Steam rose from her back and her hair. I looked down at my T-shirt to see that my body was steaming, too. A cold front had moved through, leaving behind cooler Canadian air. In time the hail grew larger, the size of marbles, and we pulled willow and alder branches down over us to protect ourselves. It thundered into the river and piled up on the ground all around us, bouncing off trees and rocks, shattering like balls of glass.

Gradually, the hail slowed and stopped, and a light rain began falling again. The thunder grew quieter in the distance, and the winds calmed. All around us, the woods glowed white, and a slushy quilt of hail floated on the river.

We stood up and stomped around in the ice. It crunched beneath our boots. If we listened carefully, we could hear the hail melting, a quiet hiss, like the leak of an air hose, all around us.

JJ said, "What now?"

"We'll just start walking downstream until we find it."

JJ looked as if she might cry.

"The river isn't that wide, and there are trees and roots sticking out all over. The boat probably didn't get far. It'll be hung up somewhere."

We followed a deer trail along the shoreline, but when the trail veered into the woods, we pushed on through the alders that grew by the water. We fought through the branches that pulled against us, and JJ had to tuck her hair inside the back of her shirt to keep it from getting tangled in the trees.

"This is bullshit," I said. "Let's walk in the water. We'll stay close to shore."

JJ stepped carefully into the river. I followed her until we were thigh-deep in the water, which now ran brown with mud and hail washed in by the storm. The cold water numbed my feet and calves, but the current pushed us forward and made the walking easier.

At each bend in the river, we'd turn the corner hopefully, only to be disappointed when we saw no dark object propped against the shoreline in the distance. We'd walk into shallower water and hold onto the branches of trees until we caught our breath. Then we'd set off again. The rain had slowed to a mist, and an eerie fog hovered over the river, decreasing our visibility to just fifteen or twenty yards ahead of us.

We stumbled upon the boat. It appeared out of the fog like a ghost, bobbing in the current, its side scraping against a small tree that had fallen completely across the river. Both of the oars were still in the locks, rising and falling in the current along with the boat. It rested in waist-deep water, and we were able to walk to it without trouble, bending our weight into the current to keep from being toppled over.

More than six inches of water and ice filled the bottom of the boat, but David's coffin remained upright, wet and dimpled by the hail, but otherwise undamaged. We splashed as much water from the boat as we could, and then JJ climbed over the bow. I climbed over the tree to the downstream side, and carefully lifted the stern of the boat over the fallen tree. The river current helped to push the boat downstream, and I carefully swung a leg over the gunwale and got back in.

With the influx of rainwater, the river ran faster now, and because the fog obscured our view, the trip became more frightening. It was as if we were sailing blindly through a twisting tunnel filled with obstacles. I tried to slow us with the oars as best I could, but often the boat shuddered to a sudden stop when we struck rocks or trees hidden by fog. My body ached, and blisters swelled along my rain-softened fingers and on the palms of my hands. JJ splashed as much water from the boat as she could, and in the front, her feet rested on the bottom of the boat. Because I weighed more, however, most of the water settled in the back, and my boots stayed ankle-deep as the water sloshed from side to side.

Many times, we ran up against large trees that had fallen completely across the river. Once, a waterlogged birch tree rode low in the water, and we stood waist-deep in the current and lifted the boat over the top, aided by the running water. Other times, we ran into large aspens or maples, uprooted by a storm some time ago, that rode too high to pass over, and too low to slide beneath, so we had to beach the boat and physically drag it along the shoreline, through tangles of willow and alders, through blackberry vines and nettle. We were soaked to the skin, our legs nets of bloody, itching scratches. Our muscles ached with fatigue. When we stopped to rest, the mist had lightened enough for the mosquitoes to attack without mercy, so we pushed on, sweat stinging our eyes.

"Pull!" JJ ordered, as we dragged the boat, inch by inch, through the trees.

"Push!" I yelled.

Branches and vines were like fingers tugging against us. Sometimes it took all our effort just to nudge the boat forward a foot.

"Rest," I said. And we stopped, briefly, dripping sweat, to get our breath. I was so tired I felt like throwing up. JJ's face was streaked with mud. Her hair looked like a thick strand of wet, dirty rope. She held it over her face and squeezed the water from it into her mouth. She flopped down on the ground next to me.

JJ stuck a finger in the mud and reached for my face. She painted muddy lines across my forehead, down my cheeks and chin. She ran her wet, muddy hands backward over my hair, slicking it back into a glistening shell.

"Do me," she said. She smiled while I traced wet clay across one cheek, over her nose, and then across the other cheek. I made thin muddy circles around her throat and neck. I finished with vertical slashes down her chin, and in a series of lines across her forehead.

We stood up and began to pull the boat through the woods again.

"Pull!" JJ yelled at me.

"Push!" I screamed.

Finally, we got the boat back into the river. We sat on our seats, too exhausted to move. Ahead on our left, we could hear water bubbling, and in the moonlight we could see the wide, wide sparkle of the main branch of the Cranberry River rushing northward, and I knew from the county map that we were now just four miles from Herbster. We skimmed over a sandbar that had formed where the fork and main branch joined, then shot through the faster current into deeper water. The boat spun around backward, but my arms were numb, and I was too tired to care. JJ and I merely turned our heads to face whatever direction we were going.

Clouds of mosquitoes found us in midstream, boring through our wet shirts into our backs, buzzing steadily in our ears. In the open meadows, bats fluttered over the river on their papery wings.

The river passed more quickly, with only a handful of stops where we had to drag the boat over sandbars. Here on the main branch, the shoreline was mostly grassland and marsh, so there were fewer trees to slow us down. The river twisted and turned, narrowed and widened, and the boat spun with it. I gave JJ one of the oars, and she helped me keep the boat away from the shoreline.

I looked down at my hands. My blisters had torn open. Blood lined the creases of my palms, and clear fluid oozed from stinging, open sores on my palms and fingers.

JJ turned the flashlight on her watch. The sudden brightness was blinding. "Almost three-thirty," she said.

Just outside of town, the river twisted through a huge boggy swamp. Wild dogwood, willow, and alder thickets sprung up all around us. Up ahead, we could see lights shining. Beyond that, above the lake, were dark clouds and open sky. We could smell it, the scent of fish, of earth meeting big water.

Frogs gulped in a cacophony all around us, and sometimes we could hear a splash up ahead where a brown trout rose for something on the surface, or where a frog leaped from the bank into the river. We rounded a bend and the river narrowed. High on the right bank, a white house stood over us, and we could see electric wires and the Ts of telephone and electric poles silhouetted against the sky. Beyond that we saw a narrow road and a concrete and steel bridge. We startled three deer feeding along the highway, and they snorted and clattered across the bridge, disappearing into the thicket on the other side of the river.

The current pushed us toward the bridge. The topography flattened into low sand dunes and swampland. Ahead, we could see open air and the darkness of open water stretching to the horizon. A cool breeze blew in off of the lake. The fog had lifted.

"Keep quiet, now," I whispered. Already a dog in town had heard us, and his yelping set off a chorus of howls and deep, throaty barking. A large red building stood along the east bank, "Cranberry Bar and Restaurant" painted on the side. Beyond that I could see signs for the Chequamegon Telephone Cooperative and Herbster Community Church. Highway 13 looked like a silver ribbon stretching east to west.

We crouched in the bottom of the boat as we passed beneath the concrete and steel bridge that covered the river on Highway 13, and we found ourselves in the grassy shallows of the Cranberry River delta.

JJ and I walked the boat through the shallows. The lake lapped against the shoreline sand, and we stopped to rest on the beach before going on.

We'd been living near Lake Superior all of that time, and we had never come to see it. I wiped my face with my hand. Even in the darkness, the lake looked beautiful. Waves rolled toward us with a sliver of foam at their peaks. And it smelled as beautiful as it looked. I knelt in the sand, cupped my hands to the water and brought it to my lips. I swallowed and cupped my hands for more, the cold water running down my chin. JJ dropped to her knees beside me and drank until she was full.

We pulled the boat into the waves. I took off my wet T-shirt and tore it in half. I wrapped each half around the grips of the oars, to cushion my hands. And with JJ in front and David between us, I began to row out toward deeper water. The boat rose and fell in the waves.

We took turns rowing at five-minute intervals until the lights in Herbster were just specks against the dark trees behind them. We both preferred rowing to sitting. Rowing at least kept us warm, and the steady rhythm of the squeaking pins in the oarlocks was more pleasant when you could control the tempo. Riding high on such a thick volume of water, our old wooden boat, which once seemed so large and heavy, now seemed insignificantly small and light. I felt as if we were ants riding the ocean on a matchstick. Water ran all the way

217

to the horizon, and to the west, we could see the lights of Duluth, tiny pin pricks in the darkness.

When JJ rowed, I reclined on my back, eyes closed, feeling the water rise and fall beneath me, the tiny push of the oars against the lake.

When I rowed, JJ stared out over the water.

"What time is it?"

JJ looked at her watch. "Almost four-thirty," she said.

"I can't row anymore." The muscles in my back and arms burned. We must have been a mile from shore, maybe more. We could already see pale light growing along the eastern horizon. I lifted the sack of wire and set it on the seat next to JJ. She held the sack open and I pulled out the two steel leaf springs and the coil of wire.

"Can't we just roll the whole thing over?" JJ asked.

"It might float." I took a deep breath and opened the casket. David rested on his back with his hands crossed, the little blue sport coat still pressed, the tie still knotted. The bones below his eyes protruded a little bit against the skin. Fortunately, it was too dark to see any more detail. JJ brushed tears from her eyes as we looked at him. I felt a hollow pain inside my stomach, but I felt too exhausted to cry.

I lifted our little brother from his small casket and gently set him across my lap. Secretly, I had feared his joints would not hold, worried his legs and arms would come off in my hands. But this didn't happen.

JJ moved the empty casket to the bow of the boat and then knelt in the bottom with the coil of wire.

"Just sort of tie it to get started," I told her, "then wrap it around."

JJ began to wind the barbed wire around David's body. I held both steel springs against his chest. She passed the coil over and under, over and under, working her way toward his feet and then back again, toward his head.

The boat rocked rhythmically, the waves lapping against it. Cold lake air swirled around us. I took the oars in my hands, balancing David on my knees, and worked them to keep the bow pointed into the waves.

By the time JJ finished, the sun had started to break in a dim spectrum of colored light on the horizon. David's body was almost completely concealed by a thick coating of wire. He looked as if he were a caterpillar encased in a prickly cocoon. The weight of the leaf springs and wire pushed against my legs. JJ wrapped the remaining wire around and around his neck and head, careful to keep the coils tight, then moved back down his neck and shoulders, until the wire was gone. Carefully, she weaved and bent the loose end through several other layers, so it would not come free.

A light fog also began to roll in again, and I felt momentary panic, fearful that we would be unable to find the shore, but I could still see the lights in Herbster.

JJ reached out for David, and I gently lowered him toward her until his shoulders rested in her hands.

She nodded, blinking tears from her eyes. I began crying, too.

We stood up carefully in the rocking boat, holding David between us. I put one knee on the seat and leaned toward the water. JJ bent out over the side. We lowered our brother's body into the lake. The waves lapped against the wire and splashed in our faces, and when the cold water swirled around him, pulling him in, we let go. Like the steel hull of a ship, David sank slowly, falling away from us into the darkness of deep, cold water.

JJ leaned over the side and watched the water for a long while. She washed the mud and blood from her hands and face, then cupped her hands and drew the lake to her lips, again and again, drinking. I washed my hands and drank as well—long, cold drinks, the water spilling from my hands down my chin and chest. The rising sun was now so bright, we could not even look to the east. To the south, across the water, we could see the shoreline bathed in light. In the distance, we could even see the northwestern shore of Minnesota, a string of gray hills stretching from Duluth into Canada. The piercing cries of seagulls echoed over the water.

"Okay, now the casket," I said. I stepped around JJ and worked the open casket over the bow and halfway into the water. I tipped it sideways, and cold water filled the inside, lapping against the ivory satin. It filled quickly and began to sink, and when it was too heavy to hold, I let go. It hung in the waves for a few moments, then drifted deeper and was gone.

We beached the boat on a gravel bar in Herbster near the mouth of the Cranberry and walked into town. We were covered with mud.

My head ached and buzzed with fatigue, and my stomach burned with hunger. I felt so tired I could hardly walk or speak.

At the corner of Highway 13 and a gravel road heading south, JJ and I sat down and waited for someone to come along. I stood when cars approached and put out my thumb, but none of them turned. They poured past us on Highway 13, heading east or west. All around us, birds fluttered and sang. Red-winged blackbirds cackled and whistled from marsh cattails, meadowlarks sang in the fields, and curious chickadees buzzed around us. Finally, a bearded man wearing a Minnesota Twins baseball cap pulled over and stopped behind us in a dirty old blue pickup truck.

He stared at us for a few seconds before saying anything. "You two all right?"

I nodded.

"I'm headed to Iron River," he said. "You need a ride that way?"

"A farm north of there. We live on Airport Road."

"Yeah, I know that area." He leaned across the seat and opened the door. We thundered down the road for a while before anyone said anything. He had country music playing on the radio, and he tapped his fingers along the steering wheel in time to the music. His hands were large and greasy. The cab of his truck smelled like cigarettes.

"Some storm last night, huh?" he said. He pointed out the window. "All up and down here, folks got windows busted, aluminum siding dented. Guy across the street from me lost his satellite dish. The wind blew it right off his roof." He pushed in the lighter on the dash and pulled a cigarette from a pack with his lips. "Lotta folks going to wake up this morning happy they took out crop insurance. That hail flattened everything."

I glanced at JJ. She looked as if she were about to fall asleep. She blinked her eyes, stared out the window, her head leaning against the glass.

"So," the man said, "what have you two been up to? You look like you've been rolling in mud."

"We were on the Cranberry River," I told him.

"Fishing?" His lighter popped out and he raised the glowing coils to the tip of his cigarette. He took a drag and blew the smoke out his window.

"Floating," I said. "In a boat."

"Down the Cranberry?" he said, his voice rising. "You can't get a boat down that river, can you? It's too narrow."

"It's wider than it looks," I said.

"You look like you've been wrestling pigs," he said. "That's what it looks like you were doing."

"It wasn't an easy trip," I told him.

"I guess not. What the hell you want to float that river for, anyway? Go out to the Brule, now that's a beautiful trip. If you like mosquitoes, you can float the White through the Bibon Swamp. It's all boggy marshland, but the brown trout in there are about as big as your leg. You need a canoe, though."

JJ and I remained silent. The man chuckled and shook his head. "A boat down the Cranberry. Goddamn if that don't beat all."

He turned onto our gravel road and accelerated, the back of the truck fishtailing in the mud. "You know why they call this Airport Road?" he asked.

I shrugged.

"It's a joke," he said. "There's no airport. When they were cutting the road through a cedar swamp, they found a little single-engine airplane. It had crashed thirty or forty years before, came down in a swamp so thick no one found it. The pilot's skeleton had been eaten by animals. All they found was his teeth." He looked over at me. "So they named it Airport Road. You want a cigarette?"

"No, thanks," I said.

We drove on in silence the rest of the way. As we approached our farm, JJ suddenly sat up in her seat and ordered the man to stop.

He hit the brakes. In the distance, through the fog, I could see flashing red-and-blue lights on the road outside of our house. A patrol car was parked sideways, blocking the road about a half mile north of our land, its lights flashing. Other squad cars were parked closer to the house, one in the driveway. The scene looked eerie, the pulsing lights muted by the fog.

"Wonder what the hell's going on up there?" the driver asked.

"That's our house," I said. "We'll get out here."

"Wait a minute," the man said. He squinted through the windshield. "Is that the church everyone's been talking about? Are you from that family with the crazy man who built a big church out of logs?"

"That's our dad, and he's not crazy. He's sort of a prophet."

"He might be crazy," JJ said. "He has machine guns."

"That's true," I said.

The man held his hands up off his steering wheel. "All right," he said. "All right. You can get out here."

I closed the door. He backed into the ditch and turned his truck around, headed north again, his tires throwing red mud and gravel into the wheel wells.

JJ and I ran into the wet woods and found a deer trail that led us closer to our house. What happened next collapsed any hope we had of saving Cal from the men who were intent on arresting him.

Chapter 21

Crawling on our stomachs through the wet woods, JJ and I made our way as close to our house as we dared, and we crouched, hidden beneath a thick stand of spruces. I peered cautiously between branches. Two squad cars were parked on the road outside of our house. Another idled in the driveway. The fourth one, empty, had been pulled across the road a half mile to the north, to block traffic. All of the cars had their lights flashing. The police were on one knee behind their cars, watching over the hood or trunk. The tips of their cigarettes glowed, illuminating their chins and noses. I could hear the faint crackle of static on walkie-talkies.

Sheriff Kalupa stood at our kitchen door. He had evidently knocked already, and seemed to be waiting for Cal to come to the door. After a few seconds, I saw him knock again, and a second or two later, the sound followed.

Suddenly, Sheriff Kalupa raised his hands over his head. Two of the men on the road stiffened and aimed rifles over the hoods of their cars.

"We can't let them do this," JJ whispered.

I put my fingertips against her mouth. "Shhh. Let's just see what happens."

Sheriff Kalupa backed off of the porch, his arms still raised. If Cal had started to open the kitchen door, I would have stood up and yelled to warn him. But the door never opened. Instead, Sheriff Kalupa turned toward the road and started running and yelling something I couldn't understand. He fell once, dropped hard, belly-first, on our driveway, then struggled back to his feet. He limped away, hunched over, waving his arms at the others, still yelling like a madman, waddling as best he could to get away from the house. And whatever he was yelling, everyone else soon understood him, because they pulled their guns down and started running, too. Car doors flew open, dark figures crawled out, and all of them flopped into the deep grass in the ditch, six men in all, and a dog. One of the men was so close to JJ and me I could hear him when he talked.

After that initial panic, nothing happened for a while. Sheriff Kalupa's car idled in the driveway, its red-and-blue lights flashing against the side of our house, reflecting off of the machine shed, illuminating the giant cross Cal had erected in the front yard.

Perhaps if JJ and I had stood up then and walked from the woods up the driveway and into the house, what happened next would not have happened, and everything would have been different. But I don't know that for certain. I don't know if anything we could have done might have made any difference.

The first flash of fire came through our kitchen window, blowing out the glass, and Sheriff Kalupa's empty squad car bloomed into a fireball with a sound more deafening than thunder. The explosion flashed and the thunderous concussion pushed the air back all the way past us. The intense light temporarily blinded me. It was like looking at the sun. The roof and doors of the squad car were blown thirty or forty feet into the air.

"Holy shit!" I whispered.

"Daddy," JJ said. "Please stop."

My ears rang, the same high-pitched whine that followed you around for hours after a rock concert.

A man in the ditch shouted, "What the fuck was that?"

Sheriff Kalupa's squad car was gone. Burning pieces of it, like the wreckage of an airplane that had come down in a fireball, lay scattered across the yard and driveway. The gravel beneath the car frame, now upside down, blazed in a concave circle like a perpetual flame belching black smoke. One of the tires, blown clear of the axle, smoked and smoldered thirty or forty yards away.

The men in the ditch stayed low. Like crabs, on their bellies, they backed away even further from the house into the woods. If I got up to my knees, I could just make out Sheriff Kalupa's hat through brush and orchard grass. We were behind him and on higher ground, with a thick stand of sumac between us, although the thought did occur to me that if Cal began shooting in the direction of Kalupa's men, JJ and I might be in danger.

The second flash of fire seemed to light up the whole inside of our house, though this time it came through a different window. One of the squad cars parked on the road—the first one in line—exploded in another thunderous fireball. Pieces of the car flew over the road into the woods, like flaming metal birds hit by a shotgun blast. Other pieces landed on the road and in the ditch. A second fire burned and smaller grass fires flared where the pieces landed.

"Jesus fucking Christ," one of Sheriff Kalupa's men said. "He's got SAMs in there, Gary. That was a Stinger or an SA7. Who the hell is this guy?"

Gunfire erupted, a rapid staccato of pistol and rifle shots exploding from the ditch. Our kitchen window shattered. Bullets left a trail of holes across the wooden siding, which splintered in dozens of tiny explosions. Through the gunfire, I could hear someone screaming.

"Hold your goddamn fire! Hold your goddamn fire!" The shooting stopped. "What the hell are you doing?" Sheriff Kalupa's voice. "There are children in that goddamned house. I told you that."

"He's blown up two of our fucking cars!" someone else shouted.

"He's not trying to hurt anyone," the sheriff said. "He could have killed me, could have killed any one of us. But he's not shooting at us."

"He assaulted a cop, Gary. For Christ's sake."

"We don't know that for certain."

"The hell we don't."

"He's got a lot on his mind," Sheriff Kalupa said.

"How are we supposed to arrest him?" someone said. "He could bring a helicopter or a plane down with the shit he's got in there."

Another flash of light came from the house, and the next squad car in line on the road erupted into flames. Cal's missile ignited the gas tank, which blew the rear end of the car up over the front end, leaving the car upside-down, burning, on the road. Flames poured upward through the broken windows and windshield.

"What should we do?" JJ whispered.

"We have to wait," I said.

"We could talk to the sheriff."

I shook my head. "Let's just wait."

The muscles in my chest quivered. My hands kept on shaking. Even my teeth were chattering. I felt cold and stiff, my eyes felt gritty from lack of sleep.

A commotion came from the ditch, and Sheriff Kalupa appeared, standing gingerly on the road facing our house. His arms were raised over his head. He started walking, limping slowly, toward the road. Illuminated by the flames from the burning cars, he cast a long shadow back into the ditch. He took a step, then paused, then took another step. When he'd covered half the distance, he stopped.

He shouted toward the house. "I don't want to hurt you. And I know you don't want to hurt me."

He waited, but there was no reply.

"I'd like you to leave that final squad car alone. I've got all these men here, and we'd like to get back to town. It's a long way for walking." He spoke slowly.

"Go!" Cal shouted from somewhere inside the house. "Don't come back!"

"We're going," Sheriff Kalupa said. "You know I can't promise we won't come back. We have to come back, you know that. But I don't want any trouble. I really don't. I'm interested in justice, Cal. Same as you. It's not an easy thing to get, I know that." He stopped talking and started walking up the road toward the remaining squad car. He kept his arms up as he slowly limped toward the car. When he reached the driver's side door, he stopped.

Sheriff Kalupa opened the door. He got in, turned on the headlights. The car made a slow, deliberate U-turn, then drove south again. He stopped across from our house. Five men, one of them leading a dog on a leash, crawled up from the ditch, crouched and ran to the car, opened the doors, and piled in. After the doors slammed closed, Sheriff Kalupa drove away. We waited until the car disappeared.

Cal appeared at the kitchen door. He stepped outside. A rifle hung from one of his arms.

"John?" he shouted. "JJ? Are you out there?"

"What do we tell him?" JJ whispered.

"I don't know," I said. I walked two steps toward the road. "We're out here," I shouted.

JJ stood up and followed me. We crashed through the brush. The remains of two of the squad cars burned in front of us. What was left of Sheriff Kalupa's squad car still smoked on our driveway.

Cal set the gun down and pulled JJ to him with such force, I thought at first he was going to hurt her. Then he hugged me tightly. He wrapped his arms around my shoulder blades and squeezed. His whole body shook as if he were freezing.

"I thought they got you kids," he said.

I felt sick to my stomach, and my hands trembled from the lack of sleep. Mud swirled like frosting in my hair. Dirt was also streaked across my legs and chest. My boots, still full of water, squished like the soles were made of sponge. Broken blisters oozed into the palms of my hands. My legs bled from thin cuts made by the brush and brambles.

JJ didn't look any better. Brown sacks hung under her eyes, and pieces of sticks and clumps of soil stuck to her tangled hair. Her hands were blackened the raspberry color of dried blood, and her legs, too, were cut and bruised.

"They came to arrest me." Cal pressed his hands against his thighs. He took a deep breath and held out a quivering hand. "Look at me," he said. "I'm shaking."

"Cal," I said. "We have to leave now. We can't stay here any longer." Cal shook his head. "Where are we going to go, John?"

"We can't stay here!"

"Sure we can."

"For God's sake, Cal," I pleaded, "think about what you're doing. Just think, okay? The next time they come, they won't leave without you. You don't have any choice now, you know that. We have to leave."

Cal shook his head and smiled calmly. "Come with me," he said. "I want to show you something."

He walked up the driveway, his rifle slung over one shoulder, and we followed. We passed the house and turned toward the church. JJ looked at me, her eyes wide. Cal opened the door and led us inside.

"Look at this," he said. David's empty tomb. Fresh dirt and sand dried on small mounds scattered around it. A beam of sunlight cut through a narrow opening in the logs of the church and fell across

Cal's chest. He smiled at us. "Do you two know what's happened here?" he asked.

"Dad," JJ began, but he raised his hand and stopped her.

"I'll tell you what's happened," Cal said. "Your brother has risen from the dead." He nodded. His face beamed. "I think he's gone to find his mother."

Chapter 22

We wandered back outside, our boots sliding and sinking in the mud. The man who'd driven us home from Herbster had been right: the hailstorm had flattened everything. Our soybeans had been driven into the earth, and most of the corn was pounded flat as well, the leaves shredded. Opaque puddles and ponds had filled in all the low places, water the color of caramel.

"The crops are a complete loss," Cal said. He smiled. "Are we terrible farmers or what? We have a lot to learn." He looked at JJ. "Where were you two last night, anyway?"

"We went for a walk," she said.

"In the middle of that storm? You picked a hell of a night for a walk."

"We couldn't sleep."

"Well, I know how that feels." He shook his head. "When the storm hit, I started reading Revelation by candlelight. Wind pounded the house, like a roar coming from the mouth of the beast. I thought maybe it was the fall of Babylon. The end of the world." He looked at me. His red-rimmed eyes flashed. "I was on my knees in the dark. The sea and all the waters had turned to blood. The men were scorched with fire, then came darkness and pain. And then Revelation chapter sixteen, verse twenty-one: 'And great hail from heaven fell upon men, each hailstone about the weight of a talent. Men blasphemed God because of the plague of hail, since that plague was exceedingly great.'"

"It was just a bad thunderstorm, Cal," I said.

"No!" He smiled and shook his head. "No, it was a lot bigger than that, John. That was the force of David's resurrection, the power of life returning to his body. Sort of like the Big Bang. There is so much energy in the creation of new life!" He staggered slightly as he moved toward the house. He looked exhausted.

"So what now?" JJ asked.

He looked back at her, took a deep breath. "Well, we'll rest a bit, then get back at it. We've got work to do."

"We should pack up what we can. Maybe the Halls will loan us a car."

"We're not leaving."

"But Cal," I said. "Please listen. You hit a cop. You blew up those cars. They're not going to let it go." JJ started crying. She stood behind me, her head against my back.

"The only thing I'm guilty of is fighting for my liberty, and for the liberty of my family. Used to be that was something that made you a hero in this country."

"But you broke a cop's arm," I said.

"He didn't give me any choice! What harm was I doing, John, tell me that? I was driving home in the dark. What did it matter how fast I was going? No one else was on the road! What did it matter that I didn't have license plates on the truck? Who was I hurting? What right did he have to stop me, to scare you half to death, to pull us out of that truck and make us stand there like criminals? None of that makes sense to me."

Cal put a hand on my shoulder. "John," he said softly, "the only kind of freedom most people are interested in fighting for is the kind that requires other people to become like they are. The freedom to have a yard full of green grass with every weed and dandelion killed by chemicals. The freedom to drive a car like everybody else drives, to paint your house some appropriately drab color the neighborhood association approves of, to get a job with two weeks' vacation that numbs your brain the other fifty weeks of the year, so you can buy a bunch of shit you don't need but saw advertised on television. The freedom to get buried in a casket that costs more than a used car, stuck inside a concrete vault you also have to pay for." He shrugged. "That's not the kind of liberty I want. And you shouldn't want it, either."

Cal looked out over the field. "We're off to a rough start, here, I'll grant you that. But we're learning. I intend to put in a pond so we can raise catfish. It won't have to be deep. Catfish don't mind a muddy bottom. We'll buy some fingerlings and let them grow, and anytime we're hungry, we'll just go out and catch dinner. Won't that be something! I plan to get some bees for the honey, too. Raise sheep, spin the wool into yarn, and make our own clothes. We are just getting started."

I slept more soundly that morning than I'd ever slept in my life. Every muscle in my body ached. I felt as if I were rising and falling on waves. I could still smell the water, could still see David's wire-clad body falling away from us toward the bottom of Lake Superior.

Cal let us sleep for just six hours, and then he put us to work. All afternoon, while JJ and I cleaned broken glass from inside the house and filled every available empty container with fresh water, Cal filled burlap sacks with dirt from the garden and carried them into the house to construct sandbag bunkers around each of the first-floor windows. He took stock of our meager food supply, supplemented only by a box of MREs in the basement.

When he finished building the bunkers, Cal sat on the roof of the house with his rifle, scanning the countryside, whistling "How Great Thou Art."

"Are you scared?" JJ asked me.

"Yes. You?"

JJ nodded. Outside, it was eighty-five degrees and still. Flies and bees buzzed against the window screens. As night descended, heat lightning flashed out over Lake Superior, and a breeze made the kitchen curtains billow and snap against the walls. We ate a supper of large bowls of salad—fresh greens from our garden, with cubed Spam stirred in—at the kitchen table around a small flickering candle. Cal didn't speak while he ate. He kept one hand on a loaded rifle he'd set across the table, the muzzle facing the door.

For two days, two long days of watching and waiting, of staying near the house even when it was ninety degrees outside and the heat shimmered like gossamer gowns over the road, nothing happened. No one came. No helicopters circled overhead, day or night. No tanks churned up the gravel road, their canons pointed ominously in our direction. Butterflies flitted from flower to flower, birds sang in the trees and, in the evenings, deer came to graze placidly on our lawn.

Through those two long, hot, peaceful nights, moths and mosquitoes buzzed through open windows into our house, attracted by the flickering light of lamps or candles. Cal refused to board up our broken windows. Doing so would have made it easier for men to sneak up on us. Once, a disoriented bat entered the house through what had once been the front picture window. It darted from room to room, narrowly missing the walls and furniture, its wings dusting the ceiling, until it found open air again and disappeared into the darkness.

With a black crayon, JJ played connect-the-dots with the bullet holes in the walls. The result looked like a giant spider web.

On the third afternoon, just before suppertime, as Cal began reading from Psalms, a puff of dust emerged far down the road and grew larger. Cal grabbed his rifle and stood up. He wore only a pair of cut-off blue jean shorts, with a crisscross of brass ammunition across the front of his chest, like some commando in an old movie about the Cuban revolution. He had not washed or slept for more than a few hours in at least three days. He smelled sour, like dirt and sweat.

"Someone's coming," he announced.

I hoped it was Mother. The three of us watched from the kitchen window, ignoring Cal's call to move to the bunkers. A small parade of cars snaked up the gravel road, sending a cloud of dust blowing east, with the prevailing winds. Cal ordered us into the bunker he'd constructed in the living room, but we stood behind him, watching the train move slowly up our road. One by one, the cars entered our driveway. In front was a rusted-out Lincoln Town Car, with a tiny old woman driving. She looked so small she could hardly see over the steering wheel. Agnes Jurasko.

"Well I'll be damned," Cal said.

Jeremiah Gibbons got out of the car and slowly made his way around the hood to open the driver's side door. Agnes stepped out of the car and took Jeremiah's hand. One by one, white-haired elderly women and balding men left the other cars and began to assemble on our driveway. Seventeen people from the Herbster Senior Center— the Herbster Grays, they called themselves—had arrived. Some of them looked to be one hundred years old. Together, they walked and shuffled slowly across our yard to the kitchen door. Cal met them on the porch.

"Hello, Reverend!" Jeremiah said. He wore baggy blue work pants and a brown short-sleeved bowling shirt. Beside him, Agnes wore a flowered dress and tennis shoes. The lenses in her glasses were as thick as the bottom of a beer mug.

"Hello, Jeremiah," Cal said.

"You got a haircut!" Jeremiah said. "You don't look like an apostle anymore."

Cal smiled and nodded. "I'm just a farmer, now."

"Not from the looks of your cornfield."

Cal laughed. "That's organic corn."

"Is that what you're calling it?" Jeremiah said. "My day we just called it stunted."

"We haven't used any fertilizer."

Jeremiah nodded. "It shows," he said. "Corn's a big feeder. Needs lots of nitrogen. My daddy used to raise sweet corn, and every summer the whole family had to piss on it. We each had our own row. If he saw you going anywhere else, he'd yell at you to piss in the cornfield." Everybody laughed. "Daddy drank a bit, made his own moonshine, and by August the corn in his row was twelve feet tall!"

Cal laughed.

Jeremiah smiled. "We heard some police cars had a little trouble up here," he said. "Looks like we heard true."

"That's right," Cal said. "Came up here to try and arrest me. They won't make that mistake again."

"People are talking about this everywhere," Agnes added. "You're pretty famous, Reverend!"

"I think you found yourself some trouble," Jeremiah said.

Cal shrugged. "Nothing I can't handle."

Jeremiah chuckled. "I like your spirit," he said. "But take it from someone who has felt the heavy hand of the Man on his black ass one too many times. When they got a boot on your throat, they aim to keep it there till you shine it with your tongue."

"I've got more than they can handle."

Jeremiah shook his head. "I don't think so. They're gathered in Iron River right now," he said. "They got Humvees. Black sedans. A helicopter. Even a tank."

"A tank?" Cal said.

Jeremiah shrugged. "G-men like their toys."

"I'm not worried."

Jeremiah said, "We're here to help. Nobody is going to hurt a bunch of old people."

Agnes nodded. "You healed us. Let us help you."

"I don't think so," Cal said.

"I can still see! Jerry can still dance—and that's not all, I don't mind saying." Agnes smiled at Jeremiah. "Eleanor is still walking straight as a sober lush, though she uses a cane when it gets slippery." A small crooked woman somewhere in the crowd of people raised her hand. "Tom's diabetes is under control." A large man with a thick neck waved a baseball cap above the crowd. "You have the spirit, Reverend," Agnes said. "None of us doubt that."

Cal shook his head. "You're mistaken."

"We brought food," Agnes added. "And beer. And guns. I've got a thirty-thirty in the trunk I used to use for deer hunting."

Cal smiled and shook his head. "How about we visit for a few hours. But no guns. Please leave your guns in the car."

From large coolers they passed out warm hot dogs and buns wrapped in plastic, bottles of beer and Pepsi, bags of potato chips. We had a picnic in the front yard. We'd barely finished eating when someone noticed another car slowly moving up the road. The blinker lit when it reached our driveway. I could not recognize who was behind the wheel, but I could tell it wasn't Mother.

"Stay back," Cal said to JJ and me.

The four horsemen of the apocalypse had returned for Cal in the solitary disguise of Sheriff Kalupa. He drove up in a 1979 Country Squire station wagon, its fake wood on the doors faded, its quarter-panels cancerous with rust, an old sticker on the pitted rear bumper that read, "Reptile Gardens Sioux City South Dakota." A tiny white statue of Jesus stood on the dashboard, arms outstretched as if he were about to hug a friend.

Chapter 23

Sheriff Kalupa got out of his car, hitched up his pants, and limped into the front yard. He wore baggy blue jeans sagging below his fat belly and hanging off his butt, a dirty Green Bay Packers T-shirt, and a Milwaukee Brewers baseball cap. Soiled rubber flip-flops on his bare feet.

"Well, looks like somebody's having a picnic!" he said.

"Gary, you're welcome to some chips and beer," Agnes said, smiling. "The hot dogs are all gone."

"I thank you," he said, "but I've come to talk to Cal. Someplace private, if you please?" Cal tipped his head toward our kitchen door. Sheriff Kalupa followed, walking bent over slightly, wincing with each step.

Cal looked warily toward the sheriff's car.

"I'm alone," Sheriff Kalupa said, "I don't have a gun. You have my word." He turned a fat hip toward Cal. The sheriff pointed a finger toward his car. "That's my ex-wife's car. Borrowed it from my kid. I figured if you were going to blow up a car, might as well be hers." He chuckled, and JJ and I smiled.

Cal led him into the house, and JJ and I followed. We stopped in the kitchen.

"Take off your shirt," Cal said.

"I'm not wired. This isn't some TV show, Cal. I've come as a friend to your family."

Cal repeated, "Take off your shirt."

Sheriff Kalupa sighed. "It won't be a pretty sight." He tugged his T-shirt out of his jeans and pulled it up over his head, knocking his cap off in the process. His arms and neck were tanned a dark brown, but the rest of his torso was a pasty white, covered in hair. His belly button stuck out like half a ping-pong ball.

Sheriff Kalupa stood facing us with his arms apart, holding the T-shirt in one hand. He looked embarrassed.

"Okay," Cal said, satisfied. "You can put your shirt back on."

Sheriff Kalupa did so and then picked up his cap and put it on his head. "Told you it wouldn't be pretty."

"You didn't lie," Cal said. He smiled. "So what do you want?"

"I just want to talk," he said. "See if your children are all right. See if there's anything I can do to make this easier on everyone."

"The children are fine."

"Can I sit down? My back is killing me."

"John," Cal said, "run out to the machine shed and bring us some rope."

I slid past Cal and walked outside. I had to dig around awhile to find something other than orange baling twine, which was rough and stringy. I found a long piece of quarter-inch cotton clothesline, a bit greasy, but weathered and soft. The ends had been trimmed and then burned to keep them from fraying.

When I got back into the house, Sheriff Kalupa sat in a kitchen chair. Cal sat on the table. The sheriff drank from a glass of water. JJ sat to his right. She smiled at me when I came in with the rope.

"You've got good water out here," he said. "Water with some flavor."

"I'm going to tie you," Cal said. "You okay with that?"

"I'm just here to talk. But sure, if that makes you feel safer, I don't mind."

"Tie his legs first," Cal said. "Then his left arm."

"I'm sorry," I said to him.

"Don't be."

I cut short pieces of rope with a knife and tied Sheriff Kalupa's thick ankles to each of the front legs of the chair. His bare feet were hairy, and the big toenails were cracked and yellowed. He smelled a bit like fried onions or cigarette smoke, the way a smoker's skin smells when he sweats.

"That okay?" I asked him.

"Fine," he said.

I wrapped the rest of the rope around and around his left arm and the armrest of the chair, and tied it.

"That's not too tight, is it?"

"It's fine, John," he said.

"Isn't this like taking a hostage or something?" JJ asked.

Sheriff Kalupa chuckled. "No crime is being committed," he said. "You asked if you could tie me and I said you could."

"So, Sheriff, why are you here?" Cal asked.

"Call me Gary," he said, "Please. The reason I'm here is I don't want this to get out of hand. You blowing up all our police cars, that was a pretty crazy thing to do. I was hoping we could change horses, you know, ride out of here at a slow, smooth canter. Take a different path, if you understand my meaning."

"Your men were trespassing."

Sheriff Kalupa smiled. "Maybe by your thinking," he answered. "But no judge in America would agree that blowing up somebody's car is a just punishment for trespassing. There has to be some understanding of justice you and me can agree on, Cal." He took a drink of water. His Adam's apple twitched in his thick neck as he swallowed. When he put the empty glass down on the table, JJ picked it up and took it to the sink to fill it for him again.

"'Evil men do not understand justice, but those who seek the Lord understand all.' Are you a religious man, Gary?"

"Depends what you mean by religious," he answered. "If you mean do I attend a church regular, or read the good book, the answer would be no. But I'm no stranger to prayer, if that's what you mean. It's personal, really. Not something I'm big on talking about." JJ put a fresh glass of water on the table. "Thank you, dear," he said.

Cal didn't say anything.

Finally, the sheriff said, "You're facing quite a list of charges, Cal. There's no way to avoid arrest any longer."

"What am I looking at?" Cal asked.

"For starters, there's a warrant out for your arrest on the charge of assaulting a state patrol officer. A felony. Dashcam video was grainy and inconclusive, but they got some digital photographs the other day, and he identified you. That'll have to go to a grand jury. And of course you fire balled over one hundred thousand dollars' worth of squad cars and equipment. That won't win you any friends in the courthouse, Cal. There are federal weapons violations in there as well."

Cal shook his head but remained silent.

Sheriff Kalupa shrugged. "And I might as well tell you, you're the only suspect in a grave robbing down in Milwaukee County, which is another felony, Class C." He nodded his head toward my side of the table. "They might want to charge the boy on that one, too."

"John had nothing to do with that," Cal said.

"I believe you."

"You're only robbing when you're taking something that's not yours," Cal said. "Isn't that true?"

"In principle," Sheriff Kalupa said. "But justice is complicated. You can't just pick the laws you want to obey and ignore the ones you don't. It doesn't work that way."

"I've heard enough."

"Cal, please listen," Sheriff Kalupa said. "I didn't come in here to judge you. I'm not on the job. I'm not wearing a uniform or driving my patrol car. I came as a friend to your children. I came as a man who has also lost someone precious in his life, though not a son as you have."

"What did you lose?"

The sheriff sighed. He took a drink of water, then set the glass down on the table. "I lost a brother when I was young. A year older than me. When I was eleven."

"What happened?"

I sat forward and met eyes with JJ. She listened intently. "It was an accident," he said.

Cal said, "What kind of accident?"

"We were hunting ducks out in the sloughs off Fish Creek." He put his free hand to his mouth, wiped his chin. "My shotgun fell sideways and it went off and shot him in the neck. I shot my brother in the neck and he died."

Cal asked, "Did they turn the law on you?"

"There was an investigation, yes," he said. "They took me in, asked me questions for hours. They wanted to know if I was mad at my brother, if we ever fought. They asked everyone we knew about us. Even asked my parents."

"What'd they say?"

"Hell yes!" he said. "Of course we fought! We were boys for God's sake, brothers, competed over everything, as boys do. But he was my brother! I'd never harm him. There's family love in there you can't explain to nobody."

"Did you go to jail?"

"No," he said. He rocked forward in his chair a bit, then sat back. "No, they ruled it an accidental shooting, which is what it was. But it didn't matter, not really. I've had to carry it around. Jail would have been easier than facing everyone. My mother cried every night. All her life. She never looked at me the same way again. She wouldn't admit it, but I knew. She blamed me. How could she not? I killed my only brother. Kids used to tease me, say I killed him because I wanted his bike, shit like that. I got into so many fights I almost got thrown out of school. I thought about killing myself." He paused and turned his free hand palm up. "I'm just saying that I understand a bit of what you're feeling. That's all. And I'm trying to keep everything from getting worse."

"What was your brother's name?" JJ asked.

"Paul," Sheriff Kalupa said softly.

"Like the apostle," Cal said.

"Well, maybe. It was my dad's name. He was named after Dad."

No one said anything for a while. JJ looked as if she were about to cry, and I felt it too, in my throat. Memories of the morning David died, and the days afterward, that burning drip of anguish in the back of my throat and chest, Cal's pain, Mother's tears.

"But you haven't lost a son," said Cal. "You haven't seen your wife lift the body of your baby boy and try to make him warm in her arms again."

"No, I haven't," Sheriff Kalupa said. "But I lost the only brother I ever had." He made his hands into fists. "And I killed him with these hands. I know what grief can do, Cal. That's all I'm saying."

"So what do you suggest?" Cal asked.

"What's fair to you?" the sheriff asked him.

"Fair is you leave and never come back, and everyone else leaves us alone."

"I'm sorry. It's too late for that."

"What isn't it too late for?"

"Well," the sheriff said, weighing his words carefully, "you could come back to town with me, uncuffed, you know, a passenger in my car. Kids would come along, too, stay at my place for a while, or we could put them up in a hotel, whatever."

"Will I be arrested?"

Sheriff Kalupa nodded. "That can't be avoided any longer."

"Prison?" Cal asked.

"You assaulted a police officer, Cal. I don't think there's any way to avoid punishment for that. So the assault, plus the fireworks with the patrol cars. I won't lie to you. You'll get some time. Prosecutors are tough on folks who hurt cops."

"Well," Cal said, "then there isn't much of a choice, is there?"

"Prison's no picnic, but it's a hell of a lot better than the alternative."

"And what's that?"

Sheriff Kalupa took a deep breath and let it out through his nose, slowly. His belly heaved up and settled as he did so. "They'll come out here and take you by force," he said. "The US Marshals, men from BATF, because of the weapons you got out here. I don't know where the hell you got that stuff, Cal, but it's not legal."

"The US Marshals are here?" Cal asked, surprised.

"They're back in town with all the others. Fifteen, twenty men. You've really kicked the hornets' nest here. Someone from the sheriff's office will come out with them. Might be me, might not. I'm not too popular with my boss right now, on account of losing those patrol cars. But I won't be able to protect you either way. The feds don't give a rat's ass about anything but bringing you in. You shoot at them, you'll think you've stumbled under a flock of seagulls shitting cannonballs. If they get a shot at you, they'll take it. And they won't miss. They got guys can shoot the dick off an ant at a half mile." He turned briefly toward JJ. "Pardon the expression. And they won't drive up like a bunch of imbeciles in patrol cars with standard-issue firearms, like I did."

"What have they got?" Cal asked, smiling. JJ's eyes widened as she looked at me.

"They're driving armored Humvees, the kind they used in Desert Storm. They got night vision shit. Sharpshooters with guns that'll send a bullet a thousand yards. Steel-jacketed bullets that can pene-trate metal plate thick as my thumb. Tear gas that'd melt the eyes out of an elephant." He paused. "And they have a tank."

"I heard," Cal said. "What kind?"

"I don't know. It's on a flatbed, probably an old Sheridan."

Cal chuckled. He got up and walked around behind Sheriff Kalupa, looked out the kitchen window, then came back over and knelt down next to Sheriff Kalupa's chair. He untied the sheriff's arm and legs.

"Thanks for coming," Cal said. "I appreciate your care for my chil-dren." The sheriff tugged on the arms of the chair and struggled to stand up. His face winced in pain, and when he reached his feet, he stood bent over.

"You can't stay here, Cal. It's too dangerous. For you and the chil-dren."

"The Lord will protect us."

"Not from this shit He won't!" the sheriff said. He grew agitated. "Cal, listen to me! You're going to get hurt. Your kids'll get hurt. All those elderly people out in the yard. You're putting all them at risk, too. Please think about this."

"I have thought about it."

"Then at least let the children come into town with me," Sheriff Kalupa said. "At least do that, Cal. I'm a dad, too. I know what that's like. I know how it feels to love a child."

Cal walked around behind JJ's chair, put his hands on her shoul-ders, and looked at me. "John?" he asked. "You want to go with him?"

I thought if I stayed, I might somehow have some influence. I thought maybe I could save us, keep the worst from happening. "No," I said. "I'm staying." JJ stared at me.

"JJ?" Cal asked.

"Go," I said to her.

JJ started crying.

"Go with him," I said. "Find Anna."

"No," she said.

"Think about this, now," Sheriff Kalupa said. "This is serious dan-ger you're facing. They won't be satisfied until your daddy goes out with them, one way or another, they really won't care."

"I'm staying," JJ said.

Sheriff Kalupa looked into my eyes and shook his head. I wanted to tell him that JJ and I started all this when we let David die, and to leave now would be to avoid responsibility for something we'd done. Surely, he could understand that. He shot his own brother, so he should know. But I looked down, didn't say anything.

"Come on," Cal said. He led Sheriff Kalupa slowly to the kitchen door. "When you get to town, you tell them David slew Goliath with a stone and a sling. I've got a hell of a lot more than stones in here."

"Please, Cal, just think about it, okay? I'll come back again tomorrow morning. You think about things over night."

"Touch his back, Cal," I said suddenly.

Cal and Sheriff Kalupa looked at me. Cal blinked his eyes. "I don't do that anymore."

"Please, Cal," I said.

Cal sighed. "Where does your back hurt?"

Sheriff Kalupa frowned. "Right side," he said. "Down low, over the hip bone. It's back spasms, Cal. I'm taking muscle relaxants, but I'm still stiff as a board."

Cal placed his right hand gently on the sheriff's back. He slid the hand down slowly.

"Here?" he asked.

"A little lower."

Cal moved his hand. "Here?"

Sheriff Kalupa nodded and winced. "Yeah. Right there." Cal rubbed his hand in a small circle against the sheriff's back for about thirty seconds, then pulled his hand away. Sheriff Kalupa reached back and touched his T-shirt. He took a deep breath, then stood erect and winced again.

"Feeling any better?" I asked.

Sheriff Kalupa crossed his forearms over his chest and twisted his torso gingerly to the left, then to the right. He raised his arms toward the ceiling. "Maybe," he said. He shook his head and looked down at Cal's hand. "I'm not sure. Cal, please. Come to town with me."

"No, thanks," Cal said. "You want anything from the garden? We've got zucchini out there the size of baseball bats."

"No, thank you," Sheriff Kalupa said. He squeezed JJ's shoulder with one meaty hand as he passed her, and caught my eyes in his and shook his head.

"I won't be able to protect you," he said softly.

"We don't need your protection," Cal answered.

Cal pushed open the kitchen door, and Sheriff Kalupa squeezed out and walked down the steps to the driveway. Cal followed him just outside, holding the door open with his hip.

"That car's a piece of junk," Cal said. He smiled. "I'd be doing you a favor if I blew it up."

"My ex wouldn't think so," Sheriff Kalupa said, chuckling. He put his baseball cap on and squinted up at us. Then he walked around to the far side of his car and opened the door. "Be careful. Think it over. I'll come out again in the morning."

Then Cal disappeared. It happened so suddenly it seemed as if he'd vanished. I never heard a gunshot. No one did. The sheriff had swung a leg into his car when Cal pitched forward off the stoop three feet down to the long grass beside the driveway. He dropped as if he'd fainted, or had somehow fallen asleep while standing up, and landed on his stomach, with his gun pinned underneath him.

"Cal!" Sheriff Kalupa screamed. "Cal!" He ran around his car and dropped to his knees at Cal's side. JJ started screaming.

Cal's dirty T-shirt was already wet with blood. It oozed from a small hole in his back, just below his left shoulder blade. He rolled from side to side with his forehead in the grass.

"Those sons of bitches!" Sheriff Kalupa shouted. "Those goddamn sons of bitches! Cal, come on, hang in there." He waved an arm at me. "You kids get around to the other side of me. They're in the woods across the road somewhere. Put me between you and them."

JJ and I looked at him, but we didn't move.

"Do it!" he shouted. "Goddamn it! Get on the other side of me or they might shoot you, too. Move slowly. Keep your hands high so they can see them. And whatever you do, don't reach for Cal's gun. John, you especially."

JJ stopped screaming and put her hands to her mouth. My arms shook as I crawled around Cal's body and stopped on the other side of Sheriff Kalupa. JJ followed, one of her hands holding my ankle.

"That's it," he said.

Slowly, Agnes and Jeremiah, and the other members of the Herbster Grays, encircled us protectively. Some of them prayed. Some of them cried.

Gently, Sheriff Kalupa put a hand on Cal's left shoulder. Blood seeped through his fingers. "He's bleeding bad here. Cal, listen to me. Can you move your legs?"

Cal kicked one of his legs. He moaned, ground his forehead into the grass.

"Okay, good," Sheriff Kalupa said. "Help me," he said to JJ and me. "Let's get him over. Come on Cal, let's get a look at you."

We rolled Cal to his back. He screamed.

"It's going to hurt, Cal," Sheriff Kalupa said. "I'm sure that bullet busted up a couple ribs, maybe worse."

Cal's eyes were open, wide and disbelieving. His nose and mouth were dripping blood. He shook mildly, as if he were cold. But he gripped his gun tightly with one hand and would not let go. Where his chest had been against the ground, the grass shined wet and crimson.

JJ rubbed her hand softly over his forehead. Sheriff Kalupa found the wound in Cal's chest and pressed one of his thick bloodied hands against it.

"Ambush," Cal said softly. With his left arm, Cal tried to swing the barrel of his rifle toward Sheriff Kalupa, but the sheriff pushed it away.

"No!" Sheriff Kalupa said. "Goddamn it, Cal. I had nothing to do with this. We have to get you to a hospital. John, get me a rag or something. Take off your shirt. No, wait, you keep that vest on. Listen, I want you to lean forward here and put your hand on this wound. Put one hand on it, then cover that hand with your other hand, okay?"

I nodded. Sheriff Kalupa pulled his hand away and I pushed my hand against the wound in Cal's chest. His blood was warm and watery. I could feel his rapid pulse and slow breathing against my palm. I covered that hand with my other hand. The edges of my fingers darkened with Cal's blood. My own heartbeat pounded in my ears.

Cal grimaced with each gasping breath. "Don't die, Dad," JJ said, sobbing, leaning her head against my shoulder.

Two men in camouflaged clothing, carrying scoped long-barreled rifles, crossed the road and walked up our driveway. They wore helmets and bulletproof vests, and one of them was talking into a radio. When he reached us, he said, "Chopper's a minute out."

Sheriff Kalupa spoke to their empty faces. "I was *not* in any danger, goddamn it. You goddamn cowboys make me sick."

Cal's eyes were still closed. One of the other men had taken Cal's rifle, but they had not peeled the bands of ammunition from his chest. I sneered at these men smugly staring down at Cal. I hated them. They were young, probably still in their twenties, strong and calm. Their faces were greased with camouflage paint in shades of green and brown. One of them had aimed a rifle at Cal from so far away that we could not even hear its report before the bullet plowed through his body.

Cal coughed. Blood bubbled from his lips.

"Where's that fucking chopper!" Sheriff Kalupa shouted. He knelt down by Cal, gently moved me aside, and covered Cal's chest wound with his own hands again.

Cal turned his head to the side and blood poured from his mouth. "Dad!" JJ shouted. "Dad!"

He opened his eyes and smiled with his bloodied teeth showing. He looked at JJ and then over at me. "I'm sorry," he said. "'The Lord is my shepherd; I shall not want.'" He looked at me, his eyes fearful. "I can't remember, John. I can't remember what comes next." He pinched his eyes closed.

The steady staccato thumping of an approaching helicopter grew louder and louder. It sprayed the house and Sheriff Kalupa's car with gravel as it landed on the road. The Herbster Grays dropped to their knees and tucked their heads into their arms. Soon a man and a woman were hooking Cal up to an IV, loading him onto a gurney, rushing him into the air for a final look down at an Eden which, in the end, had eluded him.

Chapter 24

Sheriff Kalupa and some of the Herbster Grays stayed with us through the night and over the next several days, as groups of men and women—government investigators, television and newspaper reporters, sightseers—came to New Eden to wander outside our bullet-riddled house and to inspect the wreckage of the patrol cars that our dad had blown up. The sheriff also sat with us anytime men from the FBI or the BATF asked us questions about Cal and about the various weapons they tagged and loaded into a white windowless van. When they asked if we knew where David's casket was, we said we didn't know.

More and more people came to our house. Sometimes the line of cars parked along the road stretched for a half mile. Most of the people just stood by their cars and stared through binoculars, but others walked right up the driveway. The sheriff and several other county officers kept the crowds of gawkers from getting too close to JJ and me. Some of the people bold enough to walk up the driveway wanted to see the Cathedral of David up close, and many of them brought cameras and took pictures. One of the men who looked at it was an architecture professor who had driven all the way from Minneapolis. He'd seen footage of Cal's cathedral on the evening news. He spent the entire day taking pictures and making measurements. Before he left, he told us he believed that nothing like the log cathedral Cal had built existed anywhere else in the world. Moreover, this professor said, it seemed impossible—it was not possible, he was certain—that something so complex and intricate had been designed and built by someone without any training in architecture or engineering, and without the aid of mechanical equipment.

"He learned it by dreaming about bees," I told him, though this answer did not satisfy him.

Along with the Herbster Grays, some of Sheriff Kalupa's friends came out to repair broken windows and to help us clean up the refuse and broken glass. Agnes and Jeremiah cooked for us every day and returned to Herbster in the evenings.

Each night, as I tried to sleep, I kept seeing Cal fall to the ground, kept seeing his bright blood on the palms of my hands. I wanted to remember him as he once was, before David died, when he would laugh and dance with Mother around the kitchen floor in West Allis. But I couldn't remember him that way. My brain would not yet take me there.

Late one morning Sheriff Kalupa said, "Truck coming up the road." He parted the curtain over the kitchen window.

We went outside together. JJ and I walked halfway down the driveway and shaded our eyes with our hands. A gray pickup rumbled along in the gravel, kicking up dust. The truck slowed as it approached the driveway, turned in, and stopped. Mother had come home.

She'd had her hair cut. She wore a long flowing sundress the color of the sky, and her face and arms were tanned.

"Daddy's dead," JJ said, and fell into her open arms.

Mother was crying. She already knew. She drew us both against her body, wrapped her arms around each of our necks and pulled us to her. The three of us dropped to our knees on the driveway like some sad sculpture, crying into one another's hair, until Sheriff Kalupa gently helped us to our feet.

We sat down at the kitchen table, and while Sheriff Kalupa cooked us bacon and toast and filled us glasses of cold water, we told Mother everything. The morning became afternoon, and then early evening, and Sheriff Kalupa fed us again. We ate sweet corn he pulled from broken stalks in the garden, and dilled cucumbers.

Sheriff Kalupa gently interrupted our conversation to say good-bye. He looked at Mother. "Once again, I'm sorry for your loss. Both your son and your husband. Truly sorry."

Mother nodded at him. He hugged JJ and me, then turned and walked back outside, got into his car, and drove away.

At dusk, Mother, JJ, and I wandered through our muddy corn and soybean fields. The hailstorm had destroyed everything. Even both of our heifers were dead. We found them twisted hideously in the wires of the fence, their legs broken, their bodies eaten by coyotes, covered with hornets and flies. They had panicked in the storm and had run blindly into the barbed wire.

Our soybeans were twisted and curled on the ground, driven into the mud, like someone had walked through with giant feet and stomped on them. The corn leaves were pocked with holes, and most of the stalks were broken clean through, as if they'd been hit by a shotgun blast. Our vegetable garden was no better, though some of the low-growing plants, the cucumbers, the bell peppers, the turnips, seemed to have escaped major damage. Our sweet corn still held its bruised, ripened cobs and could be harvested by hand.

JJ kept staring at Mother.

"Jennifer, is something wrong?"

"You're walking different."

"I am?"

"Yes, you are. Are you pregnant?"

"You can see it already?"

JJ nodded.

"I never got the chance to tell your father. Yes. I'm going to have a baby."

We walked silently for a while, JJ and I digesting the news. All of that Song of Solomon had produced a child. Conceived to the music of the King James Bible. It was almost too much to hold inside.

We had Cal's body cremated, and when we were strong enough, we held a small memorial service at New Eden, just the three of us. We took the urn of Cal's ashes and walked into the garden, waded through the vines of cucumber and watermelon. It was a warm, late August morning. The sky clear blue. A light breeze moved our hair and fluttered the leaves in the trees.

Mother handed the urn to me. It was made of pottery, about the size of an iced-tea pitcher, glazed in blues and metallic greens and purples. Mother swallowed once, brushed her hair from her eyes. She opened Cal's Bible and began to read. "'My beloved spoke, and said to me: Rise up my love, my fair one, and come away. For lo, the winter is past, the rain is over and gone. The flowers appear on the earth; the time of singing has come, and the voice of the turtledove is heard in our land.'"

I took the cover off of the urn and handed it to Mother. She withdrew a handful of ashes, then turned her hand toward the earth. She tipped the urn toward me. I put my hand in, felt the soft, cool powder, the tiny chunks of bone. I balled my hand into a soft fist, withdrew some ash, and let it fall into the breeze. It puffed like smoke and disappeared. JJ used both hands, cupping Cal's ashes in her palms, looking hard into them, before opening her hands and letting the ashes drift across the garden in the wind.

Mother carried the urn against her hip, bending over almost to the ground as she seeded the earth with Cal's ashes. I sprinkled mine from waist-high, and the ashes dusted the green leaves, trickled through to the shade beneath. I placed a small handful around each of the tomato plants, which were staked up off the ground, badly battered by hail, but were sprouting delicate blossoms, yellow and shaped like stars.

"Save some," I said to Mother.

She nodded and smiled at me.

From the garden, Mother, JJ, and I carried Cal's remaining ashes across the farm, through our overgrown pasture, to the small creek that crossed the far corner of our land. We stopped where the creek curled around a bend and bubbled over rocks toward the woods.

"Here?" Mother asked.

I nodded. When our shadows crossed over the water, three ghostly trout darted into the current and disappeared under the bank.

Mother tipped the urn and poured the remaining ashes and bone into the water, where they were pulled under the bank by the current in a long, feathery plume. The creek would take them to the Cranberry River, and the river would take them to Lake Superior.

Quietly, we sat down and watched the creek together, listened to the singing of water over rocks and roots, breathed in the summer air, felt the sun on our faces. One by one, we pulled off our shoes and socks, rolled up our pants. Sitting between us, Mother reached for our hands, and held them. We let our feet trail in the cold tug of the current until they ached.

* * *

Mornings, now, the grass is white with frost. It crunches beneath our feet as JJ and I cross the yard to the road to meet the bus that takes us to Northwestern High School in Maple, twenty miles from the farm. Some mornings the hoarfrost is so thick, the leafless branches of trees are puffed like pipe cleaners. You can run your fingers across them, and the crystals fall from the branches like baby teeth.

JJ has a boyfriend, a junior named Billy Shepardson, an Anishinaabe who was born on the reservation in Odanah. He looks a little bit like Little Richard, but without the makeup. Though I love her and still find her beautiful, I am no longer drawn to her the way I was, and I know that she is no longer drawn to me. She is my step-sister. She has started to comb her hair again, and I have kept mine cut short. I no longer look like an apostle, Mother says. I look like the seventeen-year-old boy I am supposed to be.

With the money Eleanor left us when she died, Mother had indoor plumbing, electricity, telephone service, and a propane gas furnace installed in our house. She bought a washer and dryer, and a refrigerator. The propane tank sits out back in front of the garden like a giant silver cocoon. Mother has also taken a job at the paper mill in Ashland. Every day at work, she says, she can look up from her desk through a small window and watch the waves rolling in on Lake Superior. She can see iron ore ships steaming out of the harbor in Duluth, heading toward the St. Lawrence Seaway to sail the Atlantic on their way to some distant place in the world.

Mother's baby is due in late January. She had an ultrasound done and learned that the baby was going to be a boy. One night at supper, she told us that this child awash in her womb would be named Jonah Calvin. She read aloud to us from Jonah, the last time I ever saw her hold Cal's Bible. The words were lovely and resonant, a summation of our past distress, and an incantation against future hardship:

"'The waters surrounded me, even to my soul; The deep closed around me; Weeds were wrapped around my head. I went down to the moorings of the mountains; The earth with its bars closed behind me forever; Yet You have brought up my life from the pit. O Lord, My God.'"

A baby named Jonah, she believed, could never drown.

We were a normal family once. We probably look like we've become normal again, but I don't think we have. Sometimes at night, during a thunderstorm, JJ, Mother, and I hear what sounds like seagulls calling our names, and the sloshing of water against the windows, and the house seems to rise and fall on the waves of Lake Superior. From Mother's room, we can hear soft humming, the melody of a lullaby. Inside her body, safely awash in sweet, amniotic fluid, Jonah Calvin waits to be born.

I've painted the ceiling of my bedroom a glossy black again, but I have not placed constellations of stars there as I had before. Instead, I have arranged them in the shape of Lake Superior, its dotted shoreline shining in the dark, its watery depths mingling the bodies of Cal and David, invisible to all but as present to us as hope or memory. When I think of Cal, I believe there are unseen constellations inside all of us. The flare of a supernova is just a spark away.

About the Author

A native of Wisconsin, Ron Rindo is the author of three short story collections, including *Love in an Expanding Universe*, which won the Minnesota Voices Prize for short fiction. His short stories and essays have also appeared in many journals and anthologies, including *The Best American Essays*. He is a professor of English at the University of Wisconsin in Oshkosh, and he lives with his wife, Jenna, and an assortment of animals on five acres in the country, where they raised a blended family of five children. This is his first novel.

CPSIA information can be obtained
at www.ICGtesting.com
Printed in the USA
LVHW040335130423
744169LV00003B/344